There was a sudd[en]

The first thing Annja saw after her eyes adj[usted was a] blue figure emblazoned in front of her. A statue. Annja caught herself as she recognized who it was.

Kali.

The goddess of death.

The statue had four arms, each wielding a different weapon. And the red eyes were supposed to suggest a certain level of intoxication, a bloodlust resulting from one of Kali's many battles.

Kali was a ferocious deity.

What the hell had Annja stumbled onto here?

The torches that had sprung to life glowed hot, casting long shadows across the chamber, but also giving enough illumination for Annja to finally see the men who held them captive. Her first impression was that there weren't nearly as many of them as she'd thought there'd been in the darkness. Only a dozen or so. All chanting.

And they looked as ferocious as their goddess Kali. Slowly, each man reached up and undid the length of black cloth that covered their faces. These scarves, knotted at each end, were handled with a degree of reverence Annja found amazing. The captors tucked them into their belts, the two knotted ends dangling over, as if ready to be drawn quickly. Perhaps they were weapons.

Thuggee. The thought struck her hard. Except...

Except that cult was supposed to have been wiped out ages ago.

Titles in this series:

ROGUE Angel

Alex Archer

FURY'S GODDESS

A GOLD EAGLE BOOK FROM
WORLDWIDE®

TORONTO • NEW YORK • LONDON
AMSTERDAM • PARIS • SYDNEY • HAMBURG
STOCKHOLM • ATHENS • TOKYO • MILAN
MADRID • WARSAW • BUDAPEST • AUCKLAND

Recycling programs
for this product may
not exist in your area.

First edition March 2012

ISBN-13: 978-0-373-62155-2

FURY'S GODDESS

Special thanks and acknowledgment to
Jon Merz for his contribution to this work.

The
LEGEND

...THE ENGLISH COMMANDER TOOK
JOAN'S SWORD AND RAISED IT HIGH.
The broadsword, plain and unadorned,
gleamed in the firelight. He put the tip against
the ground and his foot at the center of the blade.
The broadsword shattered, fragments falling
into the mud. The crowd surged forward,
peasant and soldier, and snatched the shards
from the trampled mud. The commander tossed
the hilt deep into the crowd.
Smoke almost obscured Joan, but she continued
praying till the end, until finally the flames climbed
her body and she sagged against the restraints.

Joan of Arc died that fateful day in France,
but her legend and sword are reborn....

1

"Maybe it's a tiger," Annja Creed said as she perused the latest police reports on her iPad. The translated reports had been emailed over to her as she flew from New York City to India. And she was now looking at grisly pictures of mutilated bodies that had been recovered, some of them partially eaten. The remains of Annja's in-flight meal were on the tray in front of her. But somehow, the limp turkey and Swiss cheese sandwich on stale wheat bread no longer seemed very appetizing.

If it ever had, Annja thought.

"Don't tigers tend to eat everything?" Frank asked. "Some of those bodies just look, well, sort of…picked at."

Annja looked at the big man seated next to her. His innocence seemed to be waning fast. Frank Desalvo was fresh off his stint as an intern at another cable channel and had landed the job of cameraman on this assignment. The program Annja worked on, *Chasing History's*

Monsters, had snapped Frank up for his keen eye, the producers had said. Annja suspected it was because he wasn't established enough to command a higher salary.

He was likable enough, even if he still had the arrogance of a young twentysomething. With a mop of black hair and wide brown eyes, his splotchy beard made him look a few years older than he was. Annja figured he wore a beard for that reason.

"Not necessarily, although I'm not exactly an expert on man-eating tigers," she said. "They may not have been hungry enough to devour the entire body. Or perhaps they were simply defending their territory."

She continued to scan through the reports. "Whatever the case, the locals are terrified and the police haven't been able to track or trap the offender."

"Which makes for great television."

Annja frowned. "It means more people might lose their lives."

"Well, sure. But at least it's nobody we know, right? That makes it easier."

Annja came across one very gory picture and thrust the iPad in front of Frank. "You think this is any easier for the family of this person?"

Frank blanched visibly. "I guess not."

"Try to remember that the stories we cover are about people, just the same as you and me. They're not objects. We can't disconnect from them. There's too much of that going on in the world as it is, all right?"

"You're the boss."

Annja nodded. "Yes, I am."

She took a breath and went back to reading. There had been three deaths so far. Two men and a woman.

All residents of a new luxury complex on the outskirts of Hyderabad, India's sixth most populous city.

Annja started surfing the net to find out more about the city she and Frank would be heading into. After several minutes, she started forming a picture of the place in her mind and found herself getting more excited all the time.

Hyderabad was only about five hundred years old, although recent archaeological excavations had uncovered settlements dating back to the Iron Age, around 500 BC.

I would have enjoyed being on those digs, she thought.

Hyderabad enjoyed a hot summer, a very moist monsoon season and a delightful winter between late October and early February. Annja was relieved they were going to be in the city during the winter. She'd had enough of monsoon seasons of late, and a hot summer didn't appeal much to her, either.

With 3.6 million living in the city or its outskirts, Hyderabad certainly had plenty of potential victims for a rogue tiger to choose from. Except locals had reported hearing something that didn't sound like a tiger at all, but a mysterious creature that sounded as if it was part cat and part wolf.

The combination had aroused the intense curiosity of *Chasing History's Monsters,* and naturally, Annja was dispatched to find out the truth.

But in a city as cosmopolitan as Hyderabad, was there any place a mysterious rampaging creature could hide? Or was it a case of mistaken identity or some psychopath covering his tracks by making his victims appear to have been attacked by a wild animal?

Annja went back to reading while Frank flirted with

the flight attendant. Hyderabad's primary industries were split among real estate, pharmaceuticals, information technology, tourism and filmmaking. She found that last part intriguing. She'd heard of Bollywood before, but Hyderabad apparently had Tollywood, after the major film production complex located at Telugu Cinema. Annja paused. What if someone at Tollywood was getting especially imaginative with the props department?

"Annja."

She glanced up. Frank wore a grin a mile long. "What?"

"I think I'm in love."

"Again?" Frank had been working hard to seduce anyone with breasts the entire flight, having declared at the start of their journey his intention to join the Mile-High Club the first chance he got.

So far, his membership application had been soundly denied.

"Yeah, but this is the one." Frank nodded. "I'm telling you." He unbuckled his seat belt and stood. Pausing, he leaned over Annja. "Don't wait up, okay?"

"Sure thing, Casanova." She watched him amble off down the main aisle toward the lavatories.

There's somebody for everyone, she thought with a grin. Frank wasn't ugly, per se, but there wasn't much to write home about.

Delving back into her iPad, she learned that Hyderabad's film community had the largest IMAX theater in Asia and a host of cutting-edge technology. She frowned. The sort of technology that could distort images and make people think they were seeing something when, in fact, they were not.

Interesting.

She went back to the police reports. According to the cops, the first case had come in sometime around ten o'clock only a few weeks prior to Annja's trip. Sanjeet Gupta had been taking a walk around the residential complex and had not come home. A phone call from a distraught wife brought the police running even though only a few hours had passed since the husband was last seen. They conducted a search and came across Gupta's body lying facedown near a culvert. His arm and part of his upper torso had been torn away, resulting in massive blood loss. Part of his face had been gnawed off, according to the medical examiner.

She glanced back at her quick facts on the residential complex. It catered to the extremely wealthy. The top niche of Hyderabad's social elite seemed to live in the complex. No wonder the police responded so quickly, she thought. The rich always get preferential treatment.

There was a click overhead and the public address system came on. The flight attendant started talking in what Annja thought was Hindi, but then went on to repeat her announcement in several other dialects. Annja was reminded of the fact that while Urdu and Hindi might be the popular languages of India, regional dialects ranged extensively.

At last, the attendant switched to British-accented English. "Ladies and gentlemen, the captain has advised that we are starting our descent into Hyderabad. At this time, we would like to ask you to shut off all electronic devices, put your trays into their upright position and make sure to remain in your seats with the seat belts on at all times."

She clicked the PA system off; almost on cue, the plane started to bank. Annja gripped the armrests at the suddenness of the movement.

And then they dipped lower. Annja heard the flaps coming down.

Where was Frank?

She found out a moment later when the door to the bathroom opened and he stumbled out, a wet stain across the front of his pants. Lovely.

He clambered down the aisle and slumped back into his seat. "So," Annja said, not really wanting to know, "was it everything you hoped it would be?"

Frank frowned. "They don't make airplane bathrooms all that large, do they?"

"No, they do not."

He sighed. "Stupid cable channels always make it look better than it is in real life."

"They're in the business of selling fantasy."

"She never showed, anyway."

"But your clothes—"

Frank held up his hand. "The damn plane banked and I nearly felt into the vacuum toilet. I got blue stuff all over me. So I had to wash it out of my pants." He sighed. "I'm not exactly a professional when it comes to dry cleaning."

"Looks more like you did wet cleaning."

"Funny." Frank grabbed a copy of the in-flight magazine and started fanning himself. "So, you really think this thing isn't a tiger?"

"I don't know. That's what we're here to find out."

"Where to first?"

"The hotel," she said. "I want a shower after flying

for so many hours. After a change of clothes and a quick meal, we'll head downtown and talk to the police."

Below them sprawled the city of Hyderabad—gleaming office buildings and brilliantly painted temples. Annja leaned back away from the window and nodded thoughtfully.

"If the police haven't gotten anywhere with the case, then we'll try to find this *creature* ourselves. And that means going into harm's way."

2

"Customs line is over this way," Annja said as they made their way down the concourse.

She presented her passport and visa to the customs official, a stern-looking older man with a bushy beard. His eyes seemed as sharp as a hawk's and he scanned Annja quickly before eyeballing Frank.

Annja saw the contempt in his face. He quickly cleared Annja and then frowned as he looked at Frank. "Your papers, please."

Frank handed them over and the customs official scanned them. But unlike with Annja, he didn't hand them back. "What brings you to India?"

"Huh?" Frank was still fanning his crotch. Annja groaned inwardly. The customs official glanced over his counter and saw the stain on Frank's pants. When his eyes came back up, Annja saw irritation in them.

Uh-oh.

"We hit some turbulence on the plane and I…unfortunately…got a bit wet," Frank stammered.

"So it would appear." But there was nothing friendly in the way he said it. Annja dearly wished for a hole to curl up in until this was over.

"He's with me, actually," she said. She smiled to show how harmless she was. But the official's frown told her he wasn't in the mood to be nice.

"And why are you coming to India?"

"We're members of an American television show. We're here to do some research on a spate of recent crimes in Hyderabad."

His eyes narrowed. "Which crimes are you referring to?"

"The attacks on residents in the new development on the outskirts of the city."

"Is that so?" He stared at Frank for what seemed like a very long time. Frank shifted back and forth uncomfortably. Annja willed him to stand still.

The customs official looked back at her. "And what does this…man do for your television show? Urinate in his pants?"

"I didn't urinate on myself," Frank snapped. Annja winced.

"I think," the customs official said, "that perhaps we should talk in another area of the airport."

Annja groaned. An interrogation. Great. In the country for all of twenty minutes and we're already suspected criminals.

Swell. God knew how long they were going to be treated like would-be terrorists, but Annja guessed it would be some time before they were able to get to their hotel and unwind.

"That will not be necessary," said a man with a voice that was deep and rich, like dark chocolate poured over velvet.

Annja turned and found herself staring into the dark brown eyes of man in a well-tailored three-piece suit. He smiled at her and then his eyes flashed back to the customs officer.

The effect was immediate. "Of course, sir. I just need to see your paperwork."

Without giving the customs officer much in the way of eye contact, the newly arrived man held a sheaf of papers out to him and left them on his counter. "I will take responsibility for these travelers."

"Yes, of course, sir."

He waved Annja and Frank toward him. "Please follow me."

They walked out of the bustling airport and followed him to an idling Mercedes at the curbside.

Annja stopped him as they approached the car. "What about our bags?"

He pointed at the trunk. "We took the liberty of collecting them. They're in the boot." He indicated the car. "Please, if you would—"

"Who are you?" Annja crossed her arms. "No offense intended, but I don't usually get into cars with people I don't know. Especially in foreign countries."

"My name is Inspector Ajay Pradesh." He flashed a badge. "I am with the Hyderabad City Police Special Investigations Unit."

Frank walked past Annja. "Good enough for me."

Annja stopped Frank with a hand on his arm. "Let's try not to get into too much trouble before we know what's going on here, all right?"

Frank paused.

Pradesh seemed to be smiling at her. She frowned. "Would you mind letting me see your badge?"

"Of course not." He tossed it to her and she caught it. There was a laminated photo of Pradesh and a hologram overlaid on the identification. It could have been a forgery, but Pradesh seemed genuine enough. Still, old habits were hard to fight and Annja had a few questions before she jumped into a stranger's car.

"How did you know we were coming into town?"

"Your boss in New York called us. Apparently he was concerned that you might have some trouble when you landed." He glanced quickly at Frank and then back at Annja.

Frank looked puzzled. "Why would they think that?"

Pradesh chuckled. "Perhaps this is not the first time you have made a scene in public?"

Frank glanced down. He sighed. "That Christmas party last year wasn't my fault. Seriously."

Annja shook her head. "I'm tempted to put you on the next plane back to New York."

Frank ran his hand through his mop of hair, tousling it wildly. "Please don't do that, Annja. This is a big assignment for me. If this goes right, it could be a stepping stone to better assignments. You know I can work a camera like no one's business."

Pradesh leaned against the car and folded his arms. "I think there's a flight bound for the States in another hour." He winked at Annja. "If that's really what you want to do."

Annja smirked. "Well…"

Frank fairly dived into the backseat of the Mercedes. Annja allowed herself the briefest smile.

"Well, that seems settled," Pradesh said over the roar of an airplane taking off overhead. He held the door for her. "Would you like to sit up front? It makes you look like less of a criminal."

"All right."

Annja slid into the car and waited for Pradesh to get behind the steering wheel. He adjusted his seat belt and then guided them out into the traffic's slipstream.

He was handsome and refined. She found it hard to think of him as a policeman, but she couldn't deny that his authoritative presence had certainly heeled the customs officer. Still, he didn't have the cop vibe.

"Thanks for stepping in back there at the airport."

He shrugged. "He was doing his job, of course, but unfortunately many airport officials tend to live out their power-hungry fantasies at the expense of naive travelers."

Frank didn't say a word from the backseat.

"Your timing was impeccable."

Pradesh grinned. "Actually, I was watching for a few minutes before I intervened."

"Why?"

"I wanted to see what the two of you were like. How you handled the challenge and what you might do. I'm something of an observer of people, you see. I like knowing who I'm about to get involved with."

"Get involved with?"

Pradesh nodded as he zipped the Mercedes around a large cargo truck. A blare of a horn followed them, but Pradesh seemed unmoved by it. "I've been assigned to help you."

Annja shook her head. "I don't think we need any help."

Pradesh held up one hand. "I promise I won't interfere with your investigation. There are a lot of jurisdictions involved in this case right now."

"I get the feeling this isn't a request."

Pradesh shrugged. "I have people I answer to, as well. Orders are orders, as they say."

Annja sighed. "I'm not exactly thrilled with this."

"See it from our angle, Annja. We're dealing with a crime scene. Two foreigners—one who is, forgive me, less than culturally perceptive—with a television program coming into our jurisdiction to investigate a series of crimes we haven't been able to make much headway on yet. Imagine how bad we would look if television researchers—one with *archaeology* accreditation—were able to figure it out and we were not. Such disgrace would be intolerable for us, I'm afraid."

"So, you're here to babysit us."

"If that is how you wish to view it, that is fine with me." Pradesh shrugged. "But I do sincerely wish to assist you in any way that I might. I have been intrigued with the idea of a giant tiger roaming our city since the first body was found. But my requests for additional manpower to track it have gone unanswered."

"Why?"

Pradesh pointed out a sprawling new construction project to their left. "Hyderabad is in the midst of unparalleled economic growth. Several key industries for the city have the potential to make this part of India one of the country's richest."

"I would think the powers that be would want anything that threatened it to be taken care of at once."

"It's something of a fine line." Pradesh reduced the air-conditioning. "The city leaders are publicity clamoring for action. But behind the scenes, they don't want anything to disrupt progress. And the development where these attacks have occurred belong to some of the city's wealthiest, so it's a double-edged sword. The residents obviously want the tiger—or creature—found and killed, but they don't want a stigma attached to their homes. They would lose all cachet. And that's why they bought here."

Annja shook her head. "Bizarre. They've potentially got a man-eating tiger looking for its next meal and they're worried about what their friends will say."

"I am not even close to being in that financial realm. So perhaps my perspective is somewhat different."

"More like realistic," she said.

"We will have to proceed with discretion," Pradesh said. "There are people who already think the city leaders have been too vocal about finding the tiger. For them, it would be better if the tiger was lured away to some other section of the city. If it found a poorer place to settle down and hunt, they'd be quite happy."

"Don't tell me someone actually suggested that."

Pradesh smiled. "As I said, my perspective is not nearly the same as those with money."

"I guess the sooner we figure it out, then the better it will be for everyone involved."

"Absolutely. Now, let me get you settled at your hotel. I'm certain your cameraman would like to have a shower and a fresh change of clothes."

"He would," Frank said. "Thank you very much."

"What happens next?" Annja asked.

"There's a function tonight to welcome you and Frank to our city," Pradesh explained. "I don't suppose you have an evening gown with you?"

"An evening gown?" Annja frowned. "I'm here to find a tiger, not dance."

Pradesh smiled. "This will be something of a challenge." He wheeled them toward a gleaming white hotel. "But I think we will manage."

3

The hotel was gorgeous. As Annja walked into the bedroom from the steaming-hot shower she'd just enjoyed, she couldn't help but appreciate the thick shag carpet. She curled up on the bed and gave serious thought to falling right to sleep. The flight had been long, and with the stress of having to shepherd Frank through customs, she was exhausted.

Thank goodness Pradesh showed up. She smiled. He was a handsome man, and she hadn't seen a wedding ring on his finger. Although maybe that was because he didn't wear one while he worked.

Not that she was here to flirt. She had a job to do. And finding the killer was the only important thing to her right now.

Except Pradesh was picking them up in an hour for the party in their honor.

Annja sighed. Nothing worse than having to put on a

show for people. All she wanted to do was get out to the site of the murders. Apparently that would have to wait.

Her more immediate problem was what she was going to wear. Pradesh had been correct—she hadn't brought a cocktail dress with her. Why would she? When Annja had booked her flight, the only thing she thought she'd need were a good pair of boots and her usual gear.

Mingling with high society hadn't been on the agenda. Until now.

Annja laid out her best shirt and pants. Eyeing them, she frowned. There was no way that outfit was going to pass muster with Hyderabad's elite. Not a chance.

She wondered what time the stores downstairs closed. She had the credit card from the show and she could expense a new dress. But—

A knock at her door jarred her out of her thoughts. She peered through the peephole. One of the bellhops stood outside. Annja wrapped the robe a little tighter around herself and cracked the door.

"Yes?"

"Excuse me for disturbing you, Miss Creed. This was just delivered for you."

He held out a garment bag and Annja reached for it. "Thank you." She closed the door and laid the bag on the bed. A small card was tied to the hanger. Annja opened it.

I hope you don't mind my taking the liberty of getting this for you.

—Dunraj

"Who the hell is Dunraj?" Annja asked aloud. She unzipped the garment bag.

The dress inside was gorgeous. A spaghetti-strap number in black with a line of understated jewels that wound down the dress. Annja recognized it immediately as one of Paris designer Nikolai Depue's latest designs.

It must have cost a fortune.

She slipped the bathrobe off and stepped into the dress. It fit her like a glove and she couldn't help but appreciate how good she looked in the mirror on the bathroom door, how well the dress fit her curves.

I don't suppose my boots are going to look good with this, she thought. But then she noticed that bulge at the bottom of the garment bag. A pair of simple black leather heels. She stepped into them and instantly felt like a million dollars.

And that made her very uncomfortable. She didn't even know who'd sent this outfit. She looked down at her khakis on the bed and was sorely tempted to put her own clothes on instead.

Just as she reached to unzip the dress, her phone rang. "Hello?"

"Annja? It's Frank."

Frank had a room on another floor. Annja wondered what he'd be wearing tonight. He didn't exactly seem like the designer-suit type.

"Are you ready to go?"

"Yeah. Some dude showed up at my door with a penguin suit—a freaking tuxedo. Can you believe it?"

"Actually, yes," she said. "How does it fit?"

"Uh, it fits me perfectly. I have no idea who sent it, though. And I have even less of an idea how he knew my suit size."

She studied herself in the mirror and then decided the

dress would just have to do. After all, it would only be on her a couple of hours. "Let's meet downstairs."

Annja caught the elevator, and when the doors opened to the lobby, the first person she saw was Pradesh standing near the concierge station. He wore what Annja recognized as a sleek Pathani suit.

Pradesh's eyes lit up when he saw Annja. "Forgive me for being blunt. You look incredibly beautiful."

"Blunt is not necessarily a bad thing," Annja said with a smile even though he had made her uncomfortable. "Thank you for the compliment."

Pradesh gave her a short bow and then Annja heard the elevator ding behind her. Frank walked out. The tuxedo indeed looked good on him, but he didn't have nearly the confidence to pull the look off. She could tell he felt uneasy.

"Very handsome," she said as he approached.

"Very awkward," he said quietly. "I feel like everyone is staring at me. And I don't like it." He pointed at her dress. "You look amazing."

"Thank you." Annja touched him on the arm. "You'll be fine. Just try to relax." She turned to Pradesh. "So, now what?"

"I'll drive you to the party. It's being held downtown at the offices of Dunraj Incorporated."

"Did you say Dunraj?"

Pradesh nodded. "Yes, he's one of the most influential residents of Hyderabad. He's got an estimated wealth at around one billion dollars U.S."

Frank whistled. "Wow."

"Yes, his money generally elicits that reaction from

people. It certainly seems to from the group Dunraj surrounds himself with. But there you go."

"Money's not everything," Annja said. "He didn't need to buy me this dress. I have clothes that would have been fine. Well, almost fine."

Pradesh grinned. "So, is that where that came from? I wondered, but I thought it would be rude to ask. You both do look perfectly suited for the night ahead, however, so I guess Dunraj's money was put to good use—at least in this case."

Annja glanced at him. "Suited for the night ahead? And what exactly will this night entail?"

Pradesh smiled wider. "Oh, I imagine it will involve meeting an awful lot of people who have seen your show on television and who will wish to ask you all sorts of boring questions about your work and what you do. They'll flatter you, no doubt, but each of them will want something. And they'll prattle on at length about various topics you will probably have little to no interest in. You know, the usual prattling that occurs at these tiresome things."

Annja raised her eyebrows.

He leaned forward. "I've been to one or two of these before. They get rather wearing. But such is the life of an inspector. I do my best to try to bear it, but there are times I find myself marveling at my own endurance."

He led them outside to the Mercedes. Annja noticed it had been washed and waxed since their earlier trip from the airport. She again sat up front with Pradesh, while Frank maneuvered himself into the backseat, still acting incredibly pained about his outfit.

Annja caught his eye. "Frank, let it go. You look good,

now just pretend like you know you look good and you'll be fine."

He fidgeted with his tie. "The last time I wore one of these things was my junior prom. And I hated it then. So much so, I refused to wear one for my senior prom."

"What did you wear to that?" Pradesh asked.

"Shorts. Plus a bright red blazer. I looked wild."

Annja shook her head. "That sounds like quite the night. Your date must have loved that."

"Uh, yeah. We didn't stay together for very long."

"I wish I could say I'm shocked." She laughed. "But shorts and a bright red blazer don't exactly fit the picture of what most girls want their dates to wear to the prom."

"What about what I wanted to wear?" Frank asked.

Pradesh chuckled. "From what I understand about American girls and their proms, what you wanted was never really up for discussion."

"He's right," Annja agreed. "It's all about the ladies."

"It always is," Frank grumbled. He lapsed into silence and Annja watched as the city passed outside of the window.

The sun was already below the horizon, and Annja marveled at the lights of the city. Hyderabad seemed very modern. She mentioned this to Pradesh, who nodded.

"We have a rich history, but we are also firmly embracing the future. People like Dunraj are at the forefront of this move forward. With the number of developments under way in the city limits, there is hope that we will overtake several other cities and become the economic hub of India." He tilted his head. "That's the plan, anyway. We'll see if it becomes reality or not."

"And what sort of industries are you attracting?"

"Green-power companies, technology, and we even have several movie studios that are setting up shop here. The film industry in India, as you know, is tremendously popular. And Hyderabad's climate is well suited to movies and TV. Tollywood they call our small niche."

"Does Dunraj have his hand in everything that goes on in the city?"

"To a certain extent," Pradesh said. "He prefers not to be seen as a power player, but he is one. His role is often in the background. He comes from a very old family. One with its own past and characters. But he is something of a maverick and he likes that role. He's the last of his family line, though, so sometimes he can get a bit... interesting."

"I don't understand," Annja said.

"You will."

"Well, I'm looking forward to meeting him. If only to thank him for his impeccable taste."

Pradesh eyed her. "I think perhaps he is looking forward to meeting you even more."

"He must be," Frank said from behind them. "That dress makes Annja look like a knockout."

Annja took a breath and let it out slowly. "Frank, do me a favor, will you?"

"Sure thing."

"Don't talk like that tonight. All right? This is an important function, judging by what Pradesh is telling us. And if things go well, we'll be able to work here without hassle. But if things don't go well, then we'll face all sorts of complications, which I'm not a big fan of. So remember that every time you speak tonight. What you say will have a direct impact on your future. Trust me."

"Okay, Annja." Frank sighed. "I get it."

Pradesh pointed ahead of the car. "You see that building?"

"You mean the tower with the lights?"

"That is Dunraj's corporate headquarters. From there, he oversees his rather extensive empire of business interests."

"That building must have cost him a fortune," Annja said. "You weren't joking about his personal wealth, huh?"

Pradesh nodded. "At the time, it was the most expensive building construction project in all of Hyderabad. Something along the lines of what you might see in Dubai, I'd imagine." He shrugged. "But Dunraj was determined to see it built and ended up sinking massive amounts of his own money in to fund it and make sure he finished by the deadline he'd set."

"It's quite a nice design," Annja said. She hoped Pradesh didn't take her next question the wrong way, but she wanted to get a handle on her unexpected benefactor. "Is this Dunraj guy married?"

"He is Hyderabad's most eligible bachelor. No woman in the city has attracted him enough to settle down yet. Although they all try. My, do they try. And since he is, as I said, the last of his family, I believe the pressure is on him to settle produce an heir."

"Interesting." Annja suddenly felt exposed in the dress.

Pradesh pulled the Mercedes into the outer parking area and stopped before the guard shack. He flashed his credentials and the car was waved through. Carefully manicured orange trees framed the road.

"Does he make his own orange juice, too?" Annja asked absently. She wouldn't be surprised if the guy had his own orange-juice label. He seemed to have a lot of projects under way.

Pradesh smiled. "There is very little that Dunraj is not able to do. I have no doubt if he thought orange juice was worth his time he would capture the majority market share in the city. And from there, the rest of the country."

Annja glanced back over the seat at Frank. "Are you all right back there?"

"Yeah."

Pradesh slowed the car. "We're here."

Annja took one final glance at Frank. "All right, penguin boy, let's see how smooth you can be when the stakes are high."

And then she got out and followed Pradesh into the building.

4

They took an elevator with padded leather walls up to the penthouse office suite where the doors glided back to reveal an incredible party already well under way. "And here I thought we'd be early," Annja said quietly. To her relief, the attire at the party seemed predominantly Western.

And she wasn't the only one wearing a slinky black dress and heels.

But the once-overs and glares started almost immediately. Annja rolled her eyes. All she wanted to do was get out to the development and see the crime scenes.

Now she had to play nice. Or at least she had to convince the gold diggers that she wasn't here to hook Dunraj.

Frank, at her side, whispered, "You can almost smell the money in this room. It's tangible, for crying out loud."

Pradesh seemed remarkably at ease with the environment. He might not have come from money, but he wasn't out of his depth here, either.

A waiter came by carrying a silver tray with glasses of champagne. Pradesh helped himself to two and gave one to Annja.

Annja sipped the bubbly. It must have cost roughly a thousand dollars a bottle, judging by its flavor. Frank grabbed one for himself, and Annja was relieved when he didn't knock the tray over.

A DJ was set up in one corner of the cavernous reception area. A few lights were flashing in time to the lounge music. But the volume wasn't so high that Annja had to raise her voice to be heard. A few guests closer to the DJ swayed back and forth to the beat.

Others were helping themselves to small plates of appetizers set out on a grand wooden conference table. There was food from a number of cultures. Fresh sashimi, Indian specialties, a carving station and much more. Without a doubt, this party had cost a fortune.

Then Annja spotted him. She'd had no idea what Dunraj looked like before they'd arrived, but as soon as she laid eyes on the man, working the room as effortlessly as a politician, she knew it had to be him.

Dunraj looked to be about forty-eight years old. His hair was a little long, swept back in frosted waves off his face. His tanned skin was smooth, and judging by the cut of his tuxedo, he must work out quite a bit. But he wasn't flexing his guns to impress anyone. His understated manner said enough.

She glanced over at Frank. There was no way the kid measured up. He looked as if he'd been wrestled into a straitjacket and then sent out to dance in public.

Painful for him and painful to have to watch.

Dunraj seemed to be working his way across the room. With each person he met, he would either shake their hand or give them a peck on the cheek. Annja could sense the waves of charisma rolling off him.

No wonder the women here are going bonkers, she thought. He's an incredible specimen.

Pradesh was at her ear. "He's coming to see you. Try not to gawk."

Annja shot him a look. "I don't gawk. Ever."

But Pradesh only smiled. "That's what they all say, Annja. You haven't yet met the man. I'd reserve judgment."

Annja sipped her champagne and watched Dunraj continue his arc toward where they stood. If he was trying to get to Annja, she would never have guessed it. Dunraj took his time. He never appeared hurried or impatient. It was as if he knew the world would only be too happy to wait for him.

But eventually, he seemed to materialize out of the crowd directly in front of her. His smile was the first thing she noticed. It gleamed. Annja blinked and she would have sworn that time slowed down. Like in the movies.

She blinked again. Get a grip. You don't go faint at the sight of men, not even one as obviously evolutionarily superior as this.

"You must be Annja."

Annja allowed him to sweep her hand up and then she felt his lips barely brush the back of her hand. His eyes bore into hers. The effect was potent and Annja had to take a quick breath before she could respond.

"I am," Annja said, surprised at how husky her voice sounded. "You must be Dunraj."

"I hope you'll forgive me for throwing this welcome party for you and your colleague here." He turned and shook hands with Frank. "You must be Frank. Very glad to meet you."

"Hi." Frank pumped Dunraj's hand a little too hard. But at least he didn't say anything embarrassing.

Not yet.

Dunraj refocused on Annja. "I understand you've come to our wonderful city to investigate the horrible deaths that we seem to be plagued with."

"I'm not investigating it yet. I'm here at this party. But yes, that's the purpose of our visit."

"No time for pleasure, then?"

"How do you mean?"

"We have some incredible tourist attractions here. Gardens created by kings. Fabulous restaurants. Are you sure your trip doesn't allow you to see those first? Perhaps put this unfortunate business aside while you acclimate. I'm told I'm an excellent tour guide."

"I don't doubt that for a moment." Annja smiled. "And I have no doubt Hyderabad is a wonderful place. I've been impressed so far with what we've seen. And the police are obviously very efficient."

Dunraj turned to Pradesh. "The police are fantastic here. And Pradesh is perhaps the finest of them all."

Pradesh bowed briefly. "You are too kind, sir." But while that might have sounded humble, Annja noticed that Pradesh didn't bow too low. She liked that.

"Nonsense. You've always proven to be an excellent

civil servant. Your adherence to duty and honor is something to be greatly admired."

The compliments and praise seemed to come as easily to Dunraj as breathing. Annja wondered how much of his day was spent serving up platitudes.

Not that there was anything necessarily wrong with that. Dunraj obviously needed the gift of gab to accomplish his mission. And the praise didn't seem insincere.

"Are you comfortable at the hotel?"

"The hotel? It's fine. Nothing wrong with it that I could see."

Dunraj put one hand on her shoulder. It was just a touch. A warm one. "You know, we have much nicer hotels elsewhere in the city. I could make some phone calls if the hotel isn't quite to your liking. Get you and your traveling companion here into a nice suite, perhaps? It's no trouble whatsoever."

"The hotel is fine," she repeated firmly. "I've been sleeping on the floors of forests and jungles for years. I'm used to far less comfort when I travel."

Dunraj nodded. "I'm sure you must be. What a fascinating job you have. I've seen all of your shows many times over, and you've always impressed me with your candor and knowledge of subjects that most of us simply know nothing about. You're able to convey the educational background of your assignments without talking down to your audience. You have a talent, Annja, you really do."

I'm not the only talented one in the room, she thought. But she merely smiled. "Thank you very much for saying so." She sipped her champagne. "Which episode was your favorite?"

"Pardon?"

Gotcha. "I asked which episode you liked best."

Dunraj smiled, never breaking eye contact. "The one where you were in Scotland chasing down reports of the Loch Ness monster. I really need to visit there in the autumn and experience the pleasure of drinking a beer in a pub with the peat smoke and so forth, like you did in that final segment. You were able to show that Scotland has a charm all its own, even without the Loch Ness monster."

It was Annja's turn to hesitate. She hadn't expected him to be able to recount that. Perhaps Dunraj had really seen her shows.

Interesting.

Dunraj's smile grew. "I do hope you'll forgive me, but unfortunately I need to cut our time short. I've got some other guests to attend to. Please enjoy my hospitality. I will return shortly and we can talk some more then. All right?"

"Oh. Yes. Absolutely. That would be great. I'd like that." Annja blinked and then Dunraj was gone. The crowd had swallowed him up.

And the funny thing was, she missed him.

"You okay?"

She looked at Frank. "Me? Yeah, of course, I'm fine." Annja frowned. "Why would you ask me that?"

"Because you look a little pale. Like maybe your first encounter there with Captain Amazing might have been more than you bargained for."

Annja sipped her champagne. "Nothing to worry about, Frank. I'm just tired from the flight."

Frank didn't argue the point. "We should get something to eat."

"Good idea."

As they walked to the nearest table, Annja felt eyes on them. More women sizing her up, most likely. Now that Dunraj had connected with her, they were all checking her out, trying to determine if she was a rival for Dunraj's attention. Someone they would have to sort out if it became clear Dunraj fancied her.

"I told you he was something else, didn't I?" Pradesh said at Annja's elbow. "You were mesmerized and don't even realize it. Even now when he's not around you any longer."

Annja smirked. "He is something else. I'll give you that. But is he like that with everyone?"

Pradesh gestured around the room. "Do you see anyone here who isn't equally enamored of him? The women want to be with him. The men want to be like him. Dunraj is the epitome of what many in Hyderabad aspire to become."

"What's his story?"

Pradesh shrugged. "Comes from a well-respected family, as I've said, but Dunraj was never content to rely on their reputation. He was schooled abroad in Zurich and then Oxford. He speaks a number of languages, including Mandarin, Farsi and German, and that multilingualism has enabled him to reach beyond India's borders and attract both international investment and cooperation. A lot of people say he is the unofficial mayor of Hyderabad."

"And how does the mayor feel about that?"

Pradesh brushed something she couldn't see off his lapel. "I assume she's quite happy knowing that Dunraj will pour a lot of money into her next campaign. Dunraj enjoys a wonderful relationship with the mayor, and she's always ready to approve his next construction project. He has no real political aspirations. He accomplishes all of his public-service work through his construction projects. It's very much a symbiotic relationship."

Dunraj was on the far side of the room when he picked up a microphone from the DJ and the music abruptly cut out. "Ladies and gentlemen, if I could please have your attention."

Not as if he didn't already have the attention of everyone in the room. Despite the noise level and the buzzing conversations, not one person ever had their eyes off Dunraj.

Dunraj continued. "I'm so pleased you were all able to accept my invitation to attend tonight's event. I realize this was last minute."

This was last minute? She wondered what a well-planned party would have been like.

"It humbles me to have such wonderful friends and colleagues as yourselves," Dunraj continued. "Truly. Thank you so much."

Before Annja could critique his speech to Frank for laying it on too thick, Dunraj added, "My purpose in throwing tonight's party was to welcome a visitor to our great city. An American who has always impressed me with her steadfast resolve, intellect and pursuit of truth. It's my pleasure to introduce you all to Miss Annja Creed, host of *Chasing History's Monsters.*"

Annja's gut dropped, but she managed to smile and hold up her glass in acceptance of Dunraj's praise. "Thank you."

"I hope you will all take a moment to introduce yourselves to Annja and her colleague, Frank. Tell them about our city and the role it plays in India's twenty-first-century expansion and growth. And please make sure they both understand that Hyderabad is a glowing example of India's prosperity and the new hub of our nation's incredible future. Thank you and enjoy."

A few guests clapped and Dunraj handed the microphone back to the DJ. She was about to go over to him when a throng of people suddenly appeared in front of her.

And every last one of them wanted to welcome her and Frank to Hyderabad. They were like trained dogs. She smiled politely but really wanted to get out of there.

Annja looked around the room for Dunraj. But the Indian billionaire had vanished.

5

"Where'd he go?" Annja asked as she fended off throngs of well-wishers, mostly middle-aged men.

Frank, for his part, didn't seem to mind the attention a number of young women were paying him. "Where'd who go?"

"Dunraj." Annja pushed her way through the throng, straining to see above the mass of heads. But Dunraj had indeed vanished. One moment, he'd been in his reception area, and the next, he was gone.

Pradesh had also disappeared. What was going on here? Annja turned and saw what looked to be Frank giving his telephone number. She sighed and pushed back into the women around him. "All right, Frank, let's get going. Come on, now."

"Now?" He frowned. "But I'm starting to enjoy myself. There are an awful lot of very nice young women here."

"Which is exactly why I want to get the hell out of

here before your libido turns this welcome party into an orgy."

"Would that be so terrible?" Frank pleaded.

Annja grabbed him by the arm and pulled him out of the crowd. They eventually got a second to catch their breath near the entry door close to the elevator they'd rode up on.

Frank brushed himself off. "The ladies here are so forthcoming with their intimate details. Imagine."

"I don't even want to know what that means," she said. "Can we get out of here now?"

Frank looked longingly back toward the party. "Yeah, I guess. We going to the hotel?"

"I'd like to, yes. I'm exhausted. I need serious sleep if we're going to start first thing tomorrow morning."

"Can we call a taxi? I don't see Pradesh anywhere."

Annja nodded. "Me, neither. And I don't like it when our host and our minder both disappear within seconds of each other. That strikes me as sort of weird."

Frank eyed her. "You're not going to go all 'conspiracy theory' on me now, are you?" He pushed the elevator call button, and seconds later the doors slid back. Annja and Frank stepped inside, and the car descended toward the ground.

"My father had a real thing for Indian women," Frank reminisced. "I remember one time when we were Christmas shopping and there was this woman in the music store. My father was totally captivated. I get it now."

"Well, good," Annja said. "Now you two can compare notes when you get home. Nice."

Frank sighed. "Nah, he died about ten years back. We

were just getting to be really good friends when he had a heart attack."

Annja felt badly for Frank. "I'm sorry. I didn't know."

"Yeah, don't worry about it. It just bums me out sometimes when I think about him being gone. We could have had some fun times together."

She put a hand on his arm. "If it helps, I'm sure he'd be very proud of what you've accomplished in your life. Your professional life, I mean. That stunt on the airplane—" she grinned "—probably not so much."

The elevator doors opened and they were back in the lobby. They headed for the main desk. Annja was about to beckon the security guard to call them a taxi when Frank stopped her.

"Hey, there's Pradesh."

And sure enough, the policeman came striding across the lobby. "I was wondering when you'd make your escape."

Annja studied him suspiciously. "Where'd you disappear to?"

Pradesh cocked an eyebrow. "Why, down here, of course. Once Dunraj made his introduction of you and Frank, I decided it might be a good idea to have the car waiting. Neither of you strike me as being fond of mobs of ardent admirers. Well, perhaps Frank…" He smiled as he said it and even Annja had to grin.

"You could have told us."

"Now, where would the fun be in that? I imagined you making a grand exit, throwing people aside while Frank led the way to the elevator. Was I close?"

"Not even remotely," Annja said. "Aside from us taking the elevator down here again."

"Ah, well, my powers of perception aren't in the psychic realm. I apologize if I caused you any distress." He offered Annja his arm.

"No distress," she said, taking the arm to be polite. "We were going to grab a taxi back to the hotel."

"No need. I have the Mercedes waiting."

The Hyderabad night was balmy but with enough of a breeze to make it pleasant. Pradesh kept the windows down, and as they drove away from Dunraj's office park, Annja caught the scent of the trees on the breeze and suddenly felt very tired. The trip over had been a long one.

Pradesh, for his part, seemed energized. "How about a bite to eat?"

"I'm starving," Frank chimed in from the backseat. "I didn't see very much to eat at the party."

"That's because you were too busy concentrating on the women," she said. "There was an entire conference table laid out with food."

Pradesh chuckled. "Frank, I rather doubt any of those women would be as appealing as you think they are."

"Why?" Frank asked. "They seemed, uh, ready, willing and able to me."

"No doubt they are all that."

"But?"

"Well, it's just that they're also all…" He seemed to be searching for the right term. "Gold diggers, isn't that what you call them?"

Annja nodded.

"Yes. Dunraj enjoys knowing they would fight to the death if he asked them to. And they would. I have broken up one or two fights at his parties when some of the women got territorial. They don't take kindly to strangers coming into their feeding grounds, as it were."

"I'm glad we got out of there when we did."

Pradesh looked at Annja. "I know you're tired—"

"I'm not."

Pradesh held up his hand. "I can see it on your face. But I know a nice little place where the food is excellent. It would be an honor to take you both there. We could relax and talk."

"Any chance I can get changed first?" Frank asked.

"What about you? Would you prefer to change?"

Annja shrugged. "I suppose it couldn't hurt to get into some more comfortable clothes. These heels are killing me. I miss my boots."

"Very well. We can swing by your hotel and then go from there."

They got back within ten minutes thanks to the way Pradesh maneuvered through the traffic. He leaned against the Mercedes in the roundabout outside the hotel's entrance. "I'll be here."

Annja was dressed and back down in five minutes. Frank showed up two minutes later looking significantly more relaxed than he had been earlier. He wore jeans and a loose button-down shirt. Annja was relieved he hadn't opted for some obnoxious T-shirt.

Pradesh had also changed out of his suit. "Did you strip right out here in public?" Annja asked.

He laughed. "I carry a change of clothes at all times. It enables me to react to all situations."

"Good plan," Annja said as they got into the car. "So, where are we going?"

"A family restaurant. I don't know where you may

have traveled before, Annja, but the smallest, least-known restaurants are sometimes the best. It's no different here in Hyderabad. If you'll trust me to guide you, I think you will agree the meal is something spectacular."

"Sounds good to me."

Pradesh glanced in the rearview mirror. "Is that all right, Frank?"

"Sure, I'm starving."

"You like spicy food?"

"Back home I love the Indian food at a small place near my apartment. So if it's anything like that, I'm all in."

"Probably not, but we'll see."

He slipped the Mercedes in and out of traffic before getting off the busy thoroughfare and ducking onto quieter side streets. They drove slowly through a busy neighborhood and then down another side street where the noise died down. Finally, Pradesh turned into a small lot and parked the car.

"We're here."

They got out and headed for an unmarked red door. Inside, they were hit by a waft of scents that made Annja's mouth water. "Oh, my God, it smells incredible in here."

"Ajay?"

Pradesh smiled as a rotund woman rushed up, wiping her hands on her apron. She clutched him up in a giant hug. "Oh, my boy!"

Pradesh gave her a kiss and then turned to Annja and Frank. "I'd like you to meet my mother, Peta."

"Mother?" Annja smiled. "You pulled a fast one on us."

Pradesh returned her smile. "Well, this is a restaurant, but yes, I did."

"Come," Peta said after the introductions had been made. She eyed Pradesh. "The specialties?"

Pradesh nodded. "If you wouldn't mind."

"Mind? Why would I mind? It's not every night I get to cook for my only son and his friends." She beamed at them all. "Ajay is the pride of my home. A distinguished police officer. I couldn't be happier that he's brought you all here to my humble little restaurant."

She vanished into the back, and Annja heard a cacophony of dishes banging as Peta began cooking.

Pradesh smoothly dropped onto a cushion at a low table as Annja and Frank followed his lead and sat on cushions opposite him. It took Frank some time to cross his legs awkwardly. "My father died a few years ago from a heart condition," their host said. "I try to come by at least once a week when work doesn't keep me away. It's important that we still have each other."

"You're a good son," Annja said, nodding.

"So, what are we having?" Frank asked.

Pradesh grinned. "Hyderabad is known for its regional cuisine. We call it Andhra here, and it features a lot of spicy chilies, rice, lentils, some seafood and chicken dishes. My mother's specialty is preparing pickles."

"Pickles?" Frank asked, skeptical. Annja wanted to pinch him under the table but Pradesh took it in stride.

"I think you'll like them, Frank. My mother makes an incredible avakaya. Do you know what that is?"

"No."

"It's a pickle made from green mango. She also makes one from the leaves of the gongura plant. When you taste them with the other dishes, I think you'll agree this is a far better meal than what Dunraj would have served— even with all of his money behind him."

Annja took in the one other table of diners in the far corner of the rather intimate room and replied, "I don't doubt it for one moment. I can't tell you how many incredible meals I've been fortunate enough to have when I've been abroad in the past."

"Haven't you always been a broad?" Frank smirked.

Annja shot him a look. "Keep it up and I'll separate your head from your shoulders."

Frank stretched backward and almost fell over, catching himself by the edge of the table. "Yeah, right. How you going to do that?"

"Don't ask," she said. "Or you just might find out." She winked at Pradesh and he smiled.

"If the food gets too spicy, please take some of the curd that comes with the meal. It helps to neutralize the heat and will calm your stomach."

"Is this going to be very spicy?" Annja asked.

"Oh, yes. My mother is an expert at balancing heat, however, so while you may find one dish almost unbearable, she will complement it with another milder one. She's a marvel in the kitchen."

"I'm surprised she doesn't have a bigger place," Frank said.

"She used to work at a fancy hotel, but she got tired of the class of people there. She's never been as happy as when she's working for herself."

On cue, the door to the kitchen slammed open and

Peta came out bearing the first dishes. "I hope you're hungry," she fairly sang.

They were. And when Annja saw what Peta had prepared for them, she forgot all about being exhausted.

And Dunraj.

6

It was one of the best meals Annja had had in a very long time. When they were done eating, Peta closed the restaurant and served them all a strong drink she said was an old family recipe. Annja wasn't sure if it was alcoholic or not, but it was soothing and went down extremely easily.

Peta sat with them as they relaxed, helping herself to some of the drink. Annja toasted her.

"That was amazing. I can't thank you enough for your hospitality."

Frank held his glass aloft. "I second that. You are an incredible chef."

Peta beamed at them and then put her arm around her son. "Thank you. I learned to cook when I was older. I forced myself to learn how to make the best meals for Pradesh. He studied so hard in school."

Pradesh smiled at his mother. "It was a huge help when I was so exhausted from studying."

"And now he is a famous policeman, keeping our city

safe and free from corruption." Annja saw the woman's pride. Having lost Ajay's father, it was clear that her son now occupied all of her heart.

Pradesh demurred. "Annja and Frank are here to investigate the deaths of those people in the development."

Peta frowned. "A terrible thing. To imagine a creature attacking in such a way. It's horrifying."

"What do you think the creature is?" Annja asked. "A rogue tiger, perhaps?"

Peta stared at her. "In all my years I've never heard of a tiger stalking people in a city this big." She shrugged. "But I am just a cook."

"But the development—if I'm correct—is on the outskirts," Annja said. "Perhaps it's pushing into the domain of a tiger?"

Pradesh ran a hand along his chin. "It's possible, I suppose. But we've found no tracks at the crime scenes. And a tiger large enough to take down a full-grown man would leave behind some sign."

"Is the area well paved?"

Pradesh shook his head. "In some places, yes, but the area where the bodies were found was moist from the landscaping irrigation systems. And we found hardly a trace of anything in the mud. Our best forensics people were unable to locate any hair or DNA that would confirm it was a tiger."

"Maybe it's the ghost of a tiger," Frank suggested hopefully.

"Frank," Annja said, "ghosts?"

Frank helped himself to more of the drink from the small jug Peta had placed on the table and shrugged.

"Just trying to contribute a little something to the conversation."

Pradesh sighed. "I honestly wish I had more information to share with you. As you know, it's an ongoing police investigation. All I can say is we are stumped."

"Have you increased patrols in the area?"

He nodded. "We have two teams down there covering off twenty-four hours a day. They stay in constant radio contact. But something tells me if the killer is determined, not even the presence of the police will dissuade it...or...him."

Peta got to her feet. "Just promise me you'll be careful out there." She frowned. "I can't even bear to think about losing you, too."

Pradesh stood and kissed his mother on the cheek. "I'm not going anywhere, Mother. I promise."

Peta eyed Annja. "Make sure he doesn't, would you?"

Annja was taken aback. "Uh, all right."

Peta smiled. "I see things, Annja. Even things people wish to hide. I see much about you that others do not. I know what you are capable of."

Annja had no reply for that but fortunately Pradesh nudged his mother toward the kitchen. "Yes, yes, we'll bring the dishes in."

"I'm just saying—" But Pradesh had already pushed her through the doors. When he came back, he was grinning sheepishly.

"I apologize for that. My mother sometimes gets a bit...strange when she has that drink. She's claimed for years to be psychic. I don't think there's anything to it, of course. But she insists. There's no real harm in it, I suppose."

"She might be right," Annja said. "You never know."

Pradesh frowned. "I try not to encourage it in her. I've seen what the promise of supernatural possibilities can do to people. It gets them so fixated on the possibility of escaping their place in life that they end up ignoring what they have to deal with right in front of them. It becomes a never-ending cycle of disappointment." He glanced over his shoulder. "And don't worry, I'm good at taking care of myself."

"You know mothers," Annja said. "She just wants to make sure her son is well looked after. You can't blame her for loving you."

"You sound like you speak from experience."

Annja shook her head. "I never knew my parents. I was orphaned at a very early age. You're extremely lucky to know yours."

Pradesh paused. "Yes, I am. Thank you for reminding me of that."

A sudden snore erupted from Frank. Annja glanced down and saw her cameraman had fallen back against his pillows. His mouth was ajar and each breath brought a new grinding outburst.

"Good grief."

Pradesh laughed. "It seems he appreciates my mother's cooking. She'll be pleased."

"Not sure if it's that, the trip over or that drink your mom served us. Or maybe it's all three." Annja smiled. "A potent combination."

"Help me with the dishes and I'll drive you both back to the hotel. A good night's sleep will be the best thing for all of us. We can take a drive out tomorrow and start your investigation. I'm really interested to see what you come up with."

"So am I."

"You've done this type of thing before? With other so-called monsters?"

Annja shrugged. "Most times when people think there are monsters, it turns out there's a perfectly reasonable explanation. But once or twice..." Her voice trailed off as she remembered some of the more bizarre assignments she'd been on when events didn't always add up so neatly.

"Yes, well, as I said, a good night's sleep and we'll get started." Pradesh scooped up some of the dishes and carried them into the kitchen. Annja did the same, and after several trips, they'd cleaned the dining area.

Peta herded them out of the kitchen. "I can finish here."

Pradesh helped Frank up, and between them both, they managed to get him back into the car.

Annja slid into the front seat. "Will your mom be okay?"

"She lives above the restaurant. She'll be fine. The neighbors all keep an eye on her. They love having her here. I think she's doing some catering now, as well— smaller weddings mostly. She gives them such a nice discount." He started up the Mercedes and drove back onto the main thoroughfare.

At the hotel, Pradesh waited until Annja had Frank out of the car. "How about eight o'clock tomorrow? Will that be all right? Or do you need more time?"

"Eight o'clock." Annja shifted Frank's weight. "That will be fine."

"Good night, then."

"See ya." Annja turned toward the hotel and nudged Frank into the lobby. Fortunately, it wasn't crowded and she saw few people as they made it to the elevator. She propped Frank against the wall of the elevator and pushed the button for his floor.

Frank's eyes opened immediately. "Are we all clear?"

Annja punched him in the arm. "What the hell, Frank? You were sound asleep a minute ago."

He pushed away from the wall and smiled. "Pretty good, huh?"

"I thought you were drunk."

Frank shrugged. "Listen, Annja, if there's one thing I'm good at, it's holding my booze. It takes a lot more than that drink to knock me on my ass. As delicious as it was, I don't mind telling you."

"So what's up? Why the theatrics?"

"I figured it might let Pradesh open up. Maybe he'd reveal something about the case he didn't feel comfortable saying in front of me."

"Well, he didn't."

"Yeah, I know. Can't blame a guy for trying, though."

Annja watched the numbers advance on the elevator. "Pradesh said he'd meet us here at eight. That leaves plenty of time to get some solid sleep."

"Yeah," Frank said slowly.

Annja glanced at him. "What?"

"Nothing, it's just that I didn't fly halfway around the world to get a good night's sleep. I can do that anytime back home." He winked at her. "I came here for some good story action."

"Meaning what, exactly?"

Frank looked at his watch. "It's eleven o'clock. What say you to a drive to the development now? You know, see for ourselves what's going on out there. Firsthand."

"It's pitch-dark. We won't be able to see anything. We need flashlights and gear."

"All of which I've got with me," Frank said.

"We'd have to rent a car."

"They have taxis downstairs. We can take one to a car-rental agency," Frank said. "This time of night, it shouldn't take us more than twenty minutes to reach the site."

Annja frowned. "I don't know. I feel bad about going behind Pradesh's back like this."

"You here to make friends or to uncover the truth, Annja?"

The elevator dinged as it came to a stop at Frank's floor. He looked at her. "If we get stopped by the cops, we can always tell them you couldn't sleep because of jet lag or—"

"Oh, sure, blame it on me."

"You're the pretty one. They might zap me off to some sort of stink-hole jail where you'd never hear from me again."

Frank stepped out of the elevator. "Listen, I'm going to get changed. Meet me downstairs in the lobby in twenty minutes. I really think we should check it out before we get all official tomorrow with Pradesh."

Annja pushed the button for her floor again. "I'll think about it."

Frank clapped his hands. "Awesome."

"I didn't say I—" But the elevator doors cut off the

rest of her sentence. The car descended and Annja leaned against the wall. She was tired. Full of good food.

And good drink.

Sleepy.

She was curious, of course, but her curiosity could wait until morning.

Couldn't it?

The elevator dinged again and she stepped out onto her floor. She walked down the hallway and slid her key card into the lock.

Once inside, she leaned against the door and gazed longingly at the huge bed in front of her.

It looked so utterly inviting. She could turn on the air conditioner and sink beneath the covers and be asleep within moments.

She sighed and walked into the bathroom. "I'm getting too old for this craziness."

But in another moment, she was changing her clothes to go meet Frank.

7

"Do you even know where we're going?"

Frank shot her a look. "I may never have been to Hyderabad before, but most cities are laid out logically."

Annja sniffed. "Ever been to Boston?" She paused. "Just try not to get us lost, okay? It would be embarrassing if we had to call Pradesh for help."

Frank shrugged. "Like I said, we didn't come here to make friends. We've got a story to chase down."

"Friends," Annja said, "are one of the most important things in the world. And I, for one, do not want to make Pradesh feel like we were taking advantage of him. Or his mother."

"So tell him you couldn't sleep and you dragged me out of bed to come to this place. He'll believe you... I think he likes you."

"What?" Annja looked at Frank. "And just how did you arrive at that particular theory?"

"How he looks at you. The way he smiles. It's obvious if you're paying attention."

Annja sniffed. "Frank, the only thing you pay attention to are creatures with breasts."

"Well, I had time tonight when I wasn't being mobbed by my more rabid admirers."

"Any voice mails waiting for you?"

"No," he said. "Maybe they have rules over here like they do in the States. Y'know, don't call for a day or so afterward so you don't seem too eager. Stuff like that."

"Those women were there for one thing tonight—Dunraj. The only reason they mobbed you was because Dunraj told them to. And since they'll do anything to please Dunraj, that meant they were going crazy over you."

Frank was quiet for a moment. "So, what you're really saying is that I missed my chance."

"Frank!" Annja elbowed him. "Save your fantasies. I don't want to hear about them."

"Fine."

Frank wheeled off the highway after another ten minutes. He frowned. "Okay, so this is where it will probably be tougher to navigate. Google was a little sketchy on details about this place." He peered out of the windshield and pointed at a sign. "Does that say Road Closed?"

Annja studied it. "Frank, that's written in Hindi script. I have no idea what it says. Hindi is not one of the languages I understand. Do you?"

"Uh, no." Frank sighed. "Okay, we'll just have to wing it."

"Are you still thinking this was such a good idea?"

"Of course. We're on the outskirts of the city. All we

have to do is look for a modern residential dwelling. That shouldn't be too hard to find." He ran a hand through his hair. "Now, once I got off the highway, the map said to take a left and drive for a mile."

Annja sighed. "I could be back in my hotel room sound asleep. I could be getting the rest I need to make sure this assignment is handled properly and professionally. Instead, I'm driving around a foreign city with a guy who has no idea where he's going. Spectacular ending to a weird night."

Frank pointed a finger at her. "Hey, it's not actually the city right here. These are the outskirts, so that's not the right terminology. But I know exactly where I'm going, Annja. I just like having you think I don't."

"Really?"

Frank bit his lip. "Kinda."

Annja exhaled a breath and then forced herself to suck in another quickly. "Just shut up and find the place already, would you?"

For the next fifteen minutes, Frank maneuvered his way down back roads. It was incredibly dark. She spotted smaller homes with what looked like fenced-in areas for animals. Tall, spindly trees broke up the majority of the flat landscape. Wadis and canals dotted the rural area.

"Wouldn't be too difficult to imagine a rogue tiger roaming around here looking for something to eat," she said. "We're only a few miles away from the heart of Hyderabad, but just outside that it's so rural."

"I thought tigers stuck more to the countryside."

"We're pretty country here, Frank."

"I guess."

They drove for several more minutes, the tires of the

car bouncing over small potholes in the asphalt and dirt. And then Annja saw the glow of lights in the distance. "There. You think maybe that's it?"

Frank shrugged. "I'd guess it would have to be. Are those mountains behind the development?"

Annja squinted. "Tough to see exactly, but the lights cast a glow out in that direction. We probably won't know until the sun comes up tomorrow morning."

"You mean later today."

"What?"

Frank pointed at the clock on the dashboard. "Good morning. Time for that continental-breakfast buffet downstairs."

Annja sighed. "All right, whatever. We've got bigger things to deal with right now."

"Like big, ferocious tigers. Or strange, mysterious beasts."

Annja frowned. "More like those two roving police patrols Pradesh mentioned while you were pretending to be asleep. Remember?"

Frank groaned.

"Let's find a place to park the car and go on foot." Annja peered out the window. "That probably means sneaking through drainage ditches and whatnot."

Frank slowed the car to a stop and then looked at Annja. "Uh, correct me if I'm wrong, but wouldn't places like that be exactly where a hungry tiger would creep while it's looking for meaty things to eat?"

"Absolutely."

The look on Frank's face was precious. A mixture of fear and excitement.

Annja patted him on the shoulder. "Well, we're here

now and I'm wide-awake, so it would be a waste not to use this chance to get a closer look."

Outside, the humid night air buzzed with mosquitoes, but Annja had gotten used to being ravaged by them enough over the years.

Frank, however, promptly began smacking himself silly as the hordes attacked his pale skin.

"Try to ignore them," she said. "Otherwise, they'll drive you right out of your mind."

"Easier said than done, Annja." Frank smacked another one and left a smear of blood across his cheek.

"Then think of it this way—that blood on your cheek can be smelled by a tiger, so it's probably in your best interest to not kill the bugs that have just taken your precious fluid. Got it?"

"Yeah."

Annja pointed to the trunk. "You brought the gear?"

Frank walked back to the car and popped the lid. Inside, Annja saw his small backpack. "That's it?"

"What?" Frank reached into the bag and brought out what looked like a regular DSLR camera. He held it up. "This is a Canon Eos 5D Mark II. Shoots full high-definition video and does really well in low-light conditions. It'll work just fine for tonight. And if the cops do catch us, they probably won't even realize we were shooting video footage on this."

"How much room on the memory card?"

"Plenty. Plus, I've got two extra memory cards with me. But I don't think we'll need them."

Frank rummaged through the bag and came up with something that looked like a handheld vacuum cleaner. "What the hell is that?"

"A handheld FLIR—forward-looking infrared detector. It comes in handy on nights like this when you want to scan the immediate area and make sure you aren't walking into the jaws of a hungry tiger. Or a scary monster, for that matter."

Frank switched the device on and a small LCD screen lit the night. He moved it around, aiming it into the darkness. Then he pointed at the screen. "The warmer the potential target is, the darker red it will be. The device takes an ambient-temperature reading of the air around us and then uses differences to designate heat signatures of animals and other living stuff that might be lurking in the night."

Annja smiled. "Now, that is a good piece of gear. I could have used something like this on a number of occasions."

Frank shut the trunk and handed Annja an extra flashlight. "I don't recommend using the lights unless it's absolutely necessary. Our night vision will go to hell if we switch them on."

Annja took the FLIR from Frank. "Would you prefer I take point on this excursion?"

"Well, you are the host of the show, after all," Frank said. "How would it look if the cameraman was suddenly leading these outings? I wouldn't want your reputation to suffer."

"Oh, thank you for your concern. But you're right. I'd probably look like I was scared, and we can't have that, can we?" Annja moved the FLIR around to get used to scanning with it. "I can actually see the lay of the ground in front of us with this thing, too."

Frank nodded. "It's very handy."

Annja studied him. "All right, are you ready to do this?"

"If you mean potentially run into cops, get attacked by a man-eating tiger and run afoul of the nicest guy in Hyderabad, then absolutely."

Annja smiled. "How are your nerves?"

Frank put a finger on his neck, felt for his pulse and then nodded. "Completely shot."

"That's what I like to hear," she said. "Try to stay close but not too close. Everything will be just fine. I promise."

"Really?"

"No, but it sounded good when I said it, didn't it?"

"Yeah."

Annja studied the darkness, scanned it with the FLIR and then looked back at Frank. "We're clear. Let's go."

8

The residential complex was surrounded by an undulating open ground that dipped and leveled out every few feet. To Annja, it looked as if it had once been farmland that someone had sold to the developer. She stopped. She'd never even asked if Dunraj owned this place. But it seemed like a viable assumption. He seemed to own pretty much everything else in Hyderabad, and something like this would be right up his alley: a high-end complex for the ultrawealthy.

But that didn't mean Dunraj had imported a tiger to stalk his residents. What would he get out of that? Annja shook her head and scanned the area with the FLIR again, but nothing showed up on the screen.

Moreover, she didn't…feel anything. And usually right before anything bad happened, Annja would… sense something was up. But so far on this moonless night, she felt nothing out of the ordinary.

Good.

She glanced back at Frank, who took a step and promptly fell face-first into a puddle. He came up blubbering and clawing at his face.

"Be quiet!" Annja said. "There's not much noise out here and sound carries farther at night."

"I'm fine, thanks for asking." Frank wiped the greasy muck from his face.

"Make sure you don't break that camera." Annja kept moving forward, crossing a drainage ditch and a narrow culvert. She took it slow in case she happened across a lounging tiger. But the FLIR again proved its worth and showed no signs of life except for the ever-present mosquitoes.

Annja ignored Frank's hushed grumbling and brought them within two hundred yards of the development. There, she squatted to study the layout.

The area ahead of them sloped upward out of the culvert to a fence. She initially thought it would be a problem getting through the fencing, but a quick glimpse down the wire told her it was still in the process of being installed and there were several areas where it was possible to step through.

The development itself comprised elaborate mansions in a grand style reflective of the Hindu culture. The landscaping gave them the appearance of being something out of an ancient kingdom.

A few of the homes were lit by a single light, but it was otherwise quite dark. There were streetlights, but they hadn't been finished yet. By the look of things, several residents had moved in long before the complex was completed. Probably in a rush to get in there first for bragging rights.

On the way in, she'd studied the ground for any tracks. But like Pradesh had said, there seemed to be no sign of tigers.

There were an awful lot of footprints, however. Whether they'd been made by construction workers or by someone else, Annja couldn't be sure.

Frank nudged her from behind. "What's the holdup?"

"I'm trying to see what our choices are for gaining access."

He pointed at a hole in the fence. "Seems like a good place to start right there."

She held him back. "Hold on a second, would you? We haven't seen or heard any of the police patrols yet."

"Probably asleep." He started to rise when Annja grabbed him by the sleeve and yanked him back into the dirt. She'd heard the unmistakable sound of a car engine.

"Quiet!" she whispered. And then she ducked down as the first arc of light swept the area where Frank had just been standing.

The slow thrum of the motor told Annja that the police car was on a routine patrol. The light swept over them a few times before the engine cranked up and the car moved off.

But still she held Frank down. "Wait."

"Why?"

"Trust me."

She listened and heard the motor die suddenly. As if they'd turned a corner.

Time to move.

"Okay, Frank, let's get to that hole in the fence and get

through it quickly. Make sure you pick out a spot away from the fence to hide in. The darker, the better."

Frank was up and moving even as Annja finished giving him instructions. As she made her way to the fence, she knew they were about to cross a line. Once on the other side, they'd officially be trespassing.

She wondered how Pradesh would feel about that.

Well, she thought, the trick would be to get in and get out without him ever knowing. She checked her watch. An hour on the inside just to get the lay of the land.

The chain links bit at her arms, but Annja ducked through and then hustled across the small road the police car had driven down. Across the way, Frank was huddled underneath an overhang by what looked like an administration building. He had a small piece of paper unfolded and was studying it with a red-lensed penlight.

"What's that?"

Frank looked up. "Map I made of the layout of this place. I marked the crime scenes on here."

Annja smiled. "Good move."

Frank stabbed his finger at the paper, keeping his voice low. "We're here. We need to head west and find the culvert running in that direction. That's where they found that guy Gupta."

"Hopefully, they don't have another police patrol on the scene."

"This late at night?"

Annja shrugged. "They might just be parked up to discourage curious trespassers like us."

"Ah."

"I'll take point." She held the FLIR ahead of her and got a bearing. Annja stuck close to the walls and fences of the community. She was impressed with the layout. The place had obviously been designed to grant the residents the feeling of status, but it was still homey.

She glanced behind her at Frank. He was no ninja, of course, but he might just turn out to be all right.

As much of a wannabe Casanova as he was, he seemed to realize this assignment could really help further his career. If he wasn't so focused on scoring with the ladies, they might make this a compelling piece of television.

Annja approached a corner and paused. The area around it was wide-open and offered views in each direction. They could see a lot, but Annja and Frank could also be seen. If someone was looking.

Annja paused. She and Frank needed to head west, which would put them right in line with another corner of the complex. The question was, what was waiting down there that they couldn't see? If the police were stationed there, they would see Annja and Frank.

She turned and gestured for Frank.

"What's up?"

Annja pointed. "This corner exposes us. We've got no cover for at least a hundred yards, and if the cops surprise us, we'll be caught in the open. I don't like advancing unless I've got cover and concealment."

Frank studied his map. "We'd have to go outside the fence to use the ground to conceal us."

"We can't backtrack now. We'll waste too much time." Annja looked at the map over Frank's shoulder. "What's that?"

"I don't know. I got this off the computer. Figured we'd find out once we got here."

She peered closer. It looked like an extra culvert running out of the complex, but not one that was easily accessible. So how did you get into it?

She looked at the road. And grinned. "A manhole."

Frank frowned. "A manhole?"

"Yeah. You don't happen to have any tools with you, do you?"

"Like what? Something to pry a lid off?"

"Preferably."

Frank shook his head. "No. I don't."

Annja could use her sword, of course. But how would she explain that to Frank? She never wanted anyone at work to know her secret if she could possibly avoid it. That her life had been forever changed on the day she'd brought the broken shards of Joan of Arc's sword together for the first time in hundreds of years. That the sword had become whole once again—right in front of her. That the sword of Joan of Arc had somehow chosen her and was now the sword of Annja Creed.

But they needed to get into the manhole.

Annja made a decision. "Can you go back down to the hole in the fence and see if there were any tools there?"

"What are you going to do?"

She pointed. "I'll scout ahead and see if there's anything I can use. Otherwise, I'll sneak up and see if we can avoid the manhole trip."

Annja watched him go and then moved out into the road, locating the manhole cover. It was bolted down. This was going to have to be quick.

She reached into the otherwhere and grasped the sword, which hung there, waiting for her. Holding it in her hands flooded her system with strength. The sword blade cast a grayish glow into the night, and Annja desperately hoped it wouldn't attract anyone.

She shoved the point under the lip of the cover and then pried with all of her strength. She heard the bolts give one at a time, reluctantly at first, but then they came off fast.

Once they were out, she leaned into the sword and the cover came loose.

Annja slid it back slowly, hoping the grating sound on the asphalt wasn't as loud as she thought it was.

She shoved the FLIR into the hole and scanned around. A few rats scurried for cover, splashing through the darkness.

But otherwise, it seemed deserted. Annja put the sword away and waited for Frank to return.

Another thirty seconds passed before he came hustling around the corner with a big screwdriver. He held it up like a trophy until he saw Annja squatting near the opening.

He dropped to all fours. "How the hell did you manage that?"

Annja frowned. "I found a pry bar farther up. But of course once I got the lid up, I dropped it down there somewhere. Probably never find it now."

Frank shrugged. "At least you got it open."

"Yeah."

He looked into the hole. "We really have to go in there?"

"If we want to get to the crime scenes, yes."

Frank blanched. "It stinks down there."

"And it's only going to get worse."

Frank eyed her. "Does any of this stuff ever bother you?"

Annja nodded. "All of it. Now get going."

He hesitated and then jumped. Annja heard him splash and then followed him. It was a short drop of only five feet. Annja stood and hauled the manhole cover into place. At least now they hadn't left a calling card behind.

Frank's voice cut through the darkness. "Flashlight coming on. Watch your eyes."

Red light lit up the culvert. Annja looked ahead and then behind them. "Which way?"

Frank pointed. "There."

"On we go."

9

In the darkness, even with the red flashlight illuminating part of the culvert, it was difficult to see exactly what lay ahead. Annja sloshed through the dank water and tried her best to breathe through her mouth so she wouldn't have to put up with the intense stench. There was no way she and Frank would surprise anyone, making as much noise as they were.

Behind her, Frank retched twice. "This is horrible."

"The things we do for a story," she replied. "You think this is bad? I could tell you stories that would make you run home screaming to your mother."

"Leave my mother out of this." He retched again. "How much farther?"

She shrugged. Stooped as she was it was impossible to get a good read on where they were. "Maybe a few hundred feet."

"Whose idea was it to drop into a sewer again?"

"You were the one who wanted to come along on this jaunt in the first place. You want to blame someone, blame yourself. You could be asleep right now."

"Yeah, but we wouldn't be able to see this in the morning with Pradesh."

"Exactly."

Annja thought she saw something ahead. "Turn out the flashlight."

"What? Why? I don't want to trip and fall face-first in this stuff. The puddle was bad enough."

"I think we're coming out of the tunnel. Kill that light."

Frank muttered something but shut the flashlight off. Annja stopped and peered. Yes, there was definitely an opening up ahead of them. The question was: Where did it open up? The last thing Annja wanted was to come out and be exposed.

She'd have to scout.

"Stay here."

"What? No way. I'm not staying in this stinking cesspool any longer than I have to. Let me go with you."

Annja glanced back. "You want to take this one?"

"Better than staying here in the sewer."

Annja stepped aside. "Fine. Go scout the scene but try not to make any noise, all right? I need to know that it's clear for us to proceed."

Frank mock saluted her and then pushed past. "I'll be back."

"Thanks, Arnold."

Annja watched him plod through the few remaining feet of tunnel and then disappear outside. She closed her eyes and prayed silently. Please don't screw this up.

When she opened her eyes, Frank was in front of her. "You okay?"

"Yeah," she said. "Just hoping you didn't walk into an ambush."

"Ambush?" Frank frowned. "Annja, we're not playing 'Call of Duty' here. It's just trespassing." He shrugged. "Well, plus the possibility of a monster."

"Which I take it you did not run into."

"Right." Frank turned. "The culvert ends in a ditch, and according to my map, it puts us right about where we need to be. I saw what looked like crime-scene tape a few yards away."

"Good work."

"Thanks."

Annja gestured with her hand. "All right, lead on."

He turned and Annja followed him out. Frank paused and looked around. Annja smiled. He wasn't a commando by any means, but he was developing some degree of smarts. He hadn't led them into a police checkpoint at least.

Frank pointed to his left. "Ditch is that way," he said with a whisper.

She nodded and then slipped over the edge of the drainage ditch, sticking close to the ground.

In the next instant she froze. The sound of an engine. Annja glanced back and saw that Frank was already fully exposed.

"Don't move!" she whispered.

Frank ignored her and dropped, but then kept absolutely still. It helped that they were wearing dark clothes. Annja pressed her face into the dirt and prayed the cops would drive by.

As long as we don't move, we should be fine, she thought. After all, it was movement that drew the eye at night.

The cops probably didn't expect to see two Americans slinking through a field, either, so hopefully they wouldn't notice.

Annja counted to thirty and then risked looking up. The cop car had just passed their location. She could hear the conversation of the men inside but she understood none of it. But judging from the tone, they were excited about something.

Just so long as it's not us, she thought.

The car continued on its way, and when Annja judged it safe, she waved Frank on.

They moved slowly and without sudden motions that would draw the eye.

Eventually, they reached the edge of the crime scene. Annja looked at the tape with its fancy script in bold and felt bad for what she was about to do. Then again, the forensics team would have already taken up much of the evidence. So she wasn't destroying the crime scene. More like just checking it out for anything they might have missed.

Annja slid under the tape and down into the ditch.

Of course, the body of the deceased was long gone, but Annja couldn't help feeling a little uncomfortable. Someone had died here, she thought. And I'm disturbing the place where they were killed.

Frank came tumbling into the ditch a second later, nearly colliding with Annja, who only just managed to jump out of the way at the last moment.

"Sorry."

"*Swan Lake* dancer you ain't," she said. "Be careful with that camera, too. I doubt the company would be happy if you broke it."

Frank hauled the DSLR out and turned it on. "You want to do a shot here right now?"

Annja frowned. Did she?

"What the hell."

While Frank got ready, Annja wiped the muck from her face. She'd given up a long time ago on trying to keep makeup on for shots like this.

Frank looked out from behind the camera. "Ready when you are."

Annja cleared her throat. "I hope the audio levels are okay, because I'm not about to speak in my regular voice for this."

Frank shrugged. "If not, the sound guys can amp it up when we get back to the States."

Annja saw the red light come on and knew he was recording. She looked into the camera and was just about to start talking when Frank held up his hand.

"Wait a minute."

"What's the problem?"

He slowly lowered the camera. "There's a kid behind you."

"What?"

And then she felt the indescribable sensation of a metal blade being pressed into the back of her neck.

"Does this kid have a knife, Frank?"

Frank nodded. "Uh, yeah."

"That's kind of an important piece of information. Maybe next time forget the kid part and just tell me there's someone with a knife, okay?"

"Yeah, cool."

Annja held her hands up. "Relax, okay? We're not here to hurt you."

She heard a whisper. "Turn around. Slow."

Annja shifted and then turned. The kid kept the knife pressed against her throat. He couldn't have been more than ten years old.

But he looked quite serious.

And the knife was no joke. It must have been nearly as long as his forearm and he held it with confidence. As if he knew how to use it.

"Who are you?"

"My name is Annja. That's Frank."

Frank held up a hand. "Hey, how's it going?"

"Why are you here?"

His English is good, Annja thought. School? He didn't look as if he'd live here. His clothes were in bad shape. Tattered. Full of holes.

"We mean no harm," she said. "We came here to find out about the monster."

"The monster?"

"The one that killed three people. Do you know anything about the creature that did it?"

The kid frowned. "The police are here. Maybe I should take you to them. Perhaps they will reward me."

"Or you might get into worse trouble," Annja said. "After all, you're trespassing here, too, aren't you?"

He frowned deeper. "I have to. My family is poor and I can sell some of the things these rich people discard. It helps my family. This is my job."

He looked proud when he said that last part. It tugged at her heart.

"I have a proposition for you."

"What?"

"How about we hire you to work for us?"

His eyes narrowed. "Doing what?"

"You tell us what you know about the monster, and I'll pay you for your knowledge." Annja reached into her pocket and came out with a roll of money. The boy's eyes lit up like fireworks when he saw the amount.

"This would help your family, wouldn't it?"

He nodded. "Give it to me."

Annja held it back, aware that he might try to rob her regardless. "You'll have it all if you help us, okay?"

She could see his inner debate playing out. Should he try to take the money by force?

Annja didn't let him make that decision. As soon as he let his guard down, she slapped his hand and sent the blade sprawling across the ditch. Before he could recover, Annja stepped on the knife.

"I'm offering you a job. I won't double-cross you, I promise. You give us the information we need and you get paid."

"You will not lie?"

Annja shook her head. "Absolutely not."

"All right. But I need my knife back first."

Annja eyed him. "You won't try anything with it? I'd hate to have to get mean with you."

"I won't."

Annja moved her foot and quick as a flash the boy scooped up the blade. "Now give me the money."

"First you give us the information. Tell me what you know about the monster."

The boy smiled as if she was stupid. "There is no monster."

"There isn't?"

He shook his head. "Oh, no. There's something much worse."

10

Frank moved closer. "What's your name, kid?"

The boy looked Frank over, sizing him up. Annja fought back a smile when she saw that the kid didn't seem to think much of the man. Some people just didn't command respect.

After a minute, the boy shrugged. "Deva."

"Deva, I'm Frank. This is Annja."

Deva's eyes tracked back to Annja and the roll of cash she held. "So, what do you wish to know?"

"The three people who were killed here, some people seem to think that a tiger did it. Or maybe a monster." Annja eyed him. "But you don't agree with that?"

"No."

"And you know what happened?"

"It was not a tiger."

"Was it another animal of some kind?" she asked.

"I do not know of any animal that could do the things that were done to those people," Deva said. "Except one."

"Which one?"

Deva looked at her. "Man."

Frank leaned in even closer. "You saw it happen?"

Deva shrugged. "They come to the rich houses and take people away. Then they bring them back after they are done killing them. I have seen them several times do this."

"But you didn't tell the police," Annja said. "Why?"

Deva straightened his thin body. "If I do not work, my family will have nothing. My mother is very sick, and my father already works very hard to help my brothers and sisters. If I go to the police, they will stop me from working."

Annja studied him. "How old are you, Deva?"

"Ten."

She shook her head. What happened to the innocence of childhood? It seemed intolerably cruel to expect a ten-year-old boy to have to work.

"It's all right," she said. "We won't tell them what you told us. I know what it's like to have responsibilities. Your family counts on you, don't they?"

"Yes. Very much."

Annja nodded. "I'll only ask you one more thing and then I'll give you your money. Is that all right?"

"What do you want to know?"

Annja glanced around. "Can you show us where these men come into the development?"

Deva's eyes widened. "Why do you want to know that? You might run into them if you are not careful." He thumbed at Frank. "That is how I found you. I listened. He makes too much noise."

Annja smiled. "I agree with you. He does. But he's getting better."

"Not for a long time, I think."

Frank sighed. "Well, hopefully we won't be here all that long and I won't have to learn how to move so quietly."

Deva stared at the ground and didn't say anything for a long moment. "I will show you. But then I wish to be paid."

"You got it."

Deva poked his head over the lip of the ditch. "You must be quiet and move when I move. The police cars come around here all night."

"Lead the way, Deva," said Annja. "We'll follow."

Deva nodded and then vanished over the lip. Annja started to follow him when Frank pulled her back.

"Wait."

"What is it, Frank?"

"We really doing this? Trusting a kid?"

"You have another idea? He knows the lay of the ground in this place. And if he can point us toward the proper direction for this investigation, then all the better."

"Yeah, but it feels like we're taking advantage of him."

Annja raised her eyebrows. "Taking advantage of him? Frank, did you see how much cash I'm giving him? If anyone's getting ripped off here, it's me!"

Deva poked his head back over the rim of the ditch. "What is taking you two so long? Please hurry!"

Annja scrambled out. Deva was already across the street, moving quickly down a side pathway that ran between several of the houses.

Annja glanced back and saw Frank moving across the street toward her. Once they were in the shadow of the pathway, it would be harder for the police to spot them unless they shone the light in their direction.

But Deva seemed to have a pretty good idea of the schedule the cops kept. That alone was worth the price she was paying him.

She was concerned, though. If there really were some criminals killing people, then what was the point of it? Some plot for hire? Were they assassins of some sort hired to kill residents here?

But where was the sense in that?

Annja sighed. She figured that logic and murder had very little to do with each other.

In the distance, a dog barked, shattering the silence. Deva froze.

Annja followed suit. And so did Frank.

The dog barked a few more times and then Annja could hear the sound of a door opening and shutting. Deva relaxed and continued moving forward.

Annja frowned. Now that she knew there wasn't a monster, her level of fear had increased. The night seemed to hold too many shadows. Too much potential for a dangerous encounter.

She had the sword, of course, but again, if Frank saw it… How would she explain that to him? And would he be able to keep his mouth shut back at the office?

Doubtful.

Deva came to the end of the path. Ahead of them, it was lighter, and Annja again felt the sensation of being exposed in the open. Deva crouched near the corner of a house and seemed to be waiting for something.

Annja crept closer and put her hand over his ear to whisper, "Is everything all right?"

Deva nodded. "Police."

They shrank back into the shadows as another cruiser crawled along out on the road. It passed by without incident, and Annja felt Deva's thin body slump.

"You okay?" she asked.

"There seem to be a lot of them out tonight," Deva explained. "But fortunately, we are almost there."

"Okay."

"Stay close to me," the boy said. "There is open ground ahead of us and we must move quickly."

"I like the way you think."

Deva darted out and Annja followed. Frank kept pace with them. Deva ran toward the far side of the road and then hopped a low line of bushes, pausing on the other side to wait for them to catch up.

They lay on a steep embankment that led down to another series of ditches and culverts. Deva pointed to where Annja could just make out mountains in the dark. "They come from there."

"There's a village in that direction?"

Deva looked at Annja as if she had three heads. "No. They come from the mountains. The mountains."

Frank huffed and puffed beside them. "What—like, they live inside the mountains?"

"Yes."

Frank eyed Annja. "This is getting better by the minute."

"I'll say." She looked at Deva. "So, they come in from this direction? Through the ditches and the culverts? The tunnels?"

Deva nodded. "Yes. And this is the most I can show you. Can I have my money?"

"Thank you very much for your help, Deva." She placed the roll of cash into the young boy's hand. He scampered back up the slope and vanished.

The movement was so sudden, Frank fell back in surprise. "Jeez, don't say goodbye or anything."

Annja smiled. "He's so happy to have that money, he'll go straight home. That's good. If there are murderers stalking these grounds, then he shouldn't be here. He might get hurt."

"And what about us?"

"We'll be all right."

"Yeah? You got a shotgun on you or something?"

"Something like that."

Frank shifted the camera bag. "All right, well, what's the plan? It's getting late and I don't know how much more we can do tonight. We didn't get any evidence at the crime scene. And now we've got a tenuous lead that points us in the direction of the mountains. But what should we do? Tell Pradesh about it and have him ask us all sorts of questions we probably don't want to answer?"

Annja stared off toward the mountain ridge. "You might be right. What more can we do in the dark now?"

A noise off to her left caught Annja's attention. She held a finger to her lips. Then very slowly, she raised the FLIR.

Three blobs of red appeared on the FLIR screen. Coming from the direction of the mountains. Annja frowned. She felt it.

Danger.

Were these the murderers Deva had told them about? Did the boy know they'd be coming?

Had he led Annja and Frank here deliberately?

Annja refused to believe that. Although she had to admit that Deva had seemed very anxious to get away as soon as he was paid.

She watched the screen and showed it to Frank. Frank's eyes went white and he whispered harshly, "Let's get the hell out of here. Let the cops deal with these guys."

Annja switched the FLIR off, not wanting the LCD screen to act as a beacon in the night. These men were obviously skilled at moving quietly in darkness. And they blended in perfectly with their night surroundings.

But who were they?

Frank tugged on Annja's sleeve. She let herself be pulled, and they came up out of the shrubbery together.

A face appeared before Annja's, swathed in a black scarf. She heard Frank gasp and then something hit Annja hard on the back of her head.

And she was falling back down the embankment.

Her last thought before she passed out was that whoever these men were, they were masters of the ambush.

11

Her head ached as if someone had just blown up a barrel of gunpowder inside it.

Annja cracked her eyes, momentarily afraid there would be bright light that would only make the pain even more intolerable.

But it was dark.

Black as night.

Where am I? She remembered falling down the embankment but then nothing beyond that. She must have hit a rock. And she'd hit enough rocks to know, unfortunately.

A light breeze made her shiver. The air wasn't nearly as humid as she remembered it being.

Something shifted next to her, and she tried to feel with her hands, only to then realize they had been bound behind her.

I guess this rules out someone friendly finding us, she figured. But then she remembered Frank.

Annja forced herself to crack her eyes again. It took several minutes to adjust to the darkness, but finally she saw the outline of Frank's body next to her.

"Frank?" She kept her voice quiet. It would be better if whoever was keeping them captive didn't realize she had regained consciousness.

Frank shifted and then opened his eyes slowly. "Annja?"

"Keep your voice down. We don't want them knowing we're awake just yet."

He paused. "My hands are tied. I can't move."

"Mine are, too. Just relax and we'll figure this out."

Frank choked. "I couldn't catch you when you fell. I tried to but then this guy came out of nowhere and clocked me."

"I hit my head on a rock, I think," she said.

"Who are these guys?"

Annja shook her head slowly. "I have no idea. It's probably better if we play dumb and let them do the talking."

"If they talk at all."

"They will. If they'd wanted to kill us, we'd probably already be dead. They must want something from us."

"I hope so," he said. "In the movies, though, once you give the bad guys what they want, they always kill you, anyway."

"You watch too many movies, Frank."

"Probably."

Annja tried to grin. "Just let me handle things when the time comes, all right? Can you do that?"

"Yeah. Sure."

"Try to get some rest now. Let me think."

He shifted, and Annja heard his breath deepen appreciably. This is probably the last thing the guy expected to get himself into when he jumped all over this assignment.

It came to her then. They were surely in a cave of some sort. That would account for the temperature change, the cool, dry nature of the air. But where were there caves around Hyderabad?

Annja took a breath. The mountains they'd seen in the distance.

Wonderful.

There would be no sign back at the development that Annja and Frank had been there. Not unless the police somehow managed to find Deva and get him to spill the beans.

And Annja knew the chances of that were slim. Deva was a survivor, and he wasn't about to jeopardize his family's welfare for Annja and Frank. Especially since he'd already been paid.

Annja tried to figure out how long they'd been unconscious. Unless the guys who had attacked them had vehicles nearby, they would have had to carry their victims back to the mountains. And the mountains were at least a few miles away from the development.

Annja shook her head and winced around the pain. Hours must have passed.

It might be dawn outside but she had no way of knowing that for certain. One thing she did know was that Pradesh would be losing his mind trying to figure out what the hell had happened to them.

First he'd check their rooms. Then when that didn't turn up any clues, he'd ask the hotel to run surveillance tape. That would at least bring him to the car-rental agency.

Figure another few hours before the car turned up near the development, and Pradesh would realize that she and Frank had gone off alone to try to find the monster.

And we've been successful, thought Annja. Much to my personal regret.

If Pradesh found the car, he would no doubt tear around the development looking for clues. But what clues would he find? He might follow their tracks in the daylight. They might lead him to the manhole cover and beyond to the crime scene.

But from there? Annja wasn't sure how accomplished a tracker Pradesh was, if at all. Still, he might find where they'd been ambushed.

And, God willing, he might even cast his eyes toward the mountains a few miles away.

But would he know to come here and look for them?

Annja had no idea what the mountains themselves were like. If it had been only one, then that would have narrowed things down. But with a range, the chances of him making his way to this exact location were next to none.

That meant they would have to find their way out of this mess on their own.

Great.

Annja had had less than stellar sidekicks before, but even the worst seemed to have some semblance of fighting skill. The closest Frank had probably ever gotten to fighting was on his video-game console.

Well, he was just going to have to get up to speed

pretty damned quick. If she couldn't count on him, then Frank would be going home in a pine coffin.

First things first. Annja had to figure out who their captors were.

In her mind's eye she saw the sword hanging in its usual position. Ready to be used when the situation demanded it.

And Annja had little doubt that would be soon.

She took a deep breath and willed her awareness to spread out in concentric circles, trying her best to get a feel for the makeup of the cave and the area she and Frank were being kept in.

The throbbing in her skull worsened. Twice she had to fight back a surging wave of bile.

Concussions were no fun at all.

But her captors seemed unimpressed with her injuries, which Annja supposed was at the very least a marginally good sign. If she'd been seriously hurt, they might have given her some medical attention. Wouldn't they?

Unless, as Frank suggested, they were just waiting for the right moment to kill them both.

She had a sense that the cave they were in was part of a networked series of other caverns. She had no idea how low the ceiling was, however, and she'd need to be careful about that. No sense recovering from a head injury only to stand and bang into the rock roof of a cave.

Frank, for his part, seemed unhurt.

Annja took another breath and directed her thoughts inward. She focused on the sword and tried turning its gray glow to a white glow. She remembered reading somewhere that healing oneself often involved visualization of white light.

She took several more deep breaths, willing herself to relax and find a source of the white light where the sword hung in her mind's eye. Then she felt that energy expand and encompass her body.

The thundering lessened.

A little.

"Annja?"

She sighed. So much for that. "What is it, Frank?"

"I've been trying to work on the ropes that are binding my hands. They're too tight. I can't even feel my fingers anymore."

"Don't fight it. You'll only hurt yourself."

There was a momentary silence. "All right," he finally said. And then he added, "We've got to get you to a doctor."

"I'll get medical attention when I can. But right now the most important thing is for us to learn what is going on here, then make our escape."

"If you say so."

"I do. You just stay quiet when the people who did this to us come back. Let me handle the negotiation."

"There's negotiation?"

"There will be whether they like it or not," she said with only the vaguest of smiles.

Frank didn't say anything for a moment. And then he whispered, "Have you been in this situation before?"

If only you knew, she thought. But to him she said, "I've had a few run-ins in my time. They've turned out well so far. I'm still alive."

"Yeah, well, I hope this another one of those times. I don't feel like dying this young."

"Me, neither," Annja said.

And she meant it.

12

They lay there for what seemed like hours more before Annja felt a sudden shift in the air pressure. Someone was coming into the cavern.

She felt Frank stiffen. So he felt the approach, too. Another good sign that Frank was rapidly developing the instincts necessary to survive this situation.

Annja opened her eyes and saw a masked man. He was swathed in black and his head appeared disembodied.

If we were in Japan, Annja thought, I'd think he was a ninja.

But she wasn't in Japan, and she didn't think that the ninja had chosen to invade India by way of Hyderabad.

Annja made eye contact with the man and saw intense hatred screaming out of his stare. Annja forced herself to maintain the eye contact, not giving him the pleasure of seeing her frightened.

Not this time, she thought. I guarantee you I will not be like your other victims. I won't beg for mercy.

The man maintained the eye contact as well as she did. Interesting. He didn't blanch at confrontation.

That meant he wasn't used to giving up his position. And that didn't bode well if they got into a fight. He'd probably rather die than surrender.

Annja cleared her throat to speak.

The man slapped her across the face. The blow was so sudden it took Annja by surprise, mostly because she didn't think he was that close to her.

He was telling her the rules.

And rule number one seemed to be "no talking."

All right. I'll remember that slap and make sure I repay it in kind. Just wait.

He came over and helped Annja to her feet, standing her and keeping her balanced. Her knees buckled slightly from dizziness. Her gorge rose in her throat and she forced it back down, the sour acid burning a trail back down her esophagus.

She took a breath and felt more stable. The man went to Frank and hoisted him up, as well.

Annja silently shushed Frank when he looked at her. This was the hired help. Formidable as he seemed to be, this was not the person who would hold power over whether they lived or died.

But he might be bringing them to that person.

And sure enough, Annja felt herself nudged from behind and was guided out of the cavern. It was difficult seeing in the darkness, and twice she bumped her head on the way out.

She stumbled forward, trying her best to find her footing in the unfamiliar environment.

She focused not on the area in front of her but off to

the sides. In the darkness she couldn't focus on things directly in front of her; she'd need to look out of the corner of her eyes if she had any hope of making it to their destination without causing more injury to herself.

Annja stepped down into a corridor of some sort. The walls were spaced wider apart and the tunnel seemed fairly long and straight, but it had been hewn out of the rock of the mountain. She was amazed by the amount of effort that must have gone into making this place.

Was it some sort of secret mountain fortress? Had people labored over this for centuries? Decades?

Who knew? And was there only one way to gain entrance to the caves? And if so, what chance did Pradesh have of ever finding it?

Very slight. And that meant that Annja would be the only one responsible for making sure she and Frank escaped this situation with their lives.

I've got to shake this concussion, she thought.

Behind her, she heard Frank stumble and fall. Third time. Each time he fell, the man behind them didn't dish out abuse, but instead helped Frank back to his feet, dusted him off and then nudged them forward again.

As long as they didn't talk, he seemed tolerable enough.

Annja came to a fork in the tunnel complex. Left or right? She glanced back and the man in black nodded to their left. The tunnel was much smaller here. She'd need to be careful.

"Ow!" Frank bumped his head on a low overhang that Annja had avoided. Annja braced for the slap and, when it came, Frank grunted appreciably, but managed to hold his tongue.

Don't talk, Frank, she willed into his head.

They kept walking.

She felt another breeze. However the tunnels had been laid out, constructed or designed, there seemed good air-flow. But again, the air was cool and dry and not at all similar to the humid air of Hyderabad.

Was it just because this was mountain air, or was there another reason why it seemed so fresh? There'd be time to figure that out later, thought Annja. Let's get to wherever we're going and then we'll worry about the air quality of the captors' mountain fortress.

Annja could sense other openings around them. Like branches or corridors off their route, there seemed an entire honeycombed network of caves. She wondered if people lived here or if this was simply a hideout of some sort.

After another five minutes of stumbling along, Annja saw flickering torchlight ahead. It was the first measure of illumination she'd seen in the complex at all.

But even this was miniscule. A lone torch hung on the wall and seemed to be responsible for lighting an entire chamber at least twice as large as any she'd been in yet.

The man behind them grunted and seemed to be sug-gesting they now stop.

He walked past them, leaving them alone in the cor-ridor.

Annja glanced back at Frank. "Remember, no talking unless I tell you to start, okay?"

Frank nodded. "Yeah."

Annja took a breath. "You're doing a great job, Frank. I mean that. I know this is out of the ordinary."

"Just a bit."

"But keep it together. Don't let them see you're terrified or they'll have less respect for you."

"I got it."

Annja looked around them. "Did you see anything that seemed to be an escape route on the way over?"

"It's so dark here, I don't even know how I'm able to see anything at all."

"Look out of the corners of your eyes in the dark."

Annja waited. She could sense movement all around her and then saw that other dark shapes seemed to be walking right past her and Frank.

What the hell was this place?

The filing of people around them seemed to go on for several minutes. Finally, the air stilled once more.

The torchlight cast long shadows of the people that surrounded her and Frank.

Too many here to try to take on by myself, she thought. And that was if she was able to get her hands free to draw her sword in time.

She felt a presence in front of her and then saw the same eyes of the man who had escorted them down here.

Now what?

He tugged on her shirt, and for a brief second Annja was worried that he might tear it off her. But he only wanted her to come with him.

Annja took a step forward and then another. The man guided her several steps ahead of where she'd been standing. Then he disappeared and returned a few moments later with Frank.

Annja could feel the fear emanating from her cameraman. She willed him to stay calm.

But that was easier said than done. Annja herself felt

the twinges of fear as she stood there wondering what was coming next.

This much she knew: they were in a larger chamber, and many others just like her black-clad captor surrounded them. Annja concentrated and saw the sword hanging in the otherwhere. Ready.

Her best move was to simply wait. And again, she reasoned that if they'd wanted to kill them as they might have done the others, then it would already be over.

Was it because they were Americans?

Doubtful. If anything, the fact they were Americans would have meant a very painful death in many parts of the world. No, that was not saving them.

Maybe it wasn't the right time to kill them yet. Annja frowned.

Annja felt the air shift again. The man who had escorted them down to this place seemed to slink away in the darkness.

She was getting tired of not knowing what was going on.

And that's when everything changed.

13

There was a sudden explosion of light in the chamber. And then the first thing Annja saw after her eyes adjusted was a blue figure emblazoned in front of her. A statue. Annja caught herself as she recognized who it was.

Kali.

The goddess of death often characterized in Hindu as uncontrollably angry and destructive.

The statue before Annja had four arms, each wielding a different weapon. And the red eyes were supposed to suggest a certain level of intoxication, a bloodlust resulting from one of Kali's many battles.

Kali was a ferocious deity.

What the hell had Annja stumbled onto here?

She soon got her answer. After the immediate shock of so much light where there had been none before, Annja forced herself to take in her surroundings. The torches that had sprung to life glowed hot, casting long shadows across the chamber, but also giving more than enough illumination for Annja to finally see the men who held them captive.

Her first impression was that there weren't nearly as many of them as she'd thought there were in the dark.

The dozen or so men certainly looked as ferocious as their goddess, Kali. They still had their faces shrouded in black, but slowly, each man reached up and undid the length of cloth that covered them. These scarves, knotted at both ends, were handled with a degree of reverence Annja found amazing.

She racked her brain for any information she thought might help her figure out who these men were. Obviously, they were devoted to Kali. But why? What was their cause?

One by one, the men tucked their scarves into their belts, the two knotted ends dangling over, as if ready to be drawn quickly.

And used to fight with. Weapons?

A thought struck her hard.

Thuggee.

She frowned. That cult was supposed to have been wiped out ages ago.

It didn't quite make sense. Thuggee, what the Western world derived the word *thug* from, were bands of robbers and murderers who used to prey on travelers from about the thirteenth century through the British colonial period.

Because of their fearsome reputation, the authorities had taken steps to crack down on them. And as far as Annja knew, the cult had been virtually extinguished.

So what was going on here?

The scarves that they had used to cover their faces

would be what were known as *rumal*. One of the best-known weapons used by Thuggee was the garrote. And they often used their head scarves as a weapon instead. The knotted end would help them hold the *rumal* in place until their victim was dead.

Which is why they placed an unusual degree of reverence on their *rumal,* much like a samurai respected his *katana.*

Each of the men stood in silent reverence before the statue of Kali.

And Annja wondered what was coming next.

After another few minutes, she heard footsteps and turned to see one final man enter the chamber, his head wrapped in the same *rumal* as the others. But instead of black clothing, he wore a mottled blend of brown and blue along with the black head scarf.

He passed Annja too quickly for her to even see his eyes and then stood in front of the statue, bowing low. Annja heard a low murmuring among the other men as their voices rose in a muffled prayer.

The praying went on for what felt like ten minutes. Annja could feel Frank growing impatient behind her, so she shot him a glance. Disturbing the Thuggee during the prayers they were obviously offering to Kali would no doubt be met by severe punishment.

Better to let them finish it and see where we stand, she thought.

The voices in the chamber rose to a fevered pitch and the energy grew from a quiet, intense respect to a frenzied rage. The whole place felt as if it might explode into a blood orgy.

Many of the men were swaying back and forth, caught

up in an altered state of mind. Had they done narcotics before coming to prayer?

A wave of fear washed over her. In an altered state of mind, anything could happen, and these people wouldn't even realize it. She and Frank might be gutted before their killers even knew what they were doing.

Annja looked back at Frank. He seemed absolutely terrified.

And Annja couldn't blame him. She wasn't used to feeling as helpless as this.

What if she drew her sword now? If she could somehow grasp it behind her, despite the bindings on her wrists.

There was a good chance she could free herself before the men came down from their adrenaline high long enough to clue in. And if she could keep them in front of her, rather than flanking her, she might be able to get the two of them out of here alive.

Maybe.

Annja closed her eyes.

Saw the sword.

But she couldn't reach for it—

Abruptly the chanting died.

The chamber grew quiet again. The torches flickered and died, plunging the chamber back into darkness. Annja hesitated.

She felt movement all around her. Some of the men appeared to be leaving.

Prayer time was apparently done.

A single torch sprang back to life, its glow breaking the darkness. The last man to have entered the chamber still stood in front of Kali with his back to Annja.

There were four men left besides him.

Much better odds. But only if Annja could get her sword and draw it before they knew what was happening. And unfortunately, now that the prayers had stopped, the men had their eyes firmly locked on her and Frank.

The element of surprise was gone.

Annja wondered if it had ever truly been there. They no doubt knew what to expect from their prisoners. She felt confident this had happened many times before. And they wouldn't be so foolish as to leave themselves exposed to attack.

Of course, they had never had a captive like Annja before.

The four remaining men pressed closer to them. Their eyes bore into them and Annja frowned back. But she felt Frank's fear grow.

He's close to losing it. She needed to keep him in check. If he freaked out, they'd kill him.

The man standing with his back to Annja said something quietly and the men eased back. Had he felt Frank's anxiety level spike?

Annja tried to remember more about the Thuggee, but her information was scant. She had no way of knowing if they dabbled in magic or not. She didn't think they did, but she'd already witnessed some unusual happenings here that she didn't have an answer for.

And if this man in front of her was some sort of high priest, then perhaps he might have secret knowledge.

Annja frowned. I'm being ridiculous, she thought. As many times as she supposedly witnessed something magical or otherworldly, there'd been an explanation for it.

At least, most of the time. She visualized the sword.

The man in front of her bowed low again, and another litany of syllables came out of his mouth in a strange, guttural tongue Annja couldn't understand. And even though she couldn't understand his words, they seemed sincere.

The men also murmured something, and Annja felt as though another presence had entered the chamber accompanied by a strong breeze.

Annja squinted as bits of grit blew into her face. She forced herself to try to observe what was happening, but as the wind increased, it grew increasingly tougher to see. Annja's vision swam as tears filled her eyes to combat the swirling dust and debris. She wanted to wipe them but her hands were bound. If only she wasn't tied up, she could use the sword to cut her way out of this mess.

The wind died in the next moment.

And the voices of the men along with it.

They were plunged into silence, absolute and unmoving. Even Frank had grown still, his fear having frozen him in place.

The man in front of the statue of Kali raised his hands toward the roof and said another prayer, but this one was much shorter. And when he was finished, he lowered his arms.

More silence.

Annja waited. It felt as though something would happen soon. But she didn't feel the same growing sense of dread she had earlier. There didn't seem to be a frenzied action to this group, and whatever their intentions, the man in front of the statue had absolute control.

Annja smirked. Well, at least until I get free and start

using my sword, she thought. It would be interesting to see how little control he had then.

Frank shifted, and one of the men drew his arm back and sent something flying. Annja caught the movement and willed herself to stand still as the knotted end of the *rumal* took Frank squarely on his temple.

Frank grunted as it struck home, his knees almost buckling, the impact was so staggering.

But as much as the strike had hurt Frank, he still managed to keep his feet under him. He grit his teeth.

Good. Annja nodded once.

The man in front of the statue turned to face them at last. Annja watched as he drew his hands up to the *rumal* that covered his face and started untying it. It was longer than the ones the other men wore, and it took him forever to unravel it.

But when he did, the smile on the man's face took Annja's breath away.

"Hello, again, Annja. Frank."

Dunraj.

14

The way he looked was so unlike how he'd appeared at the welcome party on the previous night. Gone was all sign of rich sophistication and bespoke suits. Of Hyderabad's most eligible bachelor.

In its place stood a man with a shadow over his face and a ferocity that seethed in his eyes.

"You're about the last person I expected to find here," Annja said. "The cover of *GQ* India, yes, but not in some maze of caves on the outskirts of a city that ostensibly belongs to you."

Dunraj cracked a smile. "I can understand how you would find my superficial personality as intriguing as other women, but I assure you that I am anything but that simple."

"Apparently. I mean, you're doing something here that defies the life you seem to lead in the city." Annja nodded at the statue. "Am I right that this is Kali?"

"Of course," Dunraj said. "She is the perhaps one of

the most important deities in the Hindu culture and religion. I have devoted my life to serving her."

"By doing what? Resurrecting an old cult?"

He snorted. "And what would you know of cults? You may have guessed at what we are, but I'll wager you have very little real information as to what it is we are all about."

"You're a bunch of thugs," she said.

The look on Dunraj's face was one for the ages. If he had expected her to not know anything about what he was doing here, he was mistaken. Annja liked not living down to people's expectations.

"How did you know about us?"

"Do you know anything about me? What I do? I'm an archaeologist, for crying out loud," Annja reminded him. "History is my business. And I have a pretty broad working knowledge."

Dunraj attempted a pained smile, as if a small child was chastening him. "Regardless, you probably only have a very limited understanding of what Thuggee is."

"Probably," she admitted. "But at least I'm not as naive as some of the women I see looking for a chance to sink their hooks into you. That's points in my book at the very least."

"Granted," Dunraj acquiesced, "but then, those women are merely part of the set that I have worked so hard to fabricate. My real work lies in the service of Kali."

"And killing people," she reminded him. "Let's not forget about the murders you've committed."

"It is not murder," he said. "It is paying tribute to my goddess. Something I came to terms with long ago."

"This isn't the old days, Dunraj. You can't go wandering around killing people just because your god tells you to."

Dunraj laughed. "What world have you been living in, Annja? Of course I can. And there are millions more people like me who do exactly that. The history of religion is always written in the blood of those it subjugates. But at least my goddess is not a hypocrite about what she craves. About what she needs. She demands sacrifice."

"Wonderful. Just what the world needs—another religious zealot. Swell."

Behind her, Frank moaned. Annja shot him a look.

Dunraj sighed. "Yes, well, I suppose it was too much to expect you to understand the goal of our work here."

"And just what is it you're up to? As far as I can see, you're getting started on some small-scale terror campaign at a development that would seem to have your fingerprints all over it."

The man shook his head. "I had nothing to do with that construction project. I protested its development vociferously. I tried every resource I had at my disposal to thwart it from the start. I was unsuccessful."

Annja shrugged. "You do have a lot of resources. So if you couldn't get it derailed, then who is behind it?"

"An outside firm interested in developing large tracts of land beyond the city limits."

"And that's where you have a problem."

"Hyderabad was once a flourishing center of Thuggee activity and Kali worship. Years ago, this region was dominated by our ancestors."

"But let me guess, the British took offense to the whole murdering travelers thing, huh?"

"Yes. They did. Thuggee was forced to go underground or risk being exterminated. Out of love for our goddess, Kali, that is exactly what happened. We went underground."

"And now you're bringing it back to the surface to combat developments on sacred land, perhaps?"

"Very good, Annja," he said. "That is exactly what these lands are. They cannot be transformed into sprawling megamalls or amusement centers or housing communities."

"And yet you transform land this way every day in Hyderabad."

"I do it where it's permitted. Where I build is not sacred land. It is not hallowed ground."

Annja sighed. "I'm surprised you weren't able to tie development up with legal injunctions or court procedurals. Don't you have a flotilla of lawyers on retainer for such a thing?"

"Sometimes all the lawyers in the world cannot prevent what is seemingly inevitable."

"But if you feel that way, then what makes you think this scheme of yours will be any better at stopping the developments?"

Dunraj crossed his arms. "Because, Annja, if there is one thing these people do understand, it is the cost of building and then not recovering the investment. If word spreads that someone is targeting these sites, then no one will buy. No store will lease space. No company will risk the wrath of the Thuggee. We will succeed in preventing the spread of modernization where none should ever be spread."

"I don't think it will work," she said. "Someone will

figure out you're behind this, or someone will catch one of your thugs and then the game will be over. It will only be a matter of time before modernization rolls over this area and puts a giant Mickey D's right where your shrine to Kali stands now."

Dunraj slapped Annja across the face and her lip burst, sending a warm stream of blood into her mouth. Dunraj shoved his face just inches from her own.

"You will not speak so rudely of my goddess, Annja Creed."

Annja spit blood on the floor of the cave. "Just letting you know what I think of your rotten plan."

Dunraj smiled, revealing those gleaming teeth. "It will be my greatest pleasure when I finally introduce you to my goddess."

"And just how are you going to do that?"

Dunraj cocked an eyebrow. "Why, you're to be sacrificed, of course. You and your cameraman there."

Frank coughed. "Hey," he spluttered. "I didn't do anything."

Dunraj shook his head. "You were at the development looking for answers. That makes you a threat. And threat must be dealt with. Surely you understand."

"What I understand is I want to live," Frank said.

Dunraj sighed. "Yes, well, we can't always be master of our own fate, now, can we?"

"I'm pretty sure I could be," Annja said. "Whether or not you introduce me to your god."

Dunraj smiled again. "When you scream for mercy and beg for the sweet release of a quick death, I shall refrain from granting you that one last wish."

"And here I thought we got off on a good foot at your party," she said.

Frank shook his head. "I've got a lot of living left to do."

"Tragically," Dunraj said, "you've got a lot more dying to do before that happens. And it will be a glorious death for you, my young friend. Your blood will spill in Kali's name so she may know of the love we have for her."

"There goes that bucket list I had drawn up."

"I don't even want to know what was on that." Annja looked at Dunraj. "Why don't we do a deal here?"

Dunraj eyed her. "You're joking."

"No," she said. "You let Frank go. He's just a child, for crying out loud. Surely your goddess wouldn't want you to kill one as young as him. It doesn't make any sense. He's got no worth to her, no life experience."

Dunraj just stared.

"But me?" Annja continued. "Well, you could get a lot more mileage out of my sacrifice than you would Frank's. So let him go and keep me. Run that blade right through me when you want to and I'll go happily. He's nothing to you. Or Kali."

Dunraj laughed. "I admire your attempt—feeble as it was—to spare the boy's life. But he's not as young as you would have me believe. And Kali appreciates every drop of blood spilled."

"Fantastic," Annja said. "So she's an equal-opportunity bloodlusting goddess. Awesome."

"You should feel honored," he insisted. "It is not often we even tell people they are to be taken in Kali's name. Mostly, my men strike the sacrifices down without their bodies ever being consummated at the altar."

"I'll try to remember to feel honored as you're killing me," Frank said sardonically. "Gee, thanks."

Dunraj studied his *rumal,* toying with one end. "Don't spoil my goodwill, Frank. You wouldn't like me when I'm angry."

"You're going to kill us, anyway," Annja said. "How could it possibly get worse?"

"I can determine how long you suffer before you finally give your miserable lives to Kali. And I can be very creative in the prolonging of pain and agony when I make cuts with the knife." He smiled. "Tomorrow, you will die in front of Kali."

15

Annja and Frank were taken back to the cavern where they'd first woken up. Once there, the thug who led them down to see Dunraj left them alone. On the floor of the cavern were small bowls of water.

With their hands tied behind their backs, they had no choice but to work out a way to drink the water. First Annja squatted and used her fingers to grab one of the bowls, which she had to hold at the small of her back. Frank had to stoop forward and drink out of that. They then repeated the process so Annja could get a drink, as well.

By the time they were finished, both of them were worn-out from all the maneuvering and sat on the floor.

"We can't stay here," Annja said. "I don't relish the idea of waiting for an ax to drop on my head."

"Might be lucky if it was an ax," Frank said. "At least that way, it would be quick. Dunraj seems intent on carving us up bit by bit. That doesn't sound like a very fun way to go."

"You should have stayed quiet," she said. "I might have gotten him to let you go."

"I doubt that. And no offense or anything, but your plan to negotiate my release kinda sucked."

Annja stretched a kink in her back as best she could. "Yeah, well, I don't hear any great plans coming out of your mouth."

"That's because you never asked me."

"I'm asking now."

Frank took a breath, started to say something and then exhaled in a rush. "Oh, hell, I don't have a clue what to do. I've never been kidnapped before. And I've certainly never been considered a decent sacrifice for anything, much less some goddess like the one they worship here."

"Kali."

"Right, yeah, Kali. Great. So, what's up this chick's butt that she has to be appeased with sacrifice?"

"Kali was the consort of Shiva, the god of destruction. There was a terrible battle—one of several Kali was involved in—and the killing grew so intense that she went into something of a berserk rage, slashing her way through thousands of demons and enemies on the battlefield. Bloodlust. Eventually, she was calmed down by Shiva, but not before she engaged in an awful lot of killing."

"And ever since her worshippers have sacrificed people to her?"

Annja stretched her fingers, which were numb because of the binding. "Most followers of Kali are not Thuggee. But from what I know about Thuggee, almost all of them worship Kali. It's the blood-and-murder thing. Thuggee use Kali as a way of justifying their acts and crimes."

"Yeah, but Dunraj seems to be actively looking to kill just to show his reverence for her."

Annja agreed. "I know. And that's the problem."

"Way I see it…us dying is a big problem."

Annja smiled. "We're not dead just yet."

"Yeah, but our hands are tied and we're in some extensive network of caves." Frank sighed. "I mean, even if we just walked out of here, would you have any idea where to go?"

"Not really." She could rely on her instincts, of course, but she wouldn't tell Frank that. If it worked out that way, she would call it blind luck rather than the fact that her intuition was sharper thanks to the sword.

"So, what now?"

Annja took a breath. "We're in a cage with no bars. Our hands are tied, however, and we've got to take care of that as soon as possible. I don't want to stay here any longer than absolutely necessary."

"You won't get any complaints from me." Frank looked around the cavern. "It amazes me how well I'm able to see now…even though we're in the dark."

Annja shook her head. "There's ambient light coming from somewhere."

Frank looked at her. "Okay. So, how do we get these bindings off? I'm not even sure I can feel my hands anymore. If we don't get free soon, I'm going to develop gangrene."

Annja stood and backed into the nearest wall. The rock was exceedingly smooth, as if it had been worn down by water over hundreds of years.

That wouldn't help them.

Annja glanced at Frank. "Stand up and try running your hands over parts of the walls. If we can find an outcropping of sharp rock, we might be able to get these bindings off."

"That's your plan?"

"Like I said earlier, if you've got a better idea, then feel free to unload it on me. If you've found a way to build some sort of teleportation machine that can just zap us out of here, I'm all ears."

"You don't have to be sarcastic."

"No, but I do need to get through that thick head of yours that we need to get going on our escape. I don't want tomorrow coming and we're still sitting here like sheep before the slaughter."

"All right," Frank said. He scrambled to his feet and started moving around the cavern.

Annja did the same, running the tips of her fingers over the rocks. But everything felt smooth to the touch and finding something that could cut seemed almost an impossible idea.

"Ouch."

Annja looked over at Frank. "What?"

"I just cut my finger."

"On what?"

"This rock."

Annja moved over to him. "Which one?"

"Turn around and run your hand over this part... right...here."

Annja felt a surge of joy as pain lanced through her hand. "Yes. I think that will work just fine."

Frank took a breath. "All right, move over and let me

in there to get these things cut off my hands. I really think I'm in bad shape."

Annja frowned. "If your hands were that bad, then you wouldn't have felt pain when you brushed against the rocks."

"Says you." Frank started sawing his wrists against the rock. "I can tell you that this is worse than any pins-and-needles thing I've ever felt. I don't think I'll ever be able to hold anything again."

"Drama queen."

He continued sawing. "Once I get free, I'll help you."

"How are you going to help me untie knots when your hands are about to fall off?"

"You know what I mean."

"Just get it done," Annja said. "We don't know how much time we have left. One of those guys could come back at any time and find out what you're doing."

"So keep watch at the opening there and warn me if anyone's coming."

Annja nodded and squatted near the entrance of their makeshift cell. In the darkness she couldn't see farther than about eight feet. But now and then the air currents would change, and she would imagine it was caused by someone moving in the maze of caves and caverns.

That was the other big question: Once they got free, how would they find their way out of this place?

True, Annja could bring the sword out and hold it aloft for some illumination, and yes, she could always rely on her instincts to help steer her out, but that wasn't guaranteed. She'd probably have to find Dunraj and force him to lead them out.

Then they'd have to find their way back down the mountain to town. So they could call Pradesh.

It wasn't much of a plan.

"Dammit."

Annja glanced back. "What's the problem, Frank?"

"The rock just broke off."

"What?"

"I was sawing too hard on it, I think. The damned thing came loose and just fell away."

Now what were they going to use to cut the bindings?

Frank walked over. "I got some of it cut but I don't think it's enough to break through the ropes."

Annja sighed. "Sit here and let me know if anyone's coming. I'll try to find another rock we can use."

"Okay."

Annja backed against the walls. She moved all over the cave and was about to give up when she felt something sharp lance her wrist.

Yes.

But again, the sharp piece of rock was small and fragile. The trick would be knowing how much pressure to exert without breaking the rock off.

It would need to be a delicate operation.

She started sawing the ropes. At first, the rock seemed to be too dull, but then Annja felt something starting to happen. She resisted the urge to push harder. As it was, the edge was barely half an inch long.

This was going to take a while.

"Did you find something?"

Annja nodded. "Yeah, but it's really small. You're going to be on guard duty for a while, pal."

"Just so long as you get free."

Annja resumed her sawing motion and prayed that she had enough time. Her future and Frank's rested on whether or not she was able to get these ropes cut.

She hadn't told Frank about how much her own hands hurt from the tightness of the bindings. Better to try to set a strong example for him to follow. If she wasn't scared, she hoped he wouldn't be, either.

Although she knew that wasn't likely to hold true for long, especially if it took them much longer to get free.

She pushed a little harder on the rock, trying to keep the sawing action constant and the friction as intense as possible. But moving her hands when they were tied behind her back was awkward and tiring.

Sweat ran down her face as she gritted her teeth and kept the sawing action up. Just a little bit more, she kept telling herself. Just keep going.

"How you doing?"

"Frank, do me a favor?"

"Yeah?"

"Stop asking me that."

"All right. Sorry."

Annja felt something give. One of the ropes was cut through. Her pulse quickened. She was one step closer to being free.

She leaned in on the rock to position the next rope.

And then the rock broke.

16

"And you told me I was doing it wrong," Frank said dejectedly.

Annja slid down the cave wall and sat on her butt. The rock had cut through one of the bindings. Would she be able to break the other?

Annja got on to her haunches and flexed her wrists. The bindings were tight, that was certain. And they'd somehow been tied in such a way that the rope snaked through itself several times over. No doubt so it couldn't be compromised as easily as simply sawing through it.

Annja concentrated on the sword in her mind, tried to visualize it flooding her body with strength. But each time she tried, the image wavered and Annja sank back down, exhausted.

"It's no use, the ropes are too tight."

Frank eyed her. "You thought you were going to be able to break out of those things?"

"Worth a shot."

Frank chuckled. "No offense, Annja, but you're not exactly the type who can rip telephone books in half."

Annja raised an eyebrow. "You'd probably be surprised at what I can do, Frank."

"Well, perhaps I'm smart enough to know that brute strength isn't going to win us the day here. What we need is something a little more subtle."

"What we need," she said, "is help from someone who can get these damned ropes off us."

"That would be another choice." He shook his head. "Of course, the odds of that happening in here are slim."

"Yeah."

"I don't suppose you have your cell phone still?"

Annja eyed him. "I've got nothing. They took it all when we were kidnapped. No way they'd leave us something like that."

"Yeah, just thought I'd ask."

Annja took a breath and exhaled it. She was tired and hungry. That was why her strength was so shot. Any other time and she felt sure she'd be able to snap those restraints and be on her way to Dunraj.

But now?

She wanted to sleep. Her eyelids felt heavy. And her muscles seemed lethargic.

"Frank."

"Yeah?"

"You sleepy?"

"Very. I was just trying to get some shut-eye when you woke me up."

"Why are we so tired all of a sudden?"

"I don't—" Frank stopped. "The water we drank. What do you want to bet they drugged it somehow?"

Annja remembered the taste but it had only registered as slightly earthy, no doubt from the bowl they'd drunk out of. And that was it. They'd been so focused on getting any water into them at all, what with having to work so hard, they'd paid no attention to the actual taste or consistency of the water.

"Annja, I'm passing out here."

"Frank! Stay with me!" But even as she said it, Annja felt herself slipping into unconsciousness. *I've got one chance to stay reasonably conscious,* she thought.

In her mind's eye, Annja saw the sword hanging there with its grayish glow illuminating everything around her. Except now, black edged the gray light.

Annja drew herself closer to the sword. As long as she felt herself surrounded by the gray light, she thought she'd be safe from the effects of the drugs. But it was difficult maintaining that discipline. The blackness drew her to its warmth, to the idea of closing her eyes and forgetting the pain in her hands, the stiffness in her back.

And where she was.

Annja bit her lip, the one that had been split when Dunraj slapped her, drawing new blood. The pain. She had to embrace it to keep her mind focused.

Annja flexed her wrists and instantly felt the pain return. It seemed to pierce the blackness, making it retreat in her mind's eye. Annja kept flexing even as she started sweating uncontrollably.

Keep going, she thought. *Keep embracing that pain.* She bent her elbows up and down, forcing herself to focus on the agony of the movement.

She moaned now as the pain raced up and down her arms. She twisted, getting her hands underneath her buttocks so she was almost sitting on her wrists. An explosion of fire rocketed through her body.

The sweat now soaked through her shirt and pants. It felt as if she'd somehow managed to open up a floodgate.

She kept twisting on the floor of the cave, and more pain shot through her limbs. Annja cried out but knew her cries would fall on deaf ears. Frank was already unconscious. And he wouldn't be back until the poison worked its way through his system.

If it did.

Was this how they initiated each sacrifice? Take their prisoners here and drug them to make them compliant and unable to mount a defense when the time came to be murdered? How many others had they killed before the development murders made the news?

Annja bit her tongue. Tasted blood. Her wrists throbbed. Annja was soaked in sweat.

Her breathing came rapidly. She was on the verge of hyperventilating. If she wasn't careful, she'd pass out.

But Annja kept going, she kept racing toward that one inevitability, toward that one overwhelming thought: pain would flush the poison.

She rolled along the ground, bumping into the cave walls and into Frank's inert body. She felt her wrists bend and pop and spasm and scream as she defied the very limits of what she thought was her breaking point.

Annja went through it.

And kept going.

She was aware of the sounds in her mind that seemed like voices melted together on the sidewalk in a hot summer sun. The miasma of screams and cries and shouts of pain. But who were they? Were they the victims of the Thuggee from hundreds of years in the past?

Had they all converged on this spot right now? Could they smell the desperation and will to live in Annja? Had they heard her pleas into the afterlife and were now here to help her?

The voices continued to moan and screech and cry out, and Annja kept struggling on the floor of the cave. She was so tired. But she knew that the only way to survive was to keep going until she had nothing left to give.

Another volley of voices crashed down on her, stretching her awareness and twisting her perceptions and making her feel as if her reality was being pierced and shattered by the spirit world.

More pain enveloped her body now. She spasmed once and then went into a seizure, convulsing on the floor of the cave. Her hands underneath her were taking the full weight of her body on the delicate joints.

But Annja no longer cared.

She only knew one reality in that cave, and as sweat and pain caught her body up in its throes, she kept convulsing, sweating, crying out.

The noise.

It wasn't the dead.

It was her.

Annja was screaming.

Her cries echoed off the cave walls and came back magnified a hundred times. There was no escape from it. She was losing the battle to break the hold of the drug coursing through her veins.

Even the pain was lessening now.

Dying.

Annja.

And then she went still.

A hush fell over the cave like a blanket thrown over the body of someone sleeping.

When her eyelids fluttered a few moments later, it took her a long moment to figure out where she was.

And then it came back to her.

The cave.

Dunraj.

She rolled over and looked at Frank. His breathing seemed regular. But he hadn't been able to fight off the drug, and it had him firmly in its grasp.

Annja sat up, aware that her clothes were fairly soaked in sweat.

The pain in her body was far less now, but still present.

Did I break my wrists? Annja flexed them and was rewarded by a twinge of pain. Not broken, she surmised. Still tied, though.

She took a deep breath and exhaled it. Her senses seemed fine and not dulled at all. At least I can still function if I need to.

"That was impressive."

The voice shattered the silence.

She looked up.

Dunraj stood there before her.

"What do you want?"

"I underestimated your abilities."

She said nothing and let Dunraj continue.

"That poison we use is a very old and very effective recipe. I've never seen anyone withstand its effect the way you just did."

"I don't like drugs," she said.

"That was fairly obvious. But I must admit I'm at a loss how you were able to flush your system the way you did. Do you have some sort of experience with narcotics?"

Annja smirked. "You're not the first person who has tried to drug me, Dunraj."

He frowned. "Is that so? Fascinating. You are truly something to marvel at, Annja Creed. I almost hate to kill you."

"So don't."

Dunraj eyed her. "And what would you have me do instead—kill your comrade here? Would you barter his life for yours?"

"You know better than to ask me that question."

"Do I? It might amaze you to know that most people I've had here would sell their most treasured love to me if it meant an escape for them. The tragedy of the human race, I suppose. We can never really trust the love of others. Betrayal is so commonplace these days."

"Something you'd know a lot about, I suppose," she said.

"Naturally."

"You really think your goddess wants blood sacrifice?"

Dunraj smiled. "Of course she does. And I'll prove it to you."

Annja hesitated before slowly, painfully struggling to her feet. "How so?"

"By showing you firsthand what Kali wants." He

helped Annja steady herself through the pain of her joints.

He led Annja out of the cave, leaving Frank behind.

17

Dunraj dragged Annja back down the network of caves. She stumbled along, doing her best to keep pace, but Dunraj knew where he was going. And Annja did not. Especially since it appeared they were heading to a different section of the fortress than they'd been in before with the statue of Kali.

Besides, she'd just put her body through unbearable pain. It would take her at least a few minutes to find any strength.

"Have you figured out your way around yet?" Dunraj asked.

"It's a maze and it's dark. I have no idea where I am in this labyrinth."

"And that's exactly the way it should be." Dunraj pulled her into another corridor, one that twisted and bent into an odd shape that finally opened up into another room.

Oh, my God, thought Annja. Not this.

Five of Dunraj's men were circled around a giant stone altar in the middle of the room. On all of the walls, images of Kali adorned the rock, emblazoned in bright colors that flickered as the torchlight from several wall sconces fell across it.

A man lay naked on the altar, stretched out with his limbs splayed apart. Judging from the fear on his face, he knew what was coming. He screamed when he saw Dunraj.

"Quiet him, please."

One of Dunraj's men stuffed a gag in the man's mouth. It muffled his screams, but the moaning continued.

Annja looked at Dunraj.

"Is this absolutely necessary?"

Dunraj stared into her eyes. "I don't think you are taking us as seriously as you need to. Do you understand what is coming for you tomorrow? That you will be taken for Kali, as well?"

"You mentioned it before, I think."

"And yet you are remarkably well composed. Certainly not the actions of someone who is afraid."

"I don't let fear paralyze me into inaction. What good would that do? I have never in my life sat back and simply let things happen. I don't intend to start now."

"You mean to escape, then?"

Annja smiled. "I just finished telling you I have no idea where I am in this godforsaken place. How could I possibly be contemplating escape?"

"If you're not thinking about escape, then how else will you save your life and the life of your cameraman?"

Annja turned the tables and stared back into Dunraj's eyes. "Why would I tell you what my plans are? You'd just go ahead and spoil them. And then we'd have no fun whatsoever."

"Fun?" Dunraj shook his head. "You think this is fun? This is a solemn occasion to mark our devotion to our goddess, Kali. This isn't some summer holiday, Annja."

"I find it difficult to imagine that any deity would demand their followers spill blood in their name. More likely, this is just a bastardized attempt to justify murder for your financial gain. To get rid of competitive developments. Murder is something I don't condone or accept."

Dunraj eyed her for a moment longer before a thin smile spread across his face. "You've killed before. Haven't you?"

"What does that have to do with anything?"

"It has a great deal to do with it, actually," he said. "And it explains the lack of fear in your eyes when you look at me. You don't see me as the one to be afraid of so much as the one who currently has the power in this relationship."

Annja said nothing. Better to let Dunraj continue on his megalomania streak than interrupt it, she figured.

"That's it, isn't it? You're not afraid because you think there's going to be an opportunity for you to change the power structure. You're biding your time until that opportunity presents itself."

Annja smiled. "I won't incriminate myself in anything. If you think you've got a theory, then I guess we'll just have to wait until it happens for it to either be proven or refuted, huh?"

Dunraj frowned. "Of course, I find myself wondering how you intend to mount this power shift when your hands are conveniently tied behind your back. You certainly present no threat to anyone while you are in that state."

"You know what they say about states."

"No, what?"

"They're meant to be changed."

Dunraj allowed himself another grin. "You do so impress me with your spirit. It's a terrible shame you must be sacrificed to Kali, although I am certain she will enjoy your soul." Dunraj came closer and drew his hand over Annja's breast. "I admit I find myself wondering if perhaps there isn't a little time before I send you to the other world to serve Kali for eternity."

Annja looked down at Dunraj's hand and then back into his eyes. She licked her lips. "Well, why don't we find out?"

Dunraj smiled wider. "You'd like that, wouldn't you? At least then your miserable life would be spared. At least until you bored me."

Annja leaned closer to Dunraj's ear. "I could make your wildest dreams come true."

"I believe you could."

Annja shrugged. "But you'd have to untie me. Otherwise, I'd just be lying there and we wouldn't have any fun at all."

Dunraj leaned back away from her. "I admire your pathetic attempt to prolong your life, but it won't work." He sighed. "It's a shame we do not have more time together. I genuinely believe we could be good for each other. I'm not the monster you think I am."

Annja shook her head. "Tell me something. Why does every bad person I've ever known feel they have to go out of their way to prove that? It gets really tiresome."

Dunraj said nothing for a moment. And then he shrugged his shoulders. "Perhaps you are right, Annja."

She didn't respond.

He drew a wicked-looking knife out from his belt. Its blade gleamed in the torchlight. "We've conversed enough, I think."

Annja nodded at the blade. "And what are you planning to do with that? Kill me now?"

Dunraj laughed. "Good heavens, no. You are scheduled for tomorrow for a reason. Tomorrow is one of the most important dates in our calendar."

He ran a finger along the edge of the blade, and Annja saw a line of blood bead up on his skin. "This is for the man behind me. In a moment, I will cut his heart out."

"Lovely. Why don't you just kill him and be done with it? There's no need to prolong his suffering."

"But his suffering is what gives us power. I wouldn't expect you to understand this process. But tomorrow, when you die, you will."

When Dunraj turned back to the man, Annja tried to kick at him. But she was held back by two more men who had come up unseen behind her. They kept her pinned in place.

If only I could get my sword, Annja thought. I could make mincemeat of these assholes.

Dunraj approached the young man on the slab of rock and held the blade in front of his eyes. The poor guy started convulsing on the rock altar, desperate to escape what was coming.

Annja shook her head. "Don't do this, Dunraj."

He glanced back at her. "It's too late for him now. He will be dead very soon."

And then with a small invocation, Dunraj plunged the knife into the man's chest. Annja saw the man's face explode in pain and then go slack.

Dunraj's back mercifully blocked the view of the man's chest, but Annja could tell by the way Dunraj bent and moved his arms that he was cutting into the chest cavity.

She fought back a rush of bile.

Dunraj worked meticulously, and after several moments, he held the heart aloft as blood flowed down his arms.

Then he turned to Annja.

"You see? You see the power this organ holds? It pulses with life. With energy. And we partake of that energy to continue our service to great goddess Kali."

Dunraj smiled.

Then he plunged his teeth directly into the heart, chewing and swallowing as the bloody mess covered his face. He held the heart out to his followers. One by one the men bit from the raw heart muscle, chewing and swallowing a piece of what had once been a part of a living human.

He held the last of it out to Annja.

She vomited.

18

Annja shook her head. "He's a monster."

She sat alone in the cell. Frank was still unresponsive to her attempts to rouse him from the narcotic-induced slumber. Annja looked at his peaceful expression and she felt jealous. Frank hadn't been exposed to the horror that Annja had seen.

She owed it to him to make sure he didn't have to die inside this horrible mountain fortress. And certainly not by some psychopath named Dunraj. If they escaped and Frank got hit by a car crossing the street, then that was fate. But dying by Dunraj's hand was unacceptable.

Annja shifted. Her hands still ached. The pain had returned after she managed to fight off the effects of the Thuggee drug. And now she was growing increasingly concerned that unless she found a way to restore her blood flow, Frank's fears would be justified and she'd be in danger of losing her hands when they got out of this.

If they got out of it.

Something about the tying method of the Thuggee made this more of a challenge than the folded steel cuffs she'd gotten out of before.

Annja ducked her head out of the cavern. As far as she could tell, there was no one around. Time to see if there was a sharp piece of rock out here she could use to saw her way through the bindings.

Annja worked her way down the corridor about ten feet. It was as smooth as the walls in the cave. She switched sides and used her back to feel this wall.

Nothing.

Annja checked back in on Frank. She was going to have to make a tough decision. She needed to get these bindings off and be able to get her sword out. But there was nothing to use around here.

She had to find a way to get through them. And that would mean leaving Frank behind while she went to search.

As far as Annja knew, there'd been only one unexpected visit to their cavern and that was by Dunraj himself right before his impromptu feast. Otherwise, Annja didn't think there had been guards posted.

Of course, it was possible that Dunraj had told his men to keep an eye on her. She was, after all, not under the effects of the drugs.

But she had to take a chance if there was any hope of getting out of this place alive.

And it had to be now.

She edged farther down the corridor, feeling her way through the maze. She reached the fork in the tunnel and tried to remember which way Dunraj had dragged her.

The left seemed right, but abruptly she decided to go to the right instead.

A good thing she did.

Moments after she ducked into a recessed part of the wall, Annja felt the air shift and then saw movement heading in her direction. She pulled her head in and stilled her breathing.

Two of Dunraj's men went past her. Annja waited thirty seconds and then moved again.

If she'd taken the left branch of the tunnel, she would have walked right into them. She followed behind them, still marveling at how easily they moved through these unlit tunnels.

Annja was adapting to the lack of light, but she still had to rely on her peripheral vision to see where she was going. And it wasn't always accurate. Twice she bumped her head and winced as the pain shot through her skull.

The last thing she needed was a concussion.

A second one.

She finally came to a point where she felt rock bite into her skin. Annja wanted to shout for joy, but kept the reaction in check. She started rubbing her bindings against the sharp outcropping.

This piece was much larger than what she and Frank had found back in their cell. And so Annja put her all into cutting through the bindings. Back and forth she sawed, until once again, her shirt was soaked from the exertion.

I need to keep going, she thought. This is the only chance I have of getting us out of here.

She felt one of the bindings give way, and it fell to the

ground. Annja's heart leaped at the thought of getting closer to being freed.

But then she heard a pebble skitter nearby, and she shrank back down into the recessed portion of the tunnel.

The same two men who had gone past her before came walking back through. Annja held her breath and waited. Once they'd gone, she returned to her original position and renewed her attempts to saw through.

I need to get this done now, Annja thought. I can't risk staying here much longer or coming back later. If they find out I've left the cave, this whole place will be alive with these guys.

And if her hands weren't free, she'd die all too quick.

Annja kept sawing. She felt another binding go slack, and she had more flexion in her wrists now.

Keep going, Annja, she thought.

The rock was doing its job well, and she sawed furiously now, almost afraid once or twice that the bindings might start to smoke and catch fire.

Annja frowned and threw her entire body weight against the rock, willing the last remaining strands to split apart.

And then she was free.

But there was little time to enjoy her freedom because as soon as she brought her hands around to the front of her body, a massive avalanche of pain came shattering down on her.

Her shoulders throbbed from being in that position for so long. Her wrists felt as if they were swelling up to three times their size as blood poured down into her hands and fingers.

Every nerve ending felt as if it was being fired in a forge. Annja bit down on her lip.

She staggered back down the tunnel. She had to get back to the cavern where Frank was.

Annja stumbled and fell against the cavern floor.

And held her breath.

Off in the distance, she heard something.

Someone.

One of Dunraj's men had heard her fall. Annja scrambled to her feet and thought about bringing the sword out.

But her hands were useless. The pain shooting up and down her arms was virtually unbearable.

I need to hide.

Annja crept farther down the tunnel and found another narrow recessed point that she curled her body into.

Dunraj's man came along seconds later. His footsteps were soft.

Stealthy.

Annja steeled herself. She wasn't in any position to fight this guy. He'd kill her far too quickly, and then her escape would have been for nothing.

Dunraj's man was anything but hurried. With each step he took, he searched the area.

Did he know there was an intruder? Or did he simply suspect something was amiss?

He continued to walk toward her, and every footstep brought him closer to Annja's hiding place.

This isn't going to go well, she thought.

He was all of ten feet away when Annja felt the air around them shift again and another man came down from the other side of Annja.

Now she was surrounded.

The second man said something to Annja's original hunter, and the two of them sprinted down the corridor.

Where were they going?

No time to wait and see, Annja thought. She needed to get back to Frank.

She came out of her recess and zipped down the corridor as fast as she could, amazed at how much more balance she had now that she could use her arms again.

If only she could use her hands, she thought.

Back the way she'd come, Annja ran as softly as she dared without compromising speed. She got turned around twice, shouted at herself in her mind and then righted the direction after trusting her gut instincts.

Then she fell into the cave and there was Frank, still sleeping soundly on the cavern floor.

"Thank God," she whispered.

She sat there with her back against the wall and massaged her hands.

The pain was still intense.

At least the toughest part is done, she thought. Now the one thing that remains to be fixed is to get my hands back into working condition so I can use the sword.

The sword.

Just the thought of being able to hold it properly and feel the power bleeding into her body energized her. It was time to get the hell out of this place and call Pradesh and his buddies in to mop up the mess.

Annja glanced at Frank. He'd be shocked to see her free. And Annja needed to get his hands untied, as well. But first things first, she had to make sure she was good to go before she tried anything with Frank.

She didn't necessarily think he was in any danger at

the moment. As long as he stayed asleep, she doubted Dunraj would consider him a threat.

But Annja would definitely qualify.

And all the more as soon as she got her hands back to normal.

She could feel the blood pulsing into her tendons now. She had some feeling back in her left hand. Her right hand still ached uncontrollably.

But Annja tried, anyway. She started deep-breathing exercises designed to calm her down and let her body take care of what it needed to. It was tougher than she expected it would be.

But then again, she'd just been through a traumatic event, and the requirements to heal her would be much greater than normal.

Normal, Annja thought with a grin. What's that like?

She stayed upright, massaging her limbs until at last she started to feel healthy again. She wondered how much longer she would have had before the damage to her hands would have been untreatable. If she hadn't restored blood flow, she would have been looking at possible amputation. Frank had indeed been correct

Frank.

She had to get his circulation flowing right now.

Annja took another deep breath and exhaled it out smoothly.

She was back.

"You are quite a woman, aren't you?" a man said. A man whose voice she hadn't heard before.

19

Annja tried to bring her hands together to summon the sword, but she was still too weak to grasp the hilt and wield the weapon.

The man who had spoken held his hands up to indicate he wasn't a threat. At least not yet. "Please do not do anything rash, Annja. If I meant you any harm, I would certainly not be sitting here relaxed, given that you have managed to free yourself."

"Who are you?"

"I am called Kormi."

In the darkness it was difficult to get any real read on his features. He was swathed in the same material as the other Thuggee members. And he was most assuredly one of Dunraj's men. Although Annja hadn't seen him at the heart feast earlier, that didn't mean he wasn't a viable threat.

She frowned at her hands. You guys need to get your act together; otherwise, I'm going to be dead.

Kormi pointed at her hands. "It takes a long time after you've been tied up for such an extended period."

Annja nodded. "Yeah, well, I'd like it to be sooner than later."

"I do not doubt that," he said. "Considering what you have seen, I do not blame you one bit."

Annja looked up at him. "So, why are you here, then? Did you swing by to torment me about my upcoming date with Dunraj's dagger?"

"I came to help you."

She narrowed her eyes. "Forgive me for seeming suspicious of such a gesture. I haven't had a very good experience with others of your kind."

"I know. I was the one who carried you back from where you fell down the embankment."

"You were?"

"You would probably have died had I not administered the aid I did when we got back. I take it your head is no longer hurting?"

Annja ran a hand over her head. The truth was, she was feeling better, minus the pain in her arms and hands. "Actually, my head feels pretty good. Thank you."

Kormi bowed low and then came up smiling. "It was seen as a foolish gesture on my part, but not all of us agree with what Dunraj is doing here. We don't want to be a part of the killing. We are here to worship Kali only. But he has somehow twisted a fervent inner cadre and bent them to his will. They are the ones who wish to continue this bloodshed agenda Dunraj has embarked on."

"I think I saw an example of those guys earlier. They ate a heart."

Kormi nodded gravely. "Dunraj calls that a way for growing closer to our goddess, but to me he is perverting the very nature of our worship. I have not yet been able to figure out why he is doing this. To what end does he wish to manipulate this group?"

"I was hoping you were going to tell me that you're an undercover cop or something and that the cavalry was on its way."

Kormi smiled. "Unfortunately, that is not the case. But we are not completely alone here. I have two friends who may help us if they feel they can succeed at overthrowing Dunraj."

"How did you guys get involved with this in the first place?"

Kormi frowned. "You do not have time to understand all of the history of the Thuggee. What Dunraj told you is true. This region was known for its activity within the Thuggee community. And this is sacred land. But as to why things begin, who can say? As modern-day practitioners or adherents of Thuggee, we are not really interested in killing at all, but in protecting what is ours. This land is one of those things we feel a need to protect. But there are people only too willing to destroy them even after we explain their historic and spiritual significance. They have been in our families for many years."

"But the murder of the residents at the nearby development," Annja said. "You can't expect to walk away from such things."

Kormi shook his head. "Those killings were not committed by myself or the men I know and trust here. That was done by Dunraj's inner core."

"You were out, though, when you took Frank and me."

Kormi nodded. "We were getting supplies back into the mountain when we came upon you. We were as surprised as you were. But we know the land well and were better able to adjust accordingly."

"You could have left us there."

Kormi nodded. "And we would have but for the injury you sustained. We were concerned also that Westerners were now investigating. Bringing you back was a way to try to convince Dunraj to stop the killings."

Annja looked past him to make sure they were still alone. "That didn't work out too well."

"No. Bloodlust now flows in his veins. He is convinced that by killing he is able to draw us all closer to the goddess."

"How come you guys don't simply turn him in to the police?"

"He is protected by his inner cadre. Plus, Dunraj has an inner knowledge of this mountain that most of us do not. He is able to be anywhere he wants within moments. We believe there is another network of caves and tunnels that only he knows about."

"But he can't be here all the time."

"Hyderabad does call him away from time to time. But he is never gone for long."

Annja frowned. How could that be? If Dunraj was on the forefront of most of the major developments in the city, how could he possibly explain his long absences in the mountains? That didn't make any sense.

"Look, we've got to get out of this place. Frank and I are scheduled to be served up for Kali's breakfast tomorrow. Can you help us escape?"

Kormi shrugged helplessly. "What good will that do?

You would never find your way back, and Dunraj would still be at large."

Annja did a double take. "So what are you suggesting?"

"You want these killings to stop, don't you?"

"Of course," she said. "They absolutely have to stop."

Kormi studied the ground, not meeting her eyes. "Then there is only one alternative. We must kill Dunraj to stop the violence."

Annja didn't even blink. I'll find a way to deliver the guy to the cops, she thought.

Kormi stared into her face. "So, he was right about you."

"What did he say?"

"He warned us when we brought you here that there was much more to you than we would be able to see. He felt certain that you had a lot of violence in your past."

Annja nodded. "I do."

"And I see that the prospect of killing a man does not affect you as it would someone who has never been forced to take a life."

"I've been forced to go to extreme ends to save myself on a number of occasions," said Annja. "But I don't relish the idea of killing. If there's another way to survive this, I'll find it."

"Dunraj will prove to be a formidable enemy," Kormi said. "I have seen him in action a number of times. When we first discussed the notion of driving the residents away, one of us stood up to him. They engaged in single combat, and Dunraj played with the man as if he were a cat batting around a mouse."

"I've fought a number of people who were excellent fighters," she replied. "And I was the one who went home."

"Do not think you are invulnerable. After all, you do not have experience fighting us, do you?"

"I try to protect good people and ancient relics. That runs me afoul of some who would profit from their desecration and destruction."

Kormi eyed her. "You sound as though you have great reverence for the past."

"I do."

"In another time and place, you might have been welcomed into our ranks."

"Perhaps. But I'm better on my own. When I have to look after other people, it gets challenging."

Kormi smiled as he bent to cut Frank's bonds. "Your cameraman means well, but he is woefully unprepared for the prospect of fighting."

"That's what I'm worried about, too," she said. "How long will that drug keep him unconscious for?"

"Until tomorrow morning. It was designed to reduce the ability of captives to mount any type of defense."

"That's going to make moving him around a real chore. Is there any way we can safely stow him someplace else in this network of caves?"

"Someplace where he won't be found?"

"Once we deal with Dunraj, then we can come back for him."

"Unless he wakes up early and starts making noise," Kormi said. "That would draw our enemies to him."

"Do we have another alternative?"

"No."

Annja nodded. "How long will it take to hide him?"

Kormi, a big man, hefted Frank onto his shoulders. He seemed very much at ease carrying Frank's weight. "I will return as soon as I'm able."

Annja watched him duck out of the cavern and then disappear into the darkness. She couldn't hear any footfalls and marveled at how silent he was even while holding two hundred pounds worth of Frank.

She sat and worked on her hands again. The pain was less now that she hadn't been thinking about it, but it was difficult to form a fist.

I need to bring my sword out, Annja thought. I need to know I can get it out if I have to.

She visualized the sword hanging in the otherworld. Its glow wrapped around her now as she reached for it. Power flowed from the blade down into the hilt and then into Annja's hands and up her arms.

Instantly, the aches vanished and Annja closed her hands about it, gripping the sword tightly.

Ready.

The sword gleamed in front of her face and lit up the cavern. Annja swung it experimentally a few times, testing the weight on her muscles. Her body responded with a renewed vigor.

It occurred to Annja that she was incredibly hungry. She should have asked Kormi for some sort of ration to see her through. Undoubtedly there was going to be a lot of fighting. And if Annja didn't have some sort of sustenance, she'd get tired.

She put the sword away again.

The exhaustion of her ordeal came thundering back down on her. She curled up near a corner in the cavern and rested her head against the wall. It wasn't comfortable by any means, but she felt better knowing that she had the sword again.

Thank God.

She wondered if Kormi would run into anyone else and, if he did, how he would explain Frank.

Annja shook her head. He would have to deal with that.

She closed her eyes.

Waited.

And fell asleep.

20

How long she slept, Annja didn't know, but she suspected that it was at least an hour before she felt the rough hands of Kormi shaking her awake. Annja rose groggily. Her need for food was almost overpowering.

Fortunately, Kormi was pushing some bread into her hands. "Take it. It's not much but it should give you strength. There's water, as well. But this hasn't been drugged."

Annja gulped down the bread, working off the rustiness of jaws that hadn't been used in some time. It was a coarse, chewy bread, and Annja relished each bite of it. She washed it down with gulps of water and felt much better.

"Thank you," she said when she was finished.

"I know you have been famished. Dunraj likes his sacrifices to be starving when they die. He feels it will make them more compliant when they reach the afterlife and enter the service of Kali."

"He really believes that?"

"Yes."

Annja eyed him. "Do you?"

Kormi smiled. "Once I did. But my reasoning has finally caught up with me, and I know that Dunraj has been blinded by his quest for power. I don't say this to excuse my past actions, some of which have been less than honorable, but rather to explain my own evolution."

Annja didn't think the time was right to debate. She stood. The nourishment caused her stomach to cramp appreciatively, but the energy she gained from the food was so worth it. "That bread helped a lot."

"It's an old recipe," Kormi said. "There are many nutrients to it that will keep you ready should the need to fight arise."

"As it most definitely will."

"Undoubtedly."

Kormi led her out of the cavern and once again down the tunnel away from her cell. The tunnels seemed less dark now, but Annja knew that danger could be lurking anywhere. As soon as it was discovered that Kormi was helping her, his life would be forfeit, and she suspected that Dunraj would stop at nothing to exact a particularly painful vengeance.

But Kormi seemed undisturbed by that prospect. As they traveled, Annja noticed that he had his *rumal* out and ready to bring to bear. But the tunnel system seemed almost deserted.

At one point, Kormi paused and knelt near an intersection, putting a finger to his lips. They waited until another man passed inches from their faces and then proceeded. Kormi seemed determined not to have to engage anyone unless they left him absolutely no alternative.

Annja kept her hands together in front of her as if she was already holding her sword.

The ground sloped upward, and Annja knew they were ascending into another part of the mountain she hadn't yet seen. More ambient light and cooler breezes found their way into the tunnel system. Kormi pointed out a few key landmarks in case they got separated, but Annja was determined not to lose her guide.

Kormi rested once and shared some of his water with Annja. "Drink as much as you need. I'm used to not having a lot."

"But you need some."

"I've been drinking water all afternoon in preparation," he explained. "It is a wonder that I have not floated away."

"How did you get wrapped up in all of this crap, Kormi?"

He smiled. "My circumstances in life dictated it. I am descended from a long line of Thuggee. My job paid little money, and to care for my family, I had to make a change."

"You have a family?"

"I did. Once."

Annja eyed him. "What happened?"

"Fire. It engulfed the small home I owned and took the lives of my wife and my two sons while I was at work. I left with their smiles and love and came home to their corpses." He shook his head. "It made me a very angry, very bitter man. And I was impressionable."

"Dunraj got ahold of you."

"He did. He is also descended from the Thuggee and used that as a means of bringing us together. There are not that many, but there are enough."

Annja saw all the weariness and despair that he carried. "I'm sorry for your loss."

Kormi nodded. "It is time we were going again. The longer we rest, the more chance there is that someone will discover you are no longer in your cell."

They rose and continued climbing. Annja asked him, "Where will this lead us?"

"There is an opening farther up that then leads to a small game trail that we have sometimes used to access the mountain. If you follow it, it will bring you back down the mountain, close to where we brought you in from the development."

"But won't Dunraj and his men be looking for me?"

"That is why you will have to run. Fast."

"Ah, wonderful."

They came abreast of another intersection, with one path leading down and the other up. Kormi pointed. "If Dunraj finds you gone, he will most likely come from that path. Remember that."

"I will."

Kormi pointed ahead. "That is where we need to go. Travel quickly. Something—"

His voice was cut off by the sound of an alarm echoing all over the mountain.

She glanced at him. "You guys have electricity?"

"Not everywhere, but Dunraj wanted us to lay lines so he could have power."

"Why would he need to have electricity in here?"

"I don't know," Kormi said. "But we have a mile left before you reach the exit. I suggest we run."

Annja followed him at a sprint, and as they dashed up the path she found her vision improving.

Light!

There was an opening somewhere up ahead, and she knew that must be the exit out into daylight. Or was it evening now? She had no idea how much time had passed since she'd been taken.

Kormi ran lightly and kept his hands up in front of him. As they rounded a corner, Annja saw him snap the *rumal* out in front of him with a whipping action that caught a single man running toward them unawares. The snap of the knotted end hit the man between his eyes, and he dropped.

Annja ran past him, not pausing to even wonder if he was dead or not. Kormi glanced back. "He is unconscious but will recover soon enough. We need to hasten our escape."

They ran faster. Behind them, Annja could hear shouts of other pursuers chasing them. The silence that had held sway over the entire underground fortress of caves seemed to now be a thing of the past.

"Run faster, Annja Creed," Kormi said. "Our path will be cut off otherwise."

And then he skidded to a sudden halt. Annja nearly bumped into him. But she righted herself and saw that the way ahead had several shadows in it.

More men.

Behind them, pursuers drew to a halt and advanced warily.

They were surrounded.

Kormi moved his *rumal* in vague circles as both teams of pursuers approached. Their shouts at Kormi seemed to echo off the walls.

Some of the men drew daggers.

Enough of this, thought Annja. She reached for the sword. Its gray, gleaming light filled the tunnel, and even Kormi blinked in surprise.

"Where in the world did you get that weapon?"

"A friend of mine loaned it to me," she said. "And it's quite an amazing blade."

Annja ducked and whipped the sword around, sending the dagger that had been thrown at her skittering off with a sharp clang. The knife disappeared into the shadows.

More men approached. Annja was startled. There seemed to be a lot more of them than she remembered seeing yesterday. Or was it earlier today?

"How many men are in this place?"

"Perhaps one hundred of us. Why?"

"I thought there were a dozen."

Kormi barked a quick laugh. "Not even close. That was the circle of twelve you saw—the higher-ranked Thuggee members. But Dunraj has many foot soldiers."

"And how many friends do you have among his ranks?"

"Not enough," he said.

"There's an understatement." A new voice in the tunnel.

Annja recognized it immediately. "I was wondering if you would show up here."

"Why wouldn't I?" Dunraj came from behind them, passing through ranks of his men that parted for him.

"You don't think I would let my prized possession escape so easily, do you?"

"I was hoping."

Dunraj smiled. "Ah, hope...such a vain enterprise." He looked at Kormi. "I must admit I'm surprised to find you here. You shame your ancestors with your betrayal."

"You shame Kali by committing the atrocities you do," Kormi replied.

"You would unseat me, Kormi? You would see me deposed? Then be the man you claim to be and engage me in combat. If you win, I will die happily."

Kormi was a big man, and Annja knew he was a capable fighter, but was he good enough to topple Dunraj?

He leaned closer to her. "You must get out of here. Do as I said and proceed down the game trail. If you are pursued, there will be many places to defend yourself, places where two men cannot stand abreast. Make your stand there and then get help. It will be the only thing that can save your friend."

"What about you?"

Kormi coiled his *rumal* and smiled. "It is time I account for my sins. But before I do, I will try my best to kill him."

"Can you?"

Kormi smiled. "One never knows until one tries." He looked at Dunraj. "I accept your challenge."

"Here and now," Dunraj said.

Kormi whispered to Annja, "When I say the word, you will cut down the men standing before your exit while I move to engage Dunraj. The combined action should give us both time to make our moves."

"Good luck to you, Kormi."

"Luck is not a part of my destiny, but it may be yours."

"Then I thank you for your kindness and wish you the very best."

Kormi looked at her with an almost wistful expression. "I would like to know that I could have called you a friend, Annja Creed."

Annja nodded. "I would be honored."

"So be it." Kormi tightened his jaw and murmured, "Are you ready?"

Annja's sword gleamed. Her heart pounded but the adrenaline felt as if she was welcoming back a long-lost friend. "I'm ready."

"Now!"

He threw himself past Annja and unleashed his *rumal* directly at Dunraj's head. But Annja was already running up the slope toward the men standing between her and the exit.

They started to mount their attack. Annja cut horizontally through the first man and then cleaved upward through the shoulder of the next. She doubled back with the sword and spun, hacking through the third.

Blood sprayed the interior of the tunnel, and Annja kept running.

At last she broke out of the mountain, stumbling into the evening light, and then checked behind her. No one.

At least not yet.

Annja ran down the game trail, leaving Kormi, Frank and the mountain in her wake.

21

Annja ran along the twisting trail, sending loose rock and dirt over the edge that loomed on her right side. She was corkscrewing around the mountain on the narrow path.

She paused and bent double to suck some wind into her lungs, and something whizzed over her head, rebounding off a rock close by.

Annja brought her sword up in the next instant, deflecting another shot of lead that had been aimed right at her.

Several of Dunraj's men stalked her from farther up the mountain. Each of them swirled their *rumals* like slingshots, unleashing a volley of lead shot.

There was no place to run. The next dip in the trail would give her pursuers the tactical advantage of higher ground. And there was no way Annja was going to give that to them.

Not unless she had no more pursuers.

Time to make a stand.

Annja spun and deflected two more volleys of the shot, each one clanging off her blade and skittering harmlessly away. She frowned. At least they're not grenades.

One of Dunraj's men came down the game trail. Judging by the look on his face, he was older and the more experienced. But Annja didn't have time to waste on pleasantries, because he was already whipping his *rumal* at her head, the weighted end unfurling, as lethal as the bite of a cobra.

Annja waited until it was almost unraveled and then ducked and slashed through the cloth.

Her sword didn't cut it.

Annja frowned. That was a first. But then she wondered if the material of their *rumal* was the same as what she'd been tied with.

Another end slammed into her side and almost made her drop the sword. The weight behind these shots was devastating. If Annja hung around and took more than a few, she'd be in trouble.

She rushed back up the slope as Dunraj's man was trying to recoil his weapon. He started shouting for backup from the other two, and they responded in kind, sending shots at Annja, but she only ducked them as they flew over her head.

And then she was on the closer man.

The fury in his eyes told Annja there was no way he'd ever go quietly. He smiled and seemed to wave her on.

Annja felt the power coursing through her veins, her heart pounding in her chest. She'd been feeling so inactive for so long that the thrill of getting back into combat actually felt…good.

Try explaining that to your regular dime-store shrink.

Dunraj's man circled Annja on the tiny game trail. Annja waited until he'd stepped outside of his comfort zone and then drove straight at his heart. As she suspected, he tried to avoid the thrust by backpedaling.

And that cost him.

The game trail ran out of space, and for a moment, the man hovered in the air before dropping off the side of the mountain. His screech stretched out for several seconds until it ended in sudden silence.

Annja had no time to waste looking over the mountain. Two more of Dunraj's men were coming down the trail faster. And they probably wouldn't fall for the same trick she'd just used.

As the first man came at her, he discarded his *rumal* and brought out a dagger that must have been a foot long. It reminded Annja of the kukri knives she'd seen in Nepal.

And as he cut in, it was obvious he knew how to use the blade. He feinted with a downward slash and then abandoned it midstroke, going instead for a straight stab aimed at Annja's heart.

She pivoted as much as she could and almost found herself without any ground under her feet. She cut upward with her sword. It rang as it collided with the knife blade, and both of them bounced away from each other.

Annja was breathing hard and enjoying the strain of exertion. The man wore a smile over a face that looked as if someone had used it to sharpen their knives on. Several vertical scars ran the length of his mug, from his eyebrows down to his neck.

Whoever this guy is, thought Annja, he knows how to fight.

He attacked again, this time opting for a quick series of slashes aimed at Annja's head. Annja brought the sword up, and the man tried to close the distance with her to render the sword's advantage of length obsolete.

But Annja shoved him away. As she did, however, she felt the knife blade cut into the back of her forearm and draw blood.

The wound was superficial, and far better to take it on the outside of her forearm than the inner part with its arteries.

But Annja had had enough. She drove the man back with a series of downward cuts that forced him to retreat to ward them off. Annja got him into a rhythm and then abruptly brought the sword back up and impaled him with a simple thrust to his stomach.

Her blade slid in far too easily, and the expression on the man's face was one of shock.

Annja jerked the blade out and let the corpse fall to the ground.

Her last opponent took a look at the dead man and frowned. He'd already seen two of his comrades killed.

"Don't do it," she said quietly.

But he did. He came flying over the corpse in a frenzied attack that forced Annja to back up three steps to absorb the weight of his attack.

And then she dropped and cut horizontally.

Cutting the man nearly in two.

He dropped, and Annja didn't wait any longer. She turned and kept moving down the game trail.

The trail seemed to widen in places and then narrow again as she came around a bend. But she kept her head low, on the lookout for any more of Dunraj's men.

The sun was dipping lower in the western sky, staining the horizon with red. She was still far too high on the mountain. To get down, find her way back to the development, call Pradesh and get the cavalry out here, she'd need a lot more time than she had. She couldn't just run down the mountain or she'd risk death.

And with Frank scheduled to be sacrificed tomorrow, she wasn't sure she could make it in time.

Around the next bend, Annja took a moment to get her breath. The sword had grown heavy, and she put it back in its resting place.

The trail ahead wandered between two higher elevations, making it look like a hidden valley. Annja got herself together and wandered into it.

And instantly, a volley of lead shot rained down on her.

Far above, she spotted more of Dunraj's men. But they were at least two hundred feet above her. There was no way she could do anything except ward off the shower of lead that was pelting her.

Annja ran through the valley and then stumbled. It felt as though her foot had caught on something and she'd twisted her ankle. She bit down to keep from crying out in pain, but the stumble didn't go unnoticed by Dunraj's men, who cheered from above.

The pelting stopped.

Annja grabbed at her leg. They'll be coming for me now, she thought. Now that they've softened me up with the lead shot, they'll take advantage of the fact that I fell to come and cut me to ribbons.

Or bring me back to Dunraj.

She tried to put weight on her ankle, but grimaced. It wasn't going to work.

Annja tried to estimate how long it would take Dunraj's men to get to her. Maybe a minute? Maybe longer?

She couldn't stay here and wait for them.

Annja edged her way toward a giant boulder she saw off to one side of the valley. The going was tough but she was thankful the valley floor was hard shale. At least she wasn't leaving signs of which way she'd gone.

If she could just get behind the giant rock, she might be in a position to fend them off or at least keep them bottled up.

She pulled herself behind the giant rock. It was darker in here, and for a moment, Annja couldn't see a thing. The sun had already dropped beyond this valley and cast no more light up here.

That would help.

She froze in the next instant as she heard the delicate and tentative approach of footfalls on the valley floor outside.

Annja held her breath.

Would they think she was still there? Or would they race ahead to see if she'd been able to hobble farther down the trail.

Annja clutched her knees together and waited in the recessed shadows of the boulder.

She could hear them speaking now. Whispering in harsh voices that told Annja there were no guarantees they'd bring her back to Dunraj alive. She'd pissed them off enough to make them want to kill her.

She pressed herself deeper into the rock, willing the ancient stone to accept her into its folds.

And then she saw the black cloth-swaddled foot appear just outside the rock. These guys were so quiet, it really annoyed her.

A face appeared next, trying to penetrate the thick darkness.

Annja stabbed him right through his head with the sword, and he sank without a sound.

So much for me hiding and them going away, Annja thought frustratedly. She steeled herself for another attack.

But after several minutes, no one else came to check on him.

Annja could hear them moving around outside of the boulder, but there was no plan to their search. They were swarming over anything they thought might be hiding Annja.

And she realized that the corpse in front of her might look as if he was simply checking under the rock.

She might have a few minutes.

At least until they decided to move on and one of them wondered why the dead man hadn't moved in several minutes.

And then the corpse was jerked out suddenly. And this time Annja knew her hiding spot was compromised.

But where could she go?

It was impossible to back up right then. The boulder pressed itself into her spine and enveloped her on three sides.

All she could do was keep her back to it and hope they could only attack one at a time.

She saw another face and stabbed at it, but missed. A wicked smile flashed in the darkness, and she felt the bite of a dagger blade on her foot. Annja kicked out and then followed up with another stab.

She pressed farther back into the rock.

Was this her last stand?

Annja could hear them shouting now, probably calling to one another that they'd found her hiding place.

They would come at her in force.

Overwhelm her.

And kill her.

Annja pressed farther back. Damned foot, she thought. If I hadn't tripped I could take them all on.

But no, I had to trip.

She was so frustrated, she shoved her back into the rock.

And was surprised—shocked—when a second later she was tumbling backward through the air into more darkness.

22

Annja hit the ground, and the wind jumped out of her lungs. She continued tumbling down a steep slope until at last she came to rest at the bottom.

In pitch-darkness.

Annja got to her feet slowly, unsure of herself at first. But the pain in her ankle had subsided, and she suspected it hadn't actually been sprained at all, just more of a strain. Her head felt a little bruised but not nearly as bad as it had been the last time she rolled down a steep embankment. This time she was conscious and able to tuck her chin into her chest to protect the back of her skull.

Thank goodness, she thought.

But where was she?

She looked around her but could see very little in the darkness. Annja materialized the sword, and instantly, she got some illumination. But the sword's grayish glow only expanded so far. And all Annja could see around her was the inside of the mountain.

Had she somehow gotten herself back into the mountain by another route? But if so, then how come Kormi hadn't told her about it?

Maybe he didn't know, she thought.

He did say something about Dunraj possibly having an entire network of tunnels that no one else knew about. But why would he need those? How come he couldn't travel like the rest of his men?

Was he up to something other than ritual murder for his beloved Kali?

She wandered gingerly back to the slope and looked up. She'd fallen almost thirty feet down the steep incline. Had it not been for that sloped path, she would have simply dropped and died when she hit the ground.

How long would it be before the rest of Dunraj's men found their way into the secret passageway? She couldn't count on them not finding it. And that meant she'd have to find her way out of here.

She certainly couldn't go back the way she'd just come, not unless she wanted to have to battle the fifty or so men who were probably crawling all over that rock.

No thanks.

Annja held the sword aloft. Its light showed that she was in a smaller cavern than many of the others she'd been in throughout the fortress. Annja hobbled from end to end and then finally saw the passageway that led out of the cavern.

Annja was confused. The entire place was hard to find and harder still to orient herself to. Where was she going? Where did this passage lead?

Nothing to do but get busy doing it, she decided. She moved into the next passage, and the air grew darker around her still. But the sword managed to shed some light.

She'd moved into a tight tunnel that she could barely stand in. The point of her sword brushed the ceiling several times, giving off a scraping sound that seemed to echo back into the other chamber.

She'd have to remember to keep the noise to a minimum. Once Dunraj's men found their way into the cavern, they'd swarm all over, looking for her.

And they wouldn't rest until Annja was dead.

Annja worried that she might have wandered into a dead end. But as the passage closed in, she spotted another opening down at the bottom and then had to crawl through it.

The good thing, she decided, was that anyone pursuing her was going to have to get past a number of hurdles and obstacles before they were able to confront her. And at any moment, they might get tired of chasing and simply give up.

Yeah, right.

She smirked. These men weren't country bumpkins. They were hardened criminals and murderers. If they wanted Annja, there wasn't much she was going to be able to do about it.

Annja dragged herself through the opening and then felt herself run right into a rock.

Dead end?

She pushed against it, but it was solid. There was no way she would have been led down this path without there being some reason for its existence. It didn't seem natural. This had been hewn out of the rock. The sides of the wall were all extremely sharp. If it had been the nature of the walls in her cell, she and Frank would have had no problem sawing their bindings off.

Annja felt around the rock that barred her way. And then into the wall itself. On the third pass, she found the hidden trip switch.

She pressed it.

And the rock barring her path suddenly swung out of the way.

Feeling pleased, Annja hauled herself through the opening, noting a sudden shift of air. The sword revealed she could once again stand at full height. She marveled at the room she'd come into.

It was decorated exactly like an expensive condominium. Comfortable sofas and chairs furnished the room. And there were even windows that let in light.

Annja frowned. She was in the mountain. How could windows be letting in light?

They had to be fake, she realized. And then it made sense. Dunraj had asked his men to lay electricity cables to bring power to the mountain. But they had no idea why.

Now she did.

Dunraj had himself a nice comfortable home here. While the rest of his men lived in much more austere conditions in their caves, Dunraj lived like a king. Annja wondered just how devoted to Kali he truly was.

It was tough maintaining that religious fervor when the life of luxury was so much easier to embrace.

And enjoy.

Annja studied one of the couches more closely in disdain. The cushions must have been handmade. She wondered exactly how Dunraj had managed to transport all of this stuff into the mountain without his men ever getting wise to it.

Then again, she'd known religious zealots who were so blind they could barely see the tips of their noses.

Annja put her sword away. The light from the fake windows was enough to see by, and Annja walked the entire layout, memorizing it. It reminded her of the building where Dunraj had hosted his welcome party. She wondered if he had a condo that looked like this on another floor back in Hyderabad.

She entered the kitchen and found her way to the refrigerator. Opening it, she helped herself to a bottle of water and a hunk of cheese.

And then she heard a noise.

She quickly hid behind one of the chairs in the living room.

Just in time.

"I don't care what it takes, make sure you find her."

Dunraj's voice echoed across the condominium. Annja saw his boots as he came into the condo and stalked across the living-room floor. He collapsed into one of the sofas and then she heard the beep of a cell-phone call being disconnected.

So he had cell-phone service, too?

Interesting.

I wonder what his men would think about their glorious leader using a cell phone to make calls. Come to think of it, I wonder what Kali would think of her most ardent supporter using such technology around sacred lands?

Dunraj let out a sigh and then Annja heard him press the buttons to make another call. There was a pause before he started speaking again.

"It's me….No. No, they haven't found her yet….Yes, I know. I've told them that. They know what must be done." Another pause. "And what about on your end? Have you dealt with him?…Why not? The longer he stays alive the more likely he is to find out. He needs to die."

Annja held her breath. Dunraj was obviously in league with someone other than the men he led.

But who?

"Well, just get it done. It's almost your turn, anyway."

Annja frowned. What the hell did that mean?

Dunraj disconnected and then got up from the sofa. He stalked out of the room, and Annja heard a door open and close.

Another way out?

Maybe it was the network of extra tunnels Kormi had hinted at. Maybe Dunraj had direct access to them from this condominium. And if so, could Annja use them to rescue Frank?

She had to try.

Slowly, she rose from behind the chair and headed in the direction Dunraj had taken.

A bedroom with a king-size bed loomed before her. He'd been in here. But where did he go?

All she saw was a bathroom off to one side and a giant walk-in closet on the other.

Two chances.

Annja chose the closet.

She walked in through the expensive suits hanging

on the racks. Why would Dunraj need such finery for living inside a mountain? It didn't make sense.

Annja pressed deeper into the closet and then found herself facing a back wall.

What were the odds this was a false door?

She ran her hands along the edge of the wood. Up near the top where the piece met the ceiling, she found the splinter of wood and pressed it in. She heard a click and pressed the door open.

And walked back into the rough interior of the mountain. Up ahead of her, about two hundred yards away, she saw Dunraj striding along a well-lit path.

Annja ducked as soon as she came through the door. Fortunately, she had cover nearby.

But Dunraj didn't even look back, intent as he was on getting somewhere.

Annja gave him ten more seconds and then rose from her hiding spot.

If she could catch up with him, then she could force him to get Frank and bring him to her. And if he had a cell phone, Annja could use it to call Pradesh and his police to come to the rescue.

That would work.

By tomorrow morning, Annja could be back at the hotel, enjoying a nice long, hot bath.

And then they could fly home. World's Greatest Monster Mystery Solved.

She hobbled faster down the path toward Dunraj. But he kept his pace brisk, and Annja found herself falling behind. The path was lit with overhead lightbulbs, and Annja wondered how much electricity this place must use.

And who was paying the bills?

Dunraj obviously had extensive connections, but what exactly was he involved with here? He'd set himself up to live like a king, complete with an army of criminals ready to kill in the name of a goddess they believed would protect them.

But Annja doubted whether Kali ever would.

Dunraj needed to be brought down.

He turned suddenly, and Annja froze, halfway expecting him to see her in the corridor. If he did, she'd have precious few moments to make her move. She was too far away from him to present much of a threat, aside from shouting an insult at him. But Dunraj paid her no attention.

And then he was gone.

Annja frowned. Where had he disappeared?

She rushed ahead, fighting off her aches. I need to see where he goes, she thought.

But when she got to where Dunraj had turned, there was nothing there.

23

Annja followed that part of the corridor around and found that it looped back on itself. This place has more hiding spots than any I've ever seen, she thought.

Dunraj had gone somewhere, but where exactly, Annja couldn't quite say. And she was rapidly tiring of chasing him. Besides, if Dunraj was still alive, that could mean Kormi was dead. *Not* something she was prepared to consider right now. She needed to get back into the mountain, find Frank and Kormi, and get the hell out of this godforsaken place.

But that was easier said than done.

Still, she studied each section of the wall, and on the third go-around she found another secret entrance.

Annja stepped through into a different area of the mountain altogether. She heard the sounds of shovels and pickaxes and the clang of steel on rock. Somewhere far off, she thought she heard what sounded like a pneumatic hammer or some type of motorized excavation.

And when she came around the corner, the sight that greeted her was the last she would have expected. A full-fledged dig was apparently happening right inside the mountain, far below where she huddled.

But what were they digging for? She crouched behind a rock and studied the scene. There were at least ten workers engaged in hauling dirt and rock away from a central focal point.

And Annja saw that there was a statue still partially covered by rock. The statue looked familiar.

Kali.

Was Dunraj digging for treasure in the mountain itself? If so, then how did the cult of Thuggee figure into things? Were these men criminals who sacrificed to cover up the fact that they were treasure hunters?

She turned back to the statue. One of the arms appeared to be solid gold. And this incarnation of Kali had ten arms. It stood at least fifty feet high and twenty feet wide. Its sheer size and weight would mean that the gold alone would be worth millions. Jewel-encrusted headpieces adorned this statue, as well.

Annja slumped back behind the rock. Dunraj was excavating artifacts from the mountain—from the very sacred land he pretended to protect with his gang of thugs.

Did the rest of his men realize this? Did they know what he was up to? And if not, then how could Dunraj keep all of this concealed from them?

Annja rose and watched the work for another five minutes. The workers were taking the dirt and stone out of the chamber that lay below. Annja had to find out where they were taking it.

She snaked her way down a walkway that led closer to where the workers were digging out the statue.

The workers themselves looked as though they were average diggers at any other site. They didn't look like the Thuggee men that Annja had run into elsewhere in the mountain.

How was it that the two sides didn't know of each other's presence?

Surely they would have passed in the tunnels, wouldn't they?

Annja saw a conveyor carrying lots of boulders and dirt away from the main dig site. It vanished around a corner.

I need to follow that, Annja thought.

She waited for a worker to walk past her position and then snuck farther along the passageway. The conveyor belt trundled next to her, and she could see the rocks bouncing on the rubber belt.

Then, around the next corner, it vanished into some type of feeder machine. Annja saw an even more spectacular operation happening here. Spray hoses wet the rocks entering the feed machine, and she could see pneumatic pumps jostling trays and separating the boulders and dirt from each other.

But what were they looking for here?

Hearing a number of voices close by, Annja huddled under one of the legs of the feeder machine, pressing herself deeper into the shadows.

She needed the entire picture if she wanted to topple Dunraj's plans.

The men moved on, and Annja clambered out from

under the feeder machine. She walked down and then saw a front loader busy loading a dump truck.

Annja stopped.

There were trucks in the mountain? How was that even possible? As far as she knew, there was no way to enter or exit the mountain in something even remotely as large as these trucks.

So how in the world had they gotten them in here?

She drew closer and the noise became deafening. The sound alone should have clued Dunraj's Thuggee men in to the fact that their boss wasn't exactly being as honest with them as he claimed to be.

The more she saw, the more Annja suspected that Dunraj was using the Thuggee to accomplish his more secular goals. Certainly he wasn't interested in the worship of Kali. Whatever he did to promote that ideal was one thing, but Dunraj was clearly focused on something much bigger.

And much more lucrative.

The excavation of the Kali statue would no doubt be worth many millions of dollars, but there was something else going on here, as well.

Annja glanced back at the feeder machine and then at the various hoses that led out of it.

She frowned.

Minerals?

Gold.

Dunraj was mining the mountain from the inside out. And he was taking whatever he could get. It had obviously once been a refuge for the Thuggee and their various treasures. Dunraj would take those, as well.

But his real goal was to strip the mountain.

And why not? Doing it this way he didn't have to apply for permits or licenses or even let the government know what he was up to.

He could clean the mountain out and leave the shell behind, and no one would know any better.

So, why employ the Thuggee? To scare the residents away? Or perhaps the residents themselves had heard noises they couldn't explain. Maybe they were complaining and threatening to expose Dunraj's operation.

Something needed to be done, and the murders were it.

So Dunraj goes and gets himself a band of religious zealots and starts up the blood worship of Kali again. The residents are terrified and can't even think about asking questions about strange mechanical noises when it's not even safe to walk around outside at night.

Annja shook her head. Certainly not the most ingenious plan she'd ever heard of, but Dunraj seemed to know what he was doing. Although eating *hearts?* How had he managed to bring himself to that—and convince others to join him?

The other question that remained disturbed her, too. How was he getting all this material excavated and out of the mountain?

She heard a rumble of a big dump truck and turned to see one bearing down on her. Annja felt the first waves of panic. Had she been seen? Was it coming to run her over?

Annja eased herself closer to the next outcropping of rock and waited. Apparently she was safe; she hadn't been seen. And as the dump truck passed by, she grabbed the metal handle and swung herself up onto the back of the truck.

She ducked down and kept herself as hidden as possible as the dump truck rumbled through the caverns. The air quality was good, too. Dust seemed almost nonexistent for some reason, but then Annja saw air blowers and extractor fans.

Dunraj was looking out for his people. Annja frowned. Yeah, right. She doubted that's why he'd had them installed. But the less complaints he received from this crew, the better they'd be able to work.

The truck continued on, and then Annja saw something ahead of her that made her blink.

An actual paved road sprawled ahead of the truck.

He's got a highway down here?

And sure enough, the dump truck trundled onto the highway entrance and then started heading for an elaborate concrete tunnel. Signs in Hindi pointed out certain routes, and the truck appeared to be speeding up.

This was her chance. Annja could ride the truck and see where it went, or she could stay behind and try to free Frank.

She looked ahead as she felt the dump truck's engine kick up a gear. There was no telling how far the truck would have to drive to dump its load. It might have to go all the way back to Hyderabad for all she knew.

And if that happened, how would she find her way back to Frank?

Annja made her decision and jumped off, tucking and rolling as the truck entered the tunnel.

The impact with the paved road hurt a lot more than

she'd thought it would, but Annja kept rolling until she'd absorbed the impact as much as possible.

Then she got up and ran for the closest cover she could find: an electrical transformer that controlled the juice for this section of the excavation.

Annja huddled there and tried to get her bearings. There were workers everywhere, and some of them seemed to be on break.

She needed to find her way back to the cave where the Thuggee were. If she could lead them down here and prove that Dunraj was double-dealing with them, then they'd turn against him.

She hoped.

And what time was it now? It had to be well after sunset. Yet, the work continued down here. Clearly Dunraj was on some sort of schedule. He had shifts going twenty-four hours a day.

That was good for him, but problematic for Annja. Somehow she had to maneuver her way through all of these guys before she was discovered.

She spotted what looked like a bathroom facility and one guy heading for it. She made her decision quickly and rose from her hiding place, striding across the ground.

As long as she walked with purpose, most people wouldn't stop her or question her right to be there.

Ahead of her, the man entered the bathroom.

Annja wrinkled her nose, already able to smell the stench of the place. But it was an opportunity she couldn't pass up.

She knocked on the portable bathroom.

Someone called out from inside.

Annja quickly grasped the door handle and opened it.

Stepping inside, she clocked the man from behind.

As he fell, she caught him and dragged him out and behind the bathroom. Then she stripped off his work clothes and helmet and put them on. She stowed him back in the bathroom, and when she closed the door she broke the handle so it wouldn't open.

It wouldn't buy her much time, but she hoped she could at least get back to the dig site without any interference.

She hoped.

As she walked, she passed other workers. She kept her head down and sped up, pretending she was late for some sort of appointment elsewhere on the site. A few people called out to her, but she ignored them and kept walking.

She made it back to the feed-machine area and took a moment to catch her breath and wipe the sweat from her eyes.

That's when she saw people running toward the bathroom.

Uh-oh.

She turned and started to head back toward the dig site.

And nearly bumped into someone.

A harsh voice barked at her. Annja's helmet came off and rolled away.

She scrambled for it.

Grabbed it and stood to replace it on her head.

And came face-to-face with Dunraj.

"You seem to turn up in the most unexpected places." Then he punched her in the head.

24

When Annja came to, her ears told her that she was still down by the excavation site. She blinked a couple times, and the light made her shut her eyes again.

"Ouch."

Dunraj's face swam into view. "Yes, that was a nasty little shot I gave you there, eh? Not bad for the inter-collegiate lightweight boxing champion at Oxford, was it?"

Annja went to rub her jaw but found she couldn't move her hands. Oh, no, she thought. Not again.

She turned her head and found that her arms were tied out on either side of her with her hands pinned palms down at her wrists. She was strapped to the conveyor belt that she'd followed down to the dump-truck area.

"I think it's time we had ourselves a talk, don't you?"

"Let me go," she said. "I don't give a damn that you're raping the mountain. Just let me go."

"'Raping the mountain.'" Dunraj rubbed his chin

thoughtfully. "You know, I quite like that. I may use that, if you don't mind."

"Sure. Knock yourself out." Annja craned her neck. The feeder machine was stopped. She knew why.

"Is this all for me?"

Dunraj smiled. "I'm quite taken with you, Annja. Truly. I didn't give you enough credit. And yet, here you are. You've managed to escape and kill an awful lot of my men. And then you somehow found your way down here, and I am at quite a loss as to how to explain it all. Not that I haven't tried, but I've really not been able to come up with anything."

"That's a shame."

"I don't suppose you'd be willing to let me in on all of your little secrets, would you?"

"Just as soon as you let me off this conveyor belt."

Dunraj clapped his hands. "Yes, well, there's that, isn't there? The problem is, of course, that you seem to have discovered an inordinate amount of information about me. And frankly, it's information I like to keep secret."

"The highway back to Hyderabad," Annja said suddenly. "You're going to create a new roadway through the mountain. That will let you open up whole new areas for development, and if anyone wants to use your new road, they'll probably have to pay you a grand sum."

Dunraj smiled even wider now. "You are a marvel. Marry me."

Annja smirked. "You're such a romantic, tying me up like this when you propose. It's so, so…"

"Twenty-first-century power couple?"

"I was thinking lunatic-asylum-bound," she replied.

Dunraj sighed. "But I could never really be sure you were trustworthy, could I? No, I suppose not. Oh, well."

"Wow, that was a quick relationship. I'd better change my status on Facebook before someone else beats me to it."

"While you're there you might consider posting a last will and testament, because I'm afraid that very shortly, you'll be bound for the afterlife."

"And here I thought that you'd want to carve me up like you did that guy earlier. You know, have another one of your heart feasts."

Dunraj shook his head. "I considered dragging you back to the other cave, but you seem to have this penchant for escaping. And it wouldn't do to have you blathering on about this dig site. Some of the men over there might grow suspicious of me and what I'm up to. I can't have that."

"So you'll kill me here?"

"Yes."

Annja jerked at the chains holding her arms in place. But they were solid steel.

"I don't think you'll find them all that easy to escape," Dunraj said. "They're layered steel."

"And what—you're going to send me into your little machine there?"

"You know what it's for?"

"I have an idea. It makes big rocks into smaller rocks."

He nodded. "It helps us extract the minerals. Sometimes we find gold, sometimes other more valuable things. But either way, it doesn't matter in your case. We've removed our rocks from the machine and have set it up especially for you."

"You're really going to too much trouble on my account," Annja said. "You could have just shot me."

"I rather fancy myself more creative than that."

Annja tested the chains again, but they were wrapped around her wrists too tight. Not good. She glanced at Dunraj. "Tell me something."

"Perhaps."

Annja shrugged. "What? You've got me strapped down to a conveyor belt, and shortly you'll send me in to be ground up into tiny pieces. You can't spare a little information?"

"Depends on the information, Annja."

"Consider it a last request."

Dunraj sighed. "We'll see."

"What's the deal with the Thuggee thing?"

Dunraj cocked his head. "What do you mean?"

"I mean, you've got them here for some reason. I don't buy for one second that you're a devotee of Kali. Even if you're eating hearts raw. You're down here desecrating her sacred lands, for crying out loud."

"And what would you know of worship and all it entails?"

"I know enough to recognize a fraud when I see one. And you are a fraud. Whatever your men believe about you, it isn't the truth."

"My men believe exactly what I want them to believe. That I am a high priest of Kali and a Thuggee leader. They should all do what I say. And everything was working perfectly well until you and your cameraman came stumbling into town."

"So, your men are simply here to help perpetrate a ruse, right? To scare the residents and what—get them to sell their homes to you so you can turn around and develop this part of the area, too?"

"Maybe."

Annja frowned. "Some last request."

"I don't really care what you think about my plans here, Annja. And a big part of me is attracted to the idea of you dying without ever knowing the answers."

"I'll come back from the dead and haunt your ass."

"Idle threats."

"Oh, you'd better believe I will. You kill me now, start counting down the minutes until I come back for you and drag you down to hell with me."

Dunraj smiled. "I enjoy our repartee. It's a refreshing change from my usual boring conversations of the day."

"Unstrap me and we can talk for hours."

"Not a chance, my dear."

"Worth a shot." She struggled again with the chains. "One more thing, if you don't mind."

"You're really getting on my last nerve. What do you want now?"

"Frank."

Dunraj looked at her. "What about him?"

"Let him go. He's had nothing to do with any of this. It's my fault he got caught up in it all."

"I admire your loyalty to your friend. But unfortunately, he's seen and heard far too much."

"Oh, for crying out loud, Dunraj. His death won't make any difference to you. And not killing him wouldn't affect you, either."

He shrugged. "That's true, I suppose. It doesn't really make much of a difference either way. But I think I'll kill him just the same. And you know why?"

"Why?"

"Because you don't want me to do it. And that alone will give me a great deal of pleasure."

Annja stared him in the eyes. "I want you to know something."

"What's that?"

"I'm going to enjoy seeing the police lock you up very, very much."

"Bold words," Dunraj said. "Considering you're about to be made into tiny little Annja Creeds. I wonder what your obituary will say? Have you ever given that any thought? What those you leave behind will say about you?"

"I've got very interesting friends. I'd rather they all come after you than write some sappy obituary."

"Touching." Dunraj checked his watch. "Unfortunately, I see our time has just about come to an end."

"Has it? I thought we were just getting warmed up."

"Tragically, no." Dunraj kissed her on her forehead. "My darling, I'm afraid I must bid you adieu."

Annja felt the conveyor belt lurch underneath her, and then she was moving along at a slow pace toward the feeder machine about two hundred feet away.

"You couldn't have put me closer? What's the deal with this? You milking the moment?"

"It gives you time to think about the inevitable. And then when the first waves of pain wash over you and you're rendered into pulverized flesh, your last thought will be that I remain alive."

Annja smiled. "I meant what I said, Dunraj."

"About what?"

"About me coming back to haunt you. You think I'm joking. But I'm not."

Dunraj smirked. "You've been impressive, Annja. No one could dispute that. But even you won't be able to escape this."

"You'd better hope not. But just in case, have you given thought to your obituary?"

"Not really. I suppose that's one more way we're alike."

Annja shook her head. "We're not alike at all, Dunraj. I have respect for things from the past. You just hope to profit from them."

"You profit from them with your TV show."

Annja glanced ahead of her. The feeder machine loomed larger, and she could see the separator trays working like giant metallic teeth. Her feet would enter them first.

Not good.

She couldn't free her hands, couldn't get a grip on the sword to cut her chains away.

What the hell was she going to do?

"Dunraj, let me out of here."

But he was already behind her now and on his way. "Farewell, Annja Creed. Godspeed and all that jazz."

I'm really starting to hate that guy's guts, she thought.

But she had no more time to dwell on Dunraj.

She looked for the sword where it waited. She visualized it in her hands, visualized it cutting the chains.

But she couldn't get a grasp on it.

Damn.

Fifty feet away, the feeder machine's hungry jaws worked tirelessly.

Ready to devour her.

25

The conveyor belt churned beneath her, carrying Annja Creed toward an extremely painful death. She struggled against the chains, but it was no use. With each passing second, the conveyor belt carried her closer to her fate.

Annja tried to manifest the sword again, but without mobility in her hands, she found herself unable to do it. She could not get the sword to materialize.

She felt each bump underneath her back as the belt rattled along. The grinding gears thundered into one another like a giant wood chipper.

There's no way I'm going to survive that, Annja thought.

She kicked out with her legs, trying to free them, as well, but the chains that held her arms also pinned her feet.

She was helpless.

Is this it? Is this how it ends at last? I've carried that sword as a weapon for good and justice for years now, and when I finally need it the most, it lets me down. She frowned. Was this God's plan? Was this how He had written her fate?

Her life?

The noise of the feeder machine was overpowering, and she knew that no one would hear her. The belt moved her closer to the machine.

Toward her death.

Another few seconds and it would be all over. Another few seconds and she'd feel those first waves of agony before she blacked out.

And then the machine switched off, freezing the separator trays in midmotion, splayed apart as if in midchew. Annja looked around furiously.

"Hiya, Annja."

She looked back. "Frank?"

He grinned.

"Your timing couldn't be better. I'd ask you how you got free, but there's no time! Hurry up and get me out of here before Dunraj comes back and finds that we're both free."

Together they got the chains off and Annja hopped off the conveyor belt. She wobbled a bit and then righted herself. Frank held her up. "Looks like you've been busy." He glanced around. "What the hell is all this stuff?"

"Never mind," she replied. "We've got to get you out of here."

"Where am I going?"

"Hyderabad. You're going to find Pradesh and tell him about this place. Have him get the police or military or whatever and come out here to shut down Dunraj."

"And what about you?"

"Me?" Annja smiled. "I'm going after Dunraj."

"Alone? Don't be foolish. He's got a ton of guys and they'll kill you."

Annja shook her head. "You're going to have to trust me on this, Frank. And believe me when I tell you that Dunraj doesn't stand a chance against me."

"You say that so confidently."

"I am confident."

Frank frowned. "I don't like it."

"You don't have to like it. Do what I say and find your way to Hyderabad. There are trucks leaving all the time, taking the dirt out of here and dumping it somewhere along the way. There's got to be an exit out of the underground tunnel. Make a note of it and tell Pradesh to use it as the entrance to get his teams in here."

Frank nodded as he listened. "All right, but how do I get out of here?"

Annja pointed farther down. "You see that truck?"

"Yeah?"

"You're hitching a ride on it. Climb into the back when it's done loading and then ride it out. Once you get out of the tunnel, continue to the dump site or jump off and get help from the locals somewhere."

"This is getting very complicated."

Annja grabbed him and shoved him toward the dump truck. "Trust me, you'll be safer this way. I couldn't bear having your death on my conscience. Go now and call Pradesh. He'll know what to do."

"But what am I supposed to tell him?"

"Tell him Dunraj is dirty. That he's digging the mountain out and that the murders are all his doing. Pradesh will be able to act on that and come back here with the support we need, okay?"

Frank nodded. "Yeah. Okay." He started running toward the dump truck. "Take care of yourself, Annja."

Annja watched him climb into the back of the nearest dump truck and huddle next to a big pile of dirt. The truck moved off, and Frank waved once before getting his head back down.

Annja gave him a thumbs-up and then turned back around.

Time to find Dunraj.

But the man standing in front of her didn't look as if he was going to let that happen.

He stood about six feet two inches, and he held a long steel pipe, roughly three feet long.

He said something to Annja and then smiled.

The meaning was pretty clear.

He's going to try to kill me. Unfortunately for him, I'm not bound.

Instantly the sword was in her hands. Its strength flowed into her arms and throughout her body.

Annja regarded the man, whose shock registered on his face. "Let's make this quick, sweetie. I've got a boss to kill."

If he was afraid of the sudden appearance of the sword, he didn't let it slow him down. His first attack was a straight thrust aimed at Annja's chest. She pivoted and cut in at his hands.

But he was quick. He backhanded her, and Annja took the side of the pipe to her rib cage. She heard the crunch and felt the stabbing pain lance through her chest.

Cracked ribs, she thought. There goes sleeping for the next few months.

She wheeled away and brought up her sword as the next swing came screaming in at her head. He's swinging for the fences.

She dropped to one knee and grimaced as her cracked ribs shouted their protest. But Annja kept going, driving in and cutting up as the man used the pipe like a staff and warded off her cuts.

Then he flipped the pipe down onto the flat of Annja's blade. The impact jarred the blade out of her hands, and Annja watched the sword skip away.

"Now! Kill her now!"

She knew that voice.

Annja looked up and saw Dunraj watching the action from a higher vantage point. She smiled. "I'll be right there."

Annja reached out and took the sword back into her hands. The man with the pipe sensed an opportunity and came in hard, swinging at her repeatedly. She backpedaled against each successive cut and launched her own counterattacks.

But Pipe Man was skilled with his weapon and knew how to defend himself against the blade. And no matter how much Annja cut at him, he was able to deflect and ward off each slice she aimed his way.

Annja jumped away out of reach of his next attack and paused to breathe. Both of them were winded. The constant back and forth was taking its toll. And Annja felt as if she was breathing fire with every gasp. Damn the broken ribs.

Pipe Man recovered quicker than she did and drove in

hard, this time coming straight down as if he was chopping wood. Annja backed away, but he kept advancing.

And then she stumbled down the slope.

Not again.

Annja rolled and came to her feet, then dived just in time to avoid the next swing of the pipe.

She cut back and felt the blade just barely score a line across the man's chest. She caught the smell of blood in the air and saw him grimace.

Annja nodded. "Now it's more even."

Pipe Man watched her guardedly now, aware that the blade could indeed reach him.

Annja felt a new wave of strength flood her limbs, and she drove at him this time, attacking with all of her spirit.

Every cut and slice was echoed by a shout and yell from her as Annja dug deep and found the strength to keep up a continuous barrage of attacks.

Now it was Pipe Man's turn to go on the defense. Annja drove him back, ever back toward the feeder machine that Frank had stalled.

The Pipe Man stumbled, and Annja cut down on his wrist, severing his hand. He screamed and fell back.

The pipe clattered away across the dirt.

Annja raised her sword and prepared to finish him off.

And then Annja felt something lance her side—heard the gunshot—and stumbled forward against the feeder machine.

Two things happened next. The conveyor belt started up again, and Pipe Man scrambled to jump off.

But the cuff of his work pants was caught up in the

separator trays and grinding gears. He screamed, and Annja turned away as he was dragged into the teeth of the machine.

He only screamed for a moment.

Annja huddled next to the machine and risked peering out from around the corner.

Another shot rang out and hit the leg of the machine. Annja ducked back.

As long as Dunraj held the higher ground, he'd be able to keep shooting at her, and eventually, he might even get lucky.

She felt her side and knew the bullet had merely grazed her. But she was bleeding.

Again.

Another shot rang out, but it was poorly aimed, and Annja watched it hit a rock across the way. The rest of the workmen had stopped and were running from the action.

Annja moved around to the other side of the machine. Bright red blood was spilling out of its extractor, and Annja saw white ground-up bits of bone and gristle.

She blanched, but then saw that Dunraj had abandoned his vantage point.

That gave her the chance to move up.

She took it.

Running as fast as her ribs and gunshot wound would allow, Annja broke for the upper level. She had to catch up with Dunraj. With Frank successfully out of the tunnel, she had little to worry about.

Kormi was most likely dead. But Annja would avenge his death when she dealt with Dunraj.

She passed the statue of Kali and paused. The place was completely deserted.

And then she heard the click behind her.

She turned.

Dunraj stood there, a smile plastered on his smug face. "This is the last time you'll be a problem for me, my dear."

He fired the gun.

26

But Annja was already moving, bringing her sword up and taking herself out of the line of the bullet. It smacked into the flat of her sword blade and bounced harmlessly away.

Dunraj saw her cutting down the distance and knew he wouldn't be able to reacquire the target, so he tossed the gun and drew his own knife. Then he went to meet Annja in a furious clanging of steel blades.

"Where did you ever get that sword?"

Annja grimaced as the force of their exchange made her arms ache. "A friend of mine lent it to me."

"Here? Who?"

Annja smirked. "Remember how I told you I was going to come back and haunt you?"

Dunraj laughed. He redoubled his attack and drove Annja back toward the statue of Kali. "Let's see how well you fare dealing with this."

He launched a series of quick, shallow swipes with

his dagger, and Annja had to use her sword in a way she hadn't before. The sword's normal length gave her the advantage of distance, but with Dunraj in so close, she had to flip it this way and that and rely on her ability to pivot within the killing zone to deflect and otherwise avoid his attacks.

I can't keep this up forever, she thought. And so she closed with Dunraj, stared him straight in the eye and then shoved him back with every ounce of strength she had left.

He flew away from her, but as he did so, his knife raked down her forearm.

Annja clamped her hand over it, trying to stem the flow of blood, but it was coming fast, and she was already feeling woozy.

Dunraj charged her again, and Annja's attempt to block him was a feeble one. He sensed the opportunity and charged again and again. It was all Annja could do to keep her blade between them to gain some time.

But Dunraj wasn't about to give her that time. He kept driving her back toward the statue of Kali, and Annja backpedaled as much as she could, but in the end she ran out of room.

Dunraj grinned and then sprang at her.

Annja moved to the side, and Dunraj's body flew past her into the hole that they'd been digging the statue of Kali out of. He screamed for a short moment and then everything was quiet.

Annja crouched at the edge of the hole and tried to use the sword's light to penetrate the darkness. But she was unable to see where Dunraj might have landed. One thing she knew for sure—he couldn't have survived.

She felt nauseous and stumbled to her feet, trying to find something to use as a bandage. She found one a short time later as she wandered the work area. No one paid her any mind. As far as they were concerned, it seemed, as long as they had their paychecks, they were still working.

Although she wondered what they would do when they found out he was dead.

She sat on a crate and finished dressing her wound. She was going to need stitches, that much was certain. But she couldn't do that until she got back to Hyderabad. She glanced at the trucks. Could she hop a ride the same way she'd sent Frank off?

It was possible, she supposed. Provided no one gave her crap about it.

She stood and then collapsed. Blackness rushed at her, and the only thought in Annja's head was *Here we go again*.

SHE CAME TO ON A COT, wrapped in blankets. Annja tried to sit up but a hand held her in place.

"Take it easy, Annja. Just rest."

She opened her eyes. Frank sat at the foot of her bed. "Hey, you made it," she said to him.

"Indeed he did," another man said. "Although I should be terribly upset with you, Annja."

She turned her head and smiled at Pradesh. "I don't blame you one bit if you are. I'm really sorry we didn't wait for you."

Pradesh put up a hand. "Forget it. The most important thing now is that we were able to reach you and get you medical attention. You had a terrible wound on your arm."

Annja nodded. "Dunraj. His knife."

"Was poisoned."

She looked up at him. "Are you serious?"

"Very. If we hadn't arrived when we did, there's every possibility you would have died from the injury."

Annja leaned back and sighed. She felt as if she was battling a flu that didn't want to relent. "I feel horrible."

"That's to be expected," Pradesh explained. "But I'm told you'll make a full recovery after the antibiotics kick in. You just have to give them some time."

Annja looked around. "Where am I?"

"In the medical facility in the mountain," Frank said. "The workers had an infirmary, so we thought it best to bring you here."

"God, I'm still in this stupid mountain?"

Pradesh smiled. "Only for a short time more, I promise you. Once the doctor gives you the okay, we'll get you out of here." He glanced at Frank. "Your cameraman does some excellent work, you know."

"Yeah?" Annja felt sleepy.

"He was able to follow the trucks to their dumping point and the exit of the secret highway." Pradesh shook his head. "It was rather remarkable that such a thing even exists. If I had not seen it with my own two eyes, I might not believe that it was real."

"But it is," she said.

"I've sent word to have the mayor come out and see it. It will cause quite a stir in the Hyderabad community."

"Just so long as people know what was happening here," she said. "That's really all I can ask."

Pradesh patted her leg. "You're a terrifically brave woman, Annja Creed. I would never have dreamed you had this much gumption."

"That's me—gumption overload."

Pradesh laughed. "Apparently so." He glanced at Frank. "I'll leave you two alone for a few minutes, all right?"

He started to turn when Annja stopped him. "Pradesh?"

"Yes."

"Thank you."

He bowed his head. "Just doing my duty." And then he ducked out of the infirmary tent.

Frank looked worried. "Seriously, how are you feeling?"

"My head aches, my body aches, my sinuses are shot to hell. It feels like someone gave me the swine flu combined with Ebola."

"Well, fortunately that's not what happened. Otherwise, you'd probably be bleeding from your eyeballs."

"Don't count that out just yet. I might still surprise you."

Frank grinned. "I'm just glad you're okay."

"What about the rest of the Thuggee? Did Pradesh round them all up?"

"Annja…" Frank hesitated.

"What is it?"

"It doesn't look like the Thuggee ever existed."

Annja tried to sit up but failed. "What are you talking about? You saw them just as much as I did."

Frank nodded. "I know, I know. And I told Pradesh that, but he got access to the tunnels, and his men did a thorough search. There's no one hiding there. No one at all. Worse, they said the place looks like it was deserted many years ago."

"So, what—they think we hallucinated everything?"

Frank shrugged. "I don't know yet."

"And what about Dunraj?"

"What about him?"

Annja grabbed his arm. "Frank, if he's alive—which I doubt—they're going to arrest him, right? This can't be legal what he's doing here."

Frank pried his arm free. "It looks like he and Pradesh made some sort of deal. Maybe he's going to plead, I don't know. I don't know how the justice system works here."

"But they were able to pull him out of the hole, right?"

Frank eyed her. "What hole?"

"The hole he fell into when we were fighting."

Frank shook his head. "Annja, Dunraj was back in Hyderabad when Pradesh went to his office. I don't know what you're talking about."

"Didn't you see Dunraj before you escaped on the truck?"

"No."

Annja shook her head, and a wave of pain enveloped her. She put a hand to her skull and moaned. "What the hell is going on here?"

Frank patted her on the thigh. "Just get some rest, and we'll talk again when the poison is out of your system."

Annja could only nod and then close her eyes while Frank left the tent.

What *was* going on here? She had sent Dunraj flying into a hole. He was either dead or seriously wounded, and yet Frank told her that Dunraj had been at his office in Hyderabad.

How could that be?

How was it that Dunraj could be in two places at once? She thought she'd figured it out with the secret highway, but now this.

Her mind trailed off into sleep. Hopefully, this will help heal me was the last thing she remembered thinking.

"How is she?"

Voices in the tent. Had she dozed off? Had time passed? She couldn't seem to open her eyes.

"Better. But she'll need time to make a full recovery."

"I feel so responsible for this."

"You can answer to the judge and explain yourself, Mr. Dunraj. All I do is enforce the law."

"Yes, of course."

Annja cracked her eyes. "Pradesh?"

"I'm here, Annja."

"Who is that with you?"

"Mr. Dunraj is here."

And then amazingly, Dunraj's face swam into her vision with that same horrible smile plastered on his face. "Hello again, Annja."

Annja sat up and swung at him.

But there was no one in the tent.

She'd been dreaming.

Annja slumped back down onto the bed with a heavy sigh. That poison must be worse than I thought.

She lay there listening to the commotion outside the tent. It didn't seem as if anything was being shut down.

In fact, it sounded as if the operation was proceeding at an even faster rate.

Annja shook her head. I need to get out of here and go home. The police can sort this all out.

Annja closed her eyes again. Sleep. That's what I need.

But then the tent flap opened.

And Pradesh entered with a smile on his face.

There was someone else behind him.

Annja sat up.

"You."

"Hi, Annja."

And this time, Dunraj was really standing there.

27

"You!"

Annja came up out of her bed exactly as she had in her dream. But this time, Pradesh was there to hold her back. "Wait, Annja! Calm down! You've got him all wrong."

Dunraj backed away from the bed and grinned sheepishly. "I suppose it's only natural to expect a reaction like that considering what she's been through."

Pradesh glanced at him. "She'll be all right. It's just going to take some time."

Dunraj nodded. "Perhaps I should wait outside, then? You know, until she's ready to discuss things?"

"That might be a good idea." Pradesh waited until Dunraj had left before turning back to Annja. "You've got to calm down. Things aren't what they seem, and we're trying to explain it all to you."

Annja felt a wave of nausea, but fortunately, she was able to check it. "How come you haven't arrested that man? He's a murderer."

"I know it seems like that—"

"Seems like that? I personally witnessed him cut a man's heart out of his chest and eat the damned thing."

Pradesh lowered his voice. "Annja, that wasn't Dunraj you saw."

"Yes, it was. I'd know that face anywhere."

Pradesh leaned closer. "Annja, listen to me—Dunraj was in Hyderabad the entire time. He has an alibi, and it checks out perfectly."

"Then who killed that man that I saw?"

"His brother."

Annja stopped. Dunraj had a brother? She took a breath. "Are you certain that he's got one?"

Pradesh nodded. "One-hundred-percent positive. In fact, you fought him, and when he fell into that hole by the statue, he died."

"I don't believe this."

Dunraj poked his head back into the tent. "I hear things have quieted down now. Would you mind if I came back in?"

Annja looked at him. He was the same suave and debonair host that she'd met at the welcome party—if somewhat subdued over the apparent death of his brother. But the man she'd killed had been as debonair, albeit with a psychopathic streak a mile long. And identical physically. A *brother?*

"Explain all this to me, if you would."

Dunraj ducked back in. "First let me just say that I am terribly sorry for all you've been through. Had I known that you were involved in this, I certainly would have taken steps to safeguard your investigation."

Annja shook her head. "You'd better back up and start

from the beginning, because my head's spinning, and I don't like thinking I'm going crazy."

Dunraj nodded. "Of course, of course." He rubbed his hands together. "You see, I have a twin. I suppose that is the best way to begin."

"Your brother was a twin?"

"Indeed." Dunraj pulled up a folding chair and sat down in it. "We determined early on that he had grave psychological problems. Sociopathic tendencies. It was heartbreaking for my family."

"All right."

"When it became clear that there was very little we could do to keep him contained, so to speak, my family had a serious decision to make. Where to put him so he could never harm the family or the general public."

"So you put him in a mountain?" Annja shook her head. "That sounds almost as insane as your brother acted."

Dunraj looked pained. "Believe me, I understand how this must look. And I'm engaged in some very serious mea culpa here, as I believe the term is used. But still, you need to look at it from my perspective. He was my brother, after all."

"I'm at a bit of a loss to understand how you thought stowing him here was a good idea."

Dunraj took a moment. "He killed the rest of our family, Annja."

Annja stared at him. "What do you mean—figuratively?"

"I was away at Oxford when I got word that he had butchered my entire family."

"So how come he's not in jail?"

Dunraj looked down at the blanket on her bed. "I prevailed upon the courts to let me do things my way." He held up his hand. "Yes, I know, I used bribery to get my way. It was wrong. But as I said, I felt I owed my brother to at least try to give him some semblance of a decent life."

"You're telling me you made a home for him in this mountain. Right?"

"Yes."

"And he lived here."

"He did."

She glanced at Pradesh. "You're listening, right? How could this possibly have gone on for so long?"

Pradesh put his hand on her shoulder. "Let him finish talking."

Annja looked at Dunraj. "Okay, so you made a home for him here."

He nodded. "I needed a way to get supplies to him, so I had a special underground road constructed that I could use to bring him things. Given my position in society, it was important no one ever find out about him. As far as the public knew, there was only one of us. Me. And if he'd behaved himself, then it would have stayed that way for many years to come."

"But he found a way out of the mountain."

"When I relocated him here, there were old tunnel systems in place. That's why I chose this place."

"It didn't strike you as cruel to put him inside a mountain?"

"He was headed to jail. Or worse," Dunraj said. "I thought I was giving him a better-than-average shot at doing something with his life."

"But he didn't, did he? He started killing people."

Dunraj shrugged. "I had no way of knowing that it was actually him. Every time I came out here to see him, things seemed perfectly reasonable."

"How can you say that? He had a band of thugs with him. They resurrected an old cult, and they were engaged in systematic terror campaigns to scare the residents away."

Dunraj nodded. "Once I figured out that he had the means to escape the mountain and was sending his emissaries out, I tried to stop him."

"And how did you do that?"

"I started excavating the mountain," he replied. "I tried to get his mind focused on doing other things while he was here. I gave him a position of power in overseeing the work crews."

"Did it work?"

Dunraj sighed. "When the crews uncovered that statue of Kali—the one you saw with the ten arms—something snapped in my brother. Kali became his overriding obsession. He felt her presence in this mountain was some sort of divine calling to him."

"And then the killings picked up."

"Yes."

"And that's when Frank and I stumbled on the scene."

"Your timing," Dunraj said, "could not have possibly been worse. My brother was at his most bizarre by then, as I think you witnessed."

"Eating hearts and stuff."

He hesitated before saying, "Yes."

Pradesh cleared his throat. "Did that really happen?"

"I'll bet if you look hard enough," Annja said, "you'll find the body somewhere in the mountain."

"Or not," Dunraj interjected. "My brother had a means of disposing the corpses, although I'm not entirely sure what it was."

Annja frowned. The feeder machine? Stowing them in the dirt the trucks hauled away?

"He's really dead, though, right?"

Dunraj stared down at his hands. "My brother? Yes. I've seen his...corpse for myself. He is most definitely dead."

"As have I," Pradesh repeated. "You've got nothing to fear from him anymore."

"Good," Annja said, adding more gently, "I'm sorry about your brother, but he was a very sick man. You trying to keep him out of prison resulted in the deaths of innocent people."

"You think I don't realize that?"

"I don't know, do you?"

"Of course. And I will go out of my way to make amends to those families affected by my poor decision."

Pradesh cleared his throat again. "Look, Annja, Dunraj didn't commit any crime."

"You can't be held responsible for abetting a criminal in India?" she demanded.

"Family responsibility is something we hold very dear."

Dunraj held up his hands. "It could certainly be argued that I was complicit in the crimes. My goal right now is to make everything better. To try to repair some of the damage that I've done through my bad decision making."

Pradesh sat in the chair beside Annja's bed. "What we're after here is a truce between you and Dunraj. He's agreed to cooperate with us in the investigation."

"In exchange for immunity?"

Dunraj was quick to explain. "I have a great many projects under way that will benefit the city and the underprivileged. If I'm prosecuted, those good things will never be fully realized. I would hate to see that."

"I don't know."

Pradesh cocked his head. "This is a lot to take in all at once. Just do me a favor and give it some thought, would you?"

"Think of the poor people who would suffer," Dunraj added. "Just one of my construction projects would greatly benefit the families living in this immediate area. That road outside? The secret highway? It will open access to Hyderabad to people who thus far could only rely on rickety old buses to ferry them into the city. This will mean better jobs, better pay and a better standard of living."

Annja remembered Deva and the fact that the small boy was responsible for providing for his family. Would Dunraj's new developments help him, too? Most likely they would.

"I'll give it some thought," Annja said.

Pradesh smiled. "Great. That's great."

"Is Frank around?"

"He sure is. Would you like me to send him in?"

"That would be *great*."

Pradesh held the tent flap back so Dunraj could leave with him. Dunraj patted Annja's bed. "Thank you for listening to me. I do appreciate it."

"Yeah," she said. "Sorry about your brother."

"Thank you."

Together, he and Pradesh walked outside. Two minutes later, Frank's face appeared.

"Hey."

Annja smiled. "Get in here, would you?"

Frank came in. "Pretty wild about that guy having a twin brother, huh?"

"Convenient. Did you see the body?"

Frank nodded. "Yeah. Spitting image of each other. No wonder we were so easily fooled. They really did look exactly alike. It was pretty freaky staring down at him and then back up at Dunraj."

Annja frowned.

"What is it?"

"I don't know. The whole situation stinks. Dunraj is going to get a free pass because it wasn't him that committed the crimes. It was his brother."

"Well, he shouldn't pay for something someone else did, Annja."

Annja shook her head. "Have you ever heard of aiding and abetting? Something still smells funny to me."

"That could be you. You're pretty grungy."

"Listen up, Frank. Here's what I want you to do."

28

It took another few hours before Annja started feeling better. The IV drip in her arm continued to administer the antibiotics to combat the poison from the knife blade. And she slept a lot. By the time evening rolled around, Annja felt as though she was through the worst of it.

Frank had gone back to Hyderabad. Annja still wasn't convinced that the danger was past at the dig site. And despite Frank's protests that he wanted to stay, Annja had warned him that he should do as she said.

"You'll be more of a help than you know just by being back at our hotel," she'd said. "I won't have to worry about your safety."

Now, after her rest, she had to admit that she was indeed feeling much better. And she wasn't sure about Dunraj, but her honest focus now was simply on getting out of the mountain and getting back to Hyderabad. She could convalesce at a hospital there, and then she could go home.

At least I've solved the mystery of the deaths here, she thought.

Pradesh entered the tent. "Oh, you're awake. Excellent."

Annja smiled. "How are you doing?"

"I'm well, thank you." He looked into her face. "You're looking a lot better, as well. How are you feeling?"

"Better."

"Good," Pradesh said. "I see the antibiotics are working. Excellent. I was worried about your having any lasting effects."

"I think I'll be fine."

Pradesh smiled. "I'll let the doctor know. Once we get his okay, we can get you out of here."

"That," Annja said, "would be very nice."

"Be right back." Pradesh vanished and then came back a moment later with the doctor, who did a quick checkup of Annja and spoke in rapid-fire Hindi to Pradesh. Pradesh nodded quite a bit and said a few words to the doctor. Then the doctor left and Pradesh smiled.

"You're all set."

"I am?"

"Yes. We're going to arrange a transport back to the city for you. Frank's already headed back, eh?"

"I sent him ahead to the hotel," Annja said.

Pradesh grinned. "He didn't seem happy about having to leave. He's quite loyal to you, you know. When he called me, all he could do was go on and on about needing to rescue you. It was rather heroic."

"He'll turn out just fine, I think."

"A friend like that…" Pradesh shook his head. "You should consider yourself very lucky."

"In more ways than one. How am I being transported back to Hyderabad?"

"We have an ambulance, if that suits you?"

"That will be fine," she said. "How long before I can get out of here?"

Pradesh glanced at his watch. "Shortly, I would think. I just need to check with the driver."

Annja closed her eyes and then heard Pradesh leave the tent. She was still tired. But she spent a lot of her time focused on the sword where it rested in the otherwhere. And each time she did, she felt more of its strength flowing into her body and limbs.

Thank God I was able to get the sword back, she thought.

If she hadn't been able to… She shuddered at the thought of the feeder machine. But she'd been saved by Frank there, not the sword. She'd have to remember to thank him for that and put in a good word for him back at the offices in New York.

She smiled to herself. Everything was going as it should. The guilty man was dead, and she was fortunately getting the hell out of this mountain.

"Annja?"

She opened her eyes. Pradesh stood there with a grin on his face. Annja wondered idly if he had a girlfriend. "Yes?"

"We're going to move you now. Is that okay?"

"Absolutely."

Two men came into the tent and each grabbed an end of Annja's cot. Then they carried her carefully outside, making sure not to jostle the cot too much. Annja was still connected to the IV, and Pradesh held that above her as they walked.

Some of the workers stopped to see what was going on but the site still buzzed with activity. Annja looked up and saw the back of the ambulance doors open. It had been a very long time since she'd ridden in the back of an ambulance. She wondered if it was the same the world over.

She'd soon find out.

The two men slid the cot into the rear of the ambulance and then shut one of the doors. They left the other door open, and Pradesh hopped into the back of the wagon.

"You okay?"

Annja nodded.

Pradesh finished hanging the IV up in the back of the ambulance. "All right. These guys are going to take you back to Hyderabad and get you squared away at the hospital. I've called Frank's room to let him know that you're on the way back to the city. I'm sure he'll be waiting for you when you get there."

"Thank you, Pradesh."

"Just doing my job, Annja."

She shook her head. "No, you've gone above and beyond the call of duty. If my breath wasn't so horrendous right now, I might give you a big kiss."

A strange look crossed his face, but he quickly smiled through it. "Well, thank you. That's very nice of you to say. I may ask you to let the mayor know that I exceeded your expectations."

"Anything you need. Just ask."

"I'll see you back at the hospital."

And then the second door closed. Annja was alone in the back of the ambulance. She closed her eyes and took a deep breath.

Rest.

That was what she needed.

Lots of rest.

She felt the ambulance shift as someone climbed into the front seat and started the engine. It thrummed, and Annja heard another door open and close. Probably the other attendant.

"I'm ready, guys," she called. "Let's get the hell out of this place."

She had no idea whether they spoke English or not, but it felt good to say it.

Then the back door opened and Dunraj jumped inside.

"What are you doing here?"

Dunraj held up a hand. "I wanted to see if it would be okay for me to hitch a ride back to the city with you."

"What, you don't have your own car?"

"Actually, no. Pradesh insisted I ride out with him in his cruiser. So, that leaves me without a way back, and I have some pressing business to attend to." He smiled. "I'd consider it a great honor if you'd let me come along."

Annja hesitated. "Sure. Whatever. I might fall asleep on you, though."

"No problem." He barked out a quick command in Hindi, and the ambulance started to roll forward. Dunraj tapped her IV bag. "You're just about empty here. Let me hook you up with a fresh one."

"You don't have to—"

"Nonsense. I trained as a volunteer paramedic in school. We used to work the motorbike races on the Isle of Wight, and let me tell you, I saw my fair share of grievous injuries." He attached the new bag and fed it into the line. "There, all set."

Annja felt every bump as the wheels rolled over the uneven ground. "Ouch."

Dunraj shifted, as well, and had to hold on to one of the supports in the back of the ambulance. "That's the problem with construction sites. They're always so full of potholes and ditches."

"How in the world did you ever manage to build an underground highway?" she asked. "It's amazing."

Dunraj smiled. "Thank you. It wasn't easy, of course. But I had a number of other projects in the area, which made hiding the construction of the highway fairly easy."

"A secret highway like this must have been a boon for your other projects." She couldn't help it—she still felt suspicious of him. Despite Pradesh's assurances.

"Absolutely. It's allowed me to save a tremendous amount of money that I've subsequently channeled into other projects."

"Not to mention your bank account."

He shrugged. "I'm not only about the money, Annja. I do a lot of good work with inner-city charities. Children who would never have a chance at a successful life now have opportunities thanks to my generous donations."

Annja nodded. "That's very kind of you. But weren't you worried that someone might find out about your road here?"

"Certainly," Dunraj said. "The key, of course, was ensuring that none of the workers ever spoke of it."

"Was that difficult?"

"I've been blessed in my life with the power of money," Dunraj replied.

"Yeah, but not everyone is so easily bought off, are they?"

Dunraj eyed her. "Oh, I didn't find it too difficult to ensure silence. A few extra bonuses here and there and the vast majority of workers were more than happy to never speak of it."

"But not all of them?"

Dunraj shrugged again. "Well, we had one or two who proved to be less than willing to go along with our plans."

"And what did you do to them?" Annja asked. "I mean, if they couldn't be bought off. How did you ensure their secrecy?"

Dunraj hesitated slightly. "I made sure they knew that if they tried to talk to reporters, I would take whatever steps I deemed necessary to protect myself."

"Including force?"

Dunraj shook his head. "Annja, I have at my disposal a veritable army of lawyers who like nothing better than to charge me exorbitant hourly fees to take care of people like the ones who threatened to expose me."

"You sued them?"

"The workers were obligated to sign a confidentiality agreement when they started working for me. If they breached that agreement, I was able to silence them with just the threat of legal action."

"So it all worked out for you," Annja said, thinking what a horrible guy he was, even if he wasn't guilty of murder. She couldn't wait to be rid of him. "That's great."

Dunraj shifted as the ambulance took a turn. "Right

up until my brother went off the rails and started jeopardizing my plans here. That was unacceptable, obviously."

"Yeah," Annja said. "A real shame about that."

"You did me a rather big favor, Annja."

She looked at him. "Did I?"

"If you hadn't killed him, I might have been forced to do it myself." He laughed. "And I so dislike the idea of getting my hands dirty."

Annja suddenly felt vulnerable, being alone with him in the back of the ambulance. Why hadn't a paramedic ridden with her—or a medic? Whoever they employed as first aid in the mountain. "I'm not sure if you're joking about this or not."

"Do you think I'm the type of man who makes a joke like that without there being something behind it?" Dunraj asked, raising his eyebrows.

"I have no idea."

"You killed my brother." Dunraj leaned closer. "And it saved me from a lengthy prison sentence. So, on that level, I must thank you."

"Uh, you're welcome?" If he got any creepier, there was always the sword. She let herself relax a bit more.

Dunraj patted her arm. "You need to rest. Believe me, there will be plenty of time to talk once we arrive."

Annja closed her eyes, but not before she saw a thin smile cross Dunraj's lips.

29

Annja woke not to the sound of a bustling hospital, but rather to the sound of hushed voices. She opened her eyes and glanced around.

Confused.

She wasn't in a hospital room.

She was in darkness.

Again.

"Where am I?"

"Annja?" Frank's voice. But he was back in Hyderabad. She'd sent him there so he would be safe.

"What are you doing here?"

"Dunraj," Frank said. "You were right, Annja. He's bad news."

Annja shook her head and tried to sit up. Her head swam as if she was wading through molasses. "I thought he said his brother was the sociopath."

She heard a laugh, but didn't recognize the voice. "That's what he wants everyone to believe."

"Who are you?"

"She's not used to the darkness yet," Frank said. "It's Kormi. Remember?"

"Kormi? My God, I thought they killed you when we were escaping. I saw them jump on you."

"Yes, and I killed a number of them with my bare hands, too," Kormi said. "But in the end, there were too many to handle on my own."

"I should have stayed. Together we could have defeated them all."

"No. It was far more important that you get away." He sighed. "Although it appears it was all for nothing if we've just ended up back in this accursed mountain again."

"Someone better clue me in on what Dunraj is up to here. First I find out he's got a nutcase twin brother, and then Dunraj is supposed to be some saint, and now it appears he was a scumbag all along? Seriously, what the hell is going on?"

"I wish we knew," Frank said. "I was on my way back to Hyderabad when the driver suddenly pulled a gun on me and drove me back to the mountain. I've been here ever since. Kormi was already here. And this time, the cell has bars on it. I guess they're not taking any chances of us escaping."

"Wonderful." Annja groaned. She was able to sit up at least. As for the poison, she felt as thought she'd gotten most of it out of her system, although she was still lethargic. "I'm assuming Dunraj drugged me with the new IV bag he administered. The jerk."

"You were unresponsive when they brought you in here," Kormi said. "We feared the worst, but your respirations have been slow and steady. So we understood that you were sleeping off a powerful sedative."

Annja sighed. "None of this makes sense. What is Dunraj up to? He could have blamed this entire thing on his brother and walked away from it all, probably all the richer to boot."

"If it's true that he had a twin brother."

"It is true," Frank said. "I saw the corpse. And believe me, they looked exactly alike. And the one I saw wasn't breathing. He was definitely a twin."

"Then was Dunraj ever here at all?"

"He must have been," Annja said. "I found a condominium built into the mountain. It looked similar to the style of the reception room that we were in at the welcome party."

"It makes sense that Dunraj would have tried to make him as comfortable as possible, given the sentence he'd imposed on him."

"Living his life out inside a mountain?" Annja shook her head. "I almost wonder who the evil one is here. I can't imagine never seeing the sun. I'm surprised Dunraj's brother didn't look albino or something."

"The fact that Dunraj had a brother would certainly have enabled him to do any number of things and appear to have a watertight alibi. If the sane brother was in Hyderabad, then whatever his crazy brother was up to, it would provide Dunraj with a wonderful excuse."

"But was it really his brother?"

Frank cleared his throat. "What do you mean?"

"I've heard reports of some dictators having clones of themselves made. Not actual clones, per se, but they have people who look approximately like they do undergo plastic surgery and then become body doubles. There have been documented cases. Saddam Hussein and Kim Jong Il are two who have reportedly used them in the past."

"I don't know that it really makes a difference," Frank said. "Whether it was a twin brother or not, the fact remains that he's dead. And that leaves Dunraj behind to do God knows what."

"That's the big question. What is he up to?"

"Would it be connected with the highway?"

"What highway?" Kormi asked.

"There's a secret highway under the mountain that connects this place to Hyderabad."

"You are joking."

"She's not," Frank said. "I rode on the damned thing. It's a marvel of engineering, that's for sure."

Kormi sighed. "When we were recruited, it seemed so honorable. We were defending the sacred lands of Kali. I see now that I have been gravely misled and used as a pawn in another man's evil scheme."

"Why were you recruited?" Annja asked. "You said that Dunraj was descended from Thuggee. But is that true?"

"I do not know now what to believe," Kormi said. "We were all told that Dunraj came from a long line of Thuggee. But that may have simply been to get us to join his cause."

"What did he tell you?"

"That the lands upon which we now sit were in danger of being destroyed by developers. We would become Kali's soldiers. We would use fear and terror to make those residents abandon their properties so the land could be turned back to Kali."

Annja frowned. "I wonder."

"About what?"

"Dunraj told me that he bought worker silence with money and confidentiality agreements. But he also mentioned there were a few people who wanted to spill the beans on his little underground highway. Wouldn't it have been easy for him to simply have his band of thugs kill them? The killers would think they were doing it in Kali's name, but they were actually taking care of a problem for Dunraj. Three less people who knew about his construction project."

"But the residential development isn't one of Dunraj's projects," Frank interrupted.

"True," she said. "But imagine if the developer couldn't sell the units because of the crime. He'd be forced to sell the property or risk foreclosure. And Dunraj could step in, buy the place for dirt cheap and then announce that he had a highway leading back to Hyderabad. The ease of commute would open up this region to a lot more development, and Dunraj would be ideally suited to capitalize on it. He'd sell out in a number of weeks and laugh all the way to the bank."

"So this was never about worshipping Kali," Kormi said quietly. "I feel like such a fool."

"You wouldn't be the first believer tricked in the name of a god," Annja said. "History is full of people preyed upon because of their beliefs."

"I feel terrible about my role in this," Kormi said. "I believed I was right, and in the end I was just a fool, easily manipulated in doing something horrible for an evil man."

"You never killed, though, Kormi." Annja grinned. "And you even tried to help me. That's got to count for something."

"I should have been smart enough to see through it," he insisted. "And now my life is forfeit for the evil I've committed on that man's behalf. Gods have mercy upon my soul."

"Calm down, Kormi. No one here is casting judgment on your actions. At least not yet. Right now, we've got to find a way out of this mess."

Frank shifted. "I think it's probably a sure bet that Dunraj will come back shortly, and when he does, I don't get the feeling he's going to invite us all up for dinner."

"He'll be looking to kill us," Annja agreed. "He's got to make sure no one ever gets word of what really happened here. Once we're dead, that won't be a problem."

"What about the workers?"

"What about them? If anyone talks, they'll either be bought off, threatened with legal action or killed. Possibly, they might even have their hearts eaten. Dunraj has all his bases covered."

"So, what can we do?" Kormi asked.

"I don't know." Annja frowned. "Where was Pradesh when all this went down, anyway?"

"Wasn't he with you?' Frank asked.

"No, he said he'd meet us back in Hyderabad. At least, I think that's what he said."

"You're not sure?"

"Frank, I was doped up, fighting off the poison that

Dunraj number one had managed to nearly kill me with. My mind wasn't exactly at its best, you know?"

"Yeah, sorry, Annja."

"Who is this man you call Pradesh?" Kormi asked.

"Sorry, he's a police officer with Hyderabad," she explained. "He came out once Frank got himself back to the city. He's been a friend of ours since we arrived."

"You are certain of this?"

"Certain of what?"

"His allegiance. You are certain he is not in league with Dunraj?"

Annja fell silent. She hated to even think of it. But she couldn't be sure. Pradesh had seemed all too ready to excuse Dunraj's crimes.

Was it possible?

She had to accept the possibility that it was. Annja sighed. "I don't know what to believe about Pradesh."

"I don't think he is," Frank said. "He seemed like too good a guy to me."

Annja shook her head.

"I've got a gut feeling about this," Frank insisted. "Whatever Dunraj is up to, I don't think Pradesh is involved."

"You really believe that?" she asked.

"Yeah," he said. "Yeah, I do."

They were silent for a moment. And then Kormi asked, "If that is so, then where is Pradesh now?"

But Frank didn't have an answer for that. "Maybe he's back in Hyderabad. Hell, maybe he found out about Dunraj, and Dunraj had him shot. He could be anywhere right now. I just know that I feel like he's on the level. I can't explain it."

"Well, I for one hope you're right, Frank," Annja said. "Because we could really use a friend on the outside right now."

"Very true," Kormi agreed. "It will only be a matter of time before Dunraj returns to exact his vengeance on all of us. Most especially me."

"Why you?" Frank asked.

"Because I helped Annja escape. It was my action that set this chain of events in motion. It is my karma to pay for what I did. For what it cost Dunraj. And his brother."

"Consider it your attempt to make up for the evil you've committed," Annja said. "I'm sure your goddess, Kali, will look upon you with favor for having the bravery to do what you did."

"But I wonder if that will be the case. Kali is not a forgiving goddess. And she may find my lack of loyalty to Dunraj loathsome. I shudder to think what she will do to me in the afterlife."

"Well, how about this?" Annja said. "Let's do our best to make sure none of us heads off to the afterlife."

"And how will we do that?"

"By fighting back. When Dunraj comes for us, he's going to get the surprise of a lifetime."

30

As they sat there, Annja's vision grew more acclimated to the darkness. Frank eyed her. "And just how the hell are you planning on mounting an offensive, Annja? I mean, I'm all for it. This guy's a real piece of crap. But I don't see what we can do. He's got us locked up."

Annja smiled. "Good point. Is this the same cell?"

"No," Kormi answered. "We are in a different part of the tunnel system. On an upper level from where you were being held before."

"But you know how to find your way around still, right?" she asked.

"Of course."

Annja felt the heavy wood of the cell door and then let her hand wander through the metal bars. "It's an old bolt lock."

Frank watched her. "I didn't know you knew anything about locks."

Annja drew her hands back through the bars. "Frank,

trust me, there are plenty of things you don't know about me…yet."

"Yet?"

Annja smiled in the darkness. "Are you guys ready to get out of here?"

Kormi looked at her. "Of course. But are you? You are still fighting off the effects of the poison and the sedative, aren't you?"

Annja flexed her muscles and did a few deep knee squats. Her heart felt strong. "I think I'm good."

Frank frowned. "Are you sure you can do this? We might have to fight."

"That's what I'm counting on," Annja said. "I'm tired of waiting for Dunraj. It's time we took the fight to him."

"But how will you get us out of this cell?" Kormi asked.

Annja reached into the otherwhere and grasped her sword. Its grayish light illuminated Frank's and Kormi's shock at its sudden appearance.

"What the hell?" Frank began.

"Goddess," Kormi said.

Annja winked at Frank. "Told you there was plenty you didn't know about me. But I'd better never catch you saying anything to anyone back at the office about this. If you do, then I might have to use it on you, you got it?"

Frank bobbed his head. "Y-yeah. Absolutely."

"How is it that you have such a weapon as this?" Kormi asked. "It is not natural."

"You're telling me," Annja said.

"How come you didn't whip that thing out before and make sushi out of Dunraj?" Frank asked.

Annja brought her hands together. "We were tied up,

remember? I couldn't take the sword while my hands were tied behind my back."

"And on the conveyor belt?"

"Same thing. My hands were stretched flat so I couldn't grip the hilt of the sword."

Frank still looked skeptical. "Yeah, but that door is pretty solid."

Annja studied it. "I'm willing to bet the sword can get us out. You want to see?"

"Hell, yes. Let's get out of here and find this Dunraj guy."

Kormi stood. "I am ready, too."

Annja smiled. "Great, stand back."

She could see the lock plate on their side. The bars would only go into the wood so far and then she ought to be able to cleave her way through the timbers. They were old and probably wouldn't put up much resistance.

But first, Annja aimed the tip of her blade directly at the lock and stabbed the sword right through it.

The cell frame shuddered and Annja frowned. The door hadn't budged.

"Must be stronger than I expected."

On the second thrust, the lock shattered. Annja grabbed at the bars and swung the door open. "All right, let's go!"

Annja glanced around them and then back at Kormi. "We need to find Dunraj before he can sic the rest of his men on us. Do you know where he might be?"

Kormi frowned. "I don't. He could be anywhere in here."

Annja had a thought. "Take us out the way you took

me. I'm willing to bet that Dunraj is hanging out in the condominium."

Frank looked at her. "He's got a condo here?"

"You wouldn't believe it."

Frank chuckled. "Annja, you just pulled a sword out of nowhere in front of me. There's probably not a whole lot left I won't believe."

Kormi took point. "This way."

THEY RAN THROUGH A TUNNEL that sloped upward. As they traveled its length, parts of it felt familiar, but it wasn't until they came to an intersection that she recognized it as the place where they'd almost been surrounded, when she'd been here with Kormi earlier.

"This is where we fought together."

He nodded. "The exit is just ahead."

But then Annja heard an alarm—the same alarm as before. "So much for the element of surprise."

Kormi pushed her ahead. "You know the way. Let's go!"

They ran toward the exit and outside, where the sun was setting again. It was déjà vu for Annja as she made her way down the game trail.

At any moment, she expected Dunraj's men to start shooting volleys of lead at her, Frank and Kormi, but nothing came raining down on them.

Annja paused. "They're not chasing us?"

Kormi looked puzzled. "That is odd. Perhaps they don't know where we are just yet."

Frank kept them moving. "Well, let's not stand here out in the open. How about we get to wherever it is we're going and try to regain some surprise, huh?"

This time, when she got to the valley with the giant boulder, Annja took care how she stepped. She didn't want to trip again and risk reinjuring her ankle. It was still causing her pain without a reinjury.

She pointed out the boulder. "The hidden door is under it."

Frank frowned. "Under it? How do you get under a rock that freakin' big?"

"There's a space. You can crawl in and then you'll find the secret entrance."

"You'd better go first," he said. "After all, you've got the big ol' sword, and if anyone is waiting on the other side, it'd be better if you met them."

This time, she found the door a little easier now that she knew it was there. She slid it open and then let herself down the steep path that brought her back into the mountain.

Behind her, she heard Frank mumbling something about secrets and the mountain. She grinned. Dunraj had certainly turned this place into an enclave that had more secrets than not.

Inside, Annja showed them the passage that led off the room. Frank shook his head. "How did you ever find this?"

"I thought Dunraj's men were going to chase me, so I kept going. I was worried that if they found me in this room, they'd be able to overwhelm me, so I followed the passageway, and this is where it leads."

"And there's another door off this one?"

Annja held her finger to her lips. "The entrance to Dunraj's condo. Or his brother's. I don't know who was using it, but it's here."

"How do we get in?"

Annja crouched on the floor of the passage and made her way to the end of the tunnel before she turned and opened the door.

Inside, the condominium was darker than before.

Annja stood and let Frank and Kormi through into the palatial surroundings. "What do you think?"

Frank brushed himself off. "Amazing that this could even be inside a mountain."

"I, too, am amazed," Kormi said. "The level of luxury here is far removed from the harsh existence we were told to endure."

"Dunraj's brother was a hypocrite," Annja said. "He was far too content telling his followers what they should do and be willing to endure while he himself—uh, or his brother—was living a life of luxury."

Frank glanced around. "So, if this is where he lives, then why isn't he here right now?"

Annja frowned. "I thought he would be."

"So, what—we wait?"

Kormi shrugged. "Dunraj may choose to come back here and take shelter while they look for us. If that happens, we will be able to catch him."

Annja agreed with Kormi's suggestion. "Yeah. Let's set up the ambush. There's another exit in the bedroom."

"Another door?"

She nodded. "Through the closet. It leads out and down to the work site. It's obviously easier to get to the work site from here than it is the other set of tunnels. That's probably why none of the Thuggee knew about this place."

Kormi shook his head. "If the others knew of this decadence, they would surely revolt."

"There will be time for that soon enough," Annja said. "Now let's get into position."

She led them into the bedroom.

"This place is incredible," Frank said. "How do the windows work?"

"Near as I can figure, he's got lightbulbs behind them that can dim or brighten depending on the hour of the day. Everything about this place is supposed to convey the idea that it's a normal apartment."

"When in reality it's a prison cell."

"For a crazy man."

"I would thank you to not talk so rudely about my kin," a man said.

The lights came on. Dunraj stood across the bedroom from them, a pistol in his hand.

Annja was about to charge him but he held up his hand. "I wouldn't be so quick to do that if I were you."

Annja stopped. Something in his voice.

And then she saw it.

There were other armed men in the room, dressed in military-style fatigues. And they each had a submachine gun.

Frank sighed. "Looks as though we walked right into a trap here."

"And you've just made my job a whole lot easier," Dunraj said, "now that I don't have to chase you through those confounded tunnels. I swear I never understood them half as well as my brother."

"So, he was your brother," Annja said.

"What I told you was the truth. My brother suffered from a mental condition his entire life."

"Until I killed him."

"Yes," Dunraj said. "Until you wandered into my city and turned my plans upside down."

Annja steeled herself.

"It's time we ended this."

31

"But you're not going to do anything with that sword, Annja," Dunraj continued. "In fact, if I even see you flinch, my men here will rake you with enough bullets to make Swiss cheese jealous."

Annja smirked. "Oh, that's cute. Did it take you all night to come up with that whopper?"

Dunraj ignored her. "I don't know where you found that sword—it's true I don't have this entire mountain explored—but I want you to throw it away. Right now."

"Throw it away?"

He nodded. "Or else I will have my men shoot."

Annja frowned. Dunraj thought she'd found this in the mountain? Excellent. She nodded. "Yeah, okay." And then she threw the sword across the room so that it slid under the bed. As it disappeared from view, she knew that it was back in the otherwhere. With any luck, Dunraj wouldn't realize his mistake.

Until it was too late.

Dunraj visibly relaxed. "Better. Much better. Now, how about we all go downstairs and have a much longer conversation. Frankly, being here in my brother's home feels a little odd now that he's dead."

They marched one by one through the walk-in closet and out beyond it into the passage that led down to the work site. As they came out of the passage, Annja gasped at what she saw.

Corpses were stacked like firewood nearby. All of them swathed in black. The members of Dunraj's brother's Thuggee army had been executed. And now Dunraj was disposing of them.

He came alongside Annja and sighed. "I just couldn't take the chance that any of them wouldn't keep their mouths shut. Given what they'd all done, it seemed only fitting that they should also answer for their crimes."

"You're erasing all evidence of what happened here," Annja said. "If it doesn't exist, you can't be held accountable."

Dunraj smiled. "I still maintain that we could be so good together, you and me. You get it immediately. I don't have to explain anything to you." He came closer. "I have to tell you, it's extremely attractive to be in the presence of a beautiful woman with such an acute and imaginative mind. Not to mention the ability to fight as well as you seem able to."

"That's got to be the most interesting pickup line I've heard over the years," she said. "But as flattered as I am, I'll have to say no. I mean, how could we ever have a relationship? You'd never trust me. You don't trust anyone. And that's your problem, isn't it? All your life you've had opportunities and chances, and yet you've never found anyone equal to you."

"Until now. I could give you everything you've ever dreamed of. And probably plenty you haven't even dared imagine yet."

"As I said, tempting. But I'm afraid we're two different people. I'm trying to make a stand for good. And you're only too willing to roll right over anyone who doesn't play by your rules."

"That's only because the rules have rolled over me more than once." Dunraj shrugged. "If I hadn't done it my way, then I'd never have gotten a fair shake in life. I had to become who I am now."

"Did you? Or is that the excuse you use to justify what you do to people? To get what you want? You should stop killing people," Annja added.

Dunraj smirked. "Well, I can't do that, can I?"

"What do you mean?"

"You, Frank and that guy over there...all of you know what happened here. That's not acceptable. Anyone who knows about this place could conceivably tell others. And I can't have that. I can't take that chance."

"More trust issues," she said. "Is that why you brought in your personal little army here?"

Dunraj looked pleased. "They're Tamil Tigers. Do you know about them?"

Annja glanced at the men in the better light and saw the hardened looks on their faces. "Yeah, I know about the Tigers. They're terrorists. The crimes they've committed make you appear to be an altar boy."

"One man's terrorists are another man's freedom fighters. And these freedom fighters just happen to be cash-strapped. Nothing like a side job to help the coffers of the revolution."

"These guys can't stand elitists like you," she said. "How the hell did you convince them to come to your aid?"

"I promised them something that they appreciated."

And as he said it, Annja saw the arm of a crane moving. Suspended from it was the giant statue of Kali with the golden arms and jewel-encrusted body. That treasure must have been worth many millions of dollars, she thought, not for the first time.

"Just like that? You're giving them a statue of something that belongs in a museum."

"It's an item of antiquity. It does nothing for me." Dunraj looked at his freedom fighters. "But apparently the Tigers like such things. When I told them what I had, they were only too willing to come to my assistance for this small job."

"And what about the other workers here? The construction workers on the highway project?"

"What about them?"

"Are you going to kill them, too?"

Dunraj paused. "I don't think I'm going to have to do that."

"Why not? Any one of them could spill the beans about your project here and the things you're doing now."

"That's true," he said. "But I'm hoping that after I illustrate how serious I am, I won't have to worry about anyone becoming chatty."

"Illustrate?"

"You'll find out very soon." He walked away toward

the crane and directed the operator to swing the statue down to a flatbed truck waiting on the lower level.

Annja glanced at Frank. "This isn't good. These guys with Dunraj are professionals. They won't hesitate to kill us without a second thought. Make sure you don't do anything stupid."

"I think it's too late for that," Frank replied. "After all, I agreed to come on this trip in the first place."

Annja took a second look at him. "Wish you were back in New York?"

"Every damned minute."

"Good, that will give you something to fight for."

"You're not doing much to inspire me with confidence here, Annja."

She nodded. "Yeah, you're going to have to find your own confidence if you hope to get out of this alive. I'm going to have my hands full dealing with the Tigers. When the time comes, you take the guy closest to you and don't stop until you hear my voice. Got it?"

"Yep."

"Tell Kormi."

"I think he knows. He's been watching you the entire time we've been here. He's just waiting for your signal."

"Okay."

Annja surveyed the scene. There were ten Tigers to deal with in her immediate vicinity. They were staggered along one side of them, carefully arranged so that if they needed to shoot, they wouldn't risk hitting one of their own.

How courteous of them, Annja thought.

The crane with the Kali statue drew closer. The statue swung precariously on the end of a giant steel cable. Even from this distance, Annja could see the incredible detail of the craftsman who had made the statue. It had been brought to this mountain for some reason, and now it was being callously removed for the purpose of paying off mercenaries.

Annja wasn't sure about her relationship with the divine, but she had to believe that a powerful deity wouldn't be thrilled about being taken from its home as tribute to some ruthless band of mercenaries.

Then again, perhaps that was up Kali's alley.

The important thing about the movement of the crane was that as it drew closer to the group, Annja, Frank and Kormi were forced to move out of its way.

Closer to the Tigers.

They all had their fingers on their trigger guards. They weren't unseasoned amateurs. If they felt the threat, they'd shoot immediately, whether Dunraj told them to or not.

As the statue swung closer, its momentum carried it directly into the line of sight of the Tigers.

That was the moment Annja was waiting for. She steeled herself, felt her heart pounding in her chest.

She reached for the sword.

"Annja!"

Frank's voice jerked her eyes back to the moment without the sword. "What is it?"

"Look."

Annja followed Frank's gaze and saw what he was seeing at the bottom of the work area.

Dunraj was leading another captive up the walkway.

"Oh, no."

"Well, at least we know he wasn't in league with these

bad guys," Frank said quietly. "That's some consolation, I suppose."

"Not much. He was my last hope for rescue."

As Annja watched, Dunraj poked Pradesh in the back with his pistol. "Get on up there with the rest of them, my good friend. You will shortly have your destiny before you."

Pradesh stumbled into line with them. He looked as though someone had beat the crap out of him. His right eye was swollen shut and he was limping badly.

"What happened to you?"

Pradesh grimaced. "I was mugged, I think. Outside my precinct. They attacked me and threw me in the back of a van and drove me here. I was getting ready to come back and mount another search for you. I've spent the entire day looking for you, Annja. When you didn't show up at the hospital—"

"Enough," Dunraj said. "You can all commiserate with one another when you get to the afterlife and figure out which one of you is coming back as a fruit fly."

Annja studied Dunraj. "I should tell you something."

"What's that?"

"Before I killed your brother, I told him something I think you'll find important to your future."

"Oh? And what was that." Dunraj looked amused.

"Come closer. I don't want to have to yell it."

Dunraj took a few steps closer to Annja. But he was careful not to come too close. "Yes? What is it?"

"I told him that if he killed me, I was going to come back and haunt him for the rest of eternity. Not just this life. But every life he'd ever hoped to live. You understand that?"

"And what did my brother say when you told him this?"

"He laughed. Until I came back from the dead and sent him to hell."

Dunraj said nothing for a moment and then smiled even wider than he had before. "I have to say it again— we could have been great together, Annja. Remember that as the first bullets pierce your flesh, will you?"

Then he turned and walked toward the Tigers.

32

Annja watched Dunraj talk to one of the men standing closest to him. Annja assumed he was the leader of the Tigers. He had a thick moustache and longer hair than the others.

Thanks for the nugget of information, Dunraj, she thought. When she made her move, he was going down first. Maybe the other Tigers would scatter if their leader went down.

Probably not. The Tigers had a notorious reputation for cruelty, and none of them ever ran from a fight.

Still, it was worth a shot trying to disrupt their morale. And Annja needed a target.

The crane continued to move the statue of Kali overhead, and Annja found herself momentarily distracted by creaking.

Dunraj looked up, as well, frowning. He barked a command at another worker nearby and sent him running over to the crane's cab.

"What's going on?" Frank asked quietly.

Annja shrugged. "I don't know. But that creaking doesn't sound like a very good thing, does it?"

"Perhaps the statue is too heavy for the cable," Pradesh said. "I've seen industrial accidents involving snapped cables. Not a very pleasant sight to behold."

Frank looked at him. "Why?"

"When that cable snaps, people standing in its path get beheaded or sliced into many pieces."

Frank stared back up at the swaying statue, his body visibly shrinking.

The crane had stopped now. But the statue continued to sway back and forth, causing the cable to creak even more. Annja studied the crane, keeping one eye on the Tigers. But all of them except their leader still had their eyes on Annja and the others.

The moment wasn't there yet.

The worker Dunraj had sent over came scrambling back and said something to his boss. Dunraj looked as if he wanted to slap the man, but restrained himself and then looked back at the Tiger leader. He said a few words and then smiled.

The worker moved off to the side and blew an air horn. The work site went eerily quiet. The crane stopped moving, the statue suspended above them all, slowly twisting from the inertia.

Dunraj watched as the workers convened below them and then spread his arms as if he was welcoming them as his family. He spoke in Hindi, but Pradesh translated for Annja and Frank.

"My wonderful workers, I would like to extend my sincere thanks to you for the incredible work that you have accomplished here. Your efforts have been gallant, and we are well ahead of schedule. For that, you will all receive a substantial bonus in your next paycheck. Along with my heartfelt gratitude."

There were cheers and applause. Annja wondered how they could possibly clap in the presence of ten heavily armed men and four people who were clearly being held again their will. But she supposed that providing for their families would make anyone look away when the time was right.

So much for counting on a popular uprising, she thought.

Dunraj continued his speech. "It is, as you all know, extremely important that the work you do here never be discussed with anyone outside of this location. You are not to tell your families or friends of this project. It is a state secret, and divulging this information would threaten the national security of our great nation."

There were more shouts of support. Dunraj smiled as the workers cheered him. "Thank you. Thank you."

And then he grew serious. "It is unfortunate that we live in troubled times. Where the loyalties of someone supposedly secure in their livelihood can be bought and sold like a carton of milk. Where people would cut one another down in the hope of gaining some advantage." He glanced back at the four of them. "Where spies lurk in our midst."

The crowd looked at Annja and the others, fury on their faces. Spies in their midst?

"Through our exhaustive investigative measures, we have found these four spying around the work site. They are all spies working in the employ of a foreign govern-ment—"

Some of the workers started shouting, "Death to Paki-stan!" but Dunraj held up his hands.

"We do not yet know who they are working for. It might well be the Americans. Or the British. What is important is that we were able to find them before they could do much damage to the hard work we have all en-deavored to bring about here. We have found the traitors before they could complete their plans."

More cheers went up and Dunraj lowered his hands. "Therefore, I have decided to make an object lesson of them. I have decided to show you how we deal with traitors. How we deal with people who talk too much. Indeed, how we deal with people who do not have the honor to stay true to the confidentiality agreements each of you signed prior to coming to work here."

He glanced back at her. "Last chance, Annja. Marry me."

"Never."

Dunraj shrugged. "In a moment, I will ask my guards to execute these spies for their treachery. I want you all to watch and understand what happens to anyone who defies the glorious nature of what we have here. I will not tolerate disloyalty. I will not tolerate treachery or es-pionage."

The workers roared their approval.

Annja frowned. Wonderful, more bloodlust. She frowned. Kali must really be proud of this.

Dunraj brought his hands up one final time. "Let us all continue to work as hard as we can on this incredible project. If we come in a week ahead of schedule, each man will get a bonus double paycheck at the conclusion of the job."

Now cheers of "Dunraj! Dunraj!" went up from the crowd. Dunraj smiled and let the workers carry on for several long moments. Finally, he shushed them.

He turned and walked back to Annja. "Anything else to say to me?"

"Nice speech?"

"You speak Hindi?"

Pradesh chimed in from behind Annja. "I translated."

Dunraj nodded. "Kind of you."

Annja cocked her head to one side. "It sounded a little Communist to me. 'Glorious work?' The idea of communal labor for the betterment of all? I don't know, if I was a betting woman, I'd say you have socialist tendencies."

Dunraj frowned. "I'm one-hundred-percent capitalist, thank you. In case you hadn't figured it out by now, what with the million-dollar condominium and expensive cars."

Annja shrugged. "Yeah, the KGB used to have all those toys, too."

Dunraj looked as if he was about to say something, but instead spun on his heel and stalked away. Annja glanced at Frank and Pradesh. Kormi drew closer behind her.

"We're not going to get a better chance, so be ready."

"When?" Pradesh asked.

"You'll know."

Dunraj reached the Tiger leader and called back, "I hope you enjoy your journey to hell, Annja Creed."

Annja nodded. "If you get there first, save a seat for me, would you?"

And then she reached into the otherwhere and grasped the sword. She threw it straight at the cable holding the giant statue of Kali. And severed the creaking cable.

"Get down!" Annja shouted.

A scream went up from the crowd of workers as the cable snapped and whipped back down into their midst. The statue plummeted to the ground, bursting apart, sending fragments into the group of Tigers.

Dust rained down on Annja and the others. But Annja was already on her feet, sword in hand.

She charged the line of Tigers, cutting through one who had stumbled under a rain of rocks. And then she reached the first few shooters.

A few barks of gunfire sounded, but Annja was in their midst cutting through bone, flesh and gun alike. In her peripheral vision, she saw Pradesh already in the melee, disarming one of the Tigers and reversing the gun, shooting him.

And then Frank was in the thick of it, as well, wielding his giant hands like Thor's hammer. He was almost by Annja's side when one of the Tigers stabbed him in the shoulder.

As Frank fell to his knees, Annja was flying through the air, trying her best to cut the distance down before the Tiger could execute Frank.

But she was going to be too late. The Tiger reared back, ready to drive the knife into the base of Frank's skull.

Annja heard the shot and saw the Tiger spin away, dead.

Pradesh nodded at her, and Annja barely had time to

smile a quick thanks before she jerked to the ground as a volley of bullets cut the air where she'd been standing.

Annja wheeled around and cut horizontally, but she only sliced air. The shooter was too far away.

She allowed the momentum to carry the sword over her head, and then she threw it screaming through the air like a missile.

It sank into the Tiger's body, right through his heart.

In an instant Annja had the sword back in her hands. She saw Kormi fighting two men, and for a moment it looked as though they were going to get the better of him. But even as they piled on top and he went down, Annja saw him surge back and toss both men as if they were weightless.

Annja jumped in the air, narrowly avoiding a hacking slash by one of the Tigers who had abandoned his gun in favor of a more close-quarters weapon: his huge knife.

Annja backhanded him across the face and he stumbled back, but instead of recoiling, he smiled. Annja could see his hatred and he came at her, slashing and stabbing in a series of fluid movements that forced Annja to backpedal to gain some distance.

She waited for the pause in the rhythm of his attack and then drove straight in, forcing her attacker on the defensive. Annja kept up the pressure, cutting down and back and forward.

As Annja launched her final series of attacks, she knew she had him. He tried to block one of her strikes but she snapped his blade and sent it skittering away. Then she drove her sword into his sternum, before jerking it out again. The man slid to the ground already dead.

Annja took stock. Dunraj and the leader of the Tigers were both nowhere to be seen.

Pradesh had just dispatched another Tiger. "Where is Dunraj?" she asked him.

He shook his head. "I lost sight of him during the fighting."

Frank was on his feet, clutching his wounded shoulder. "I didn't notice where he went."

"Kormi?"

But Kormi only shrugged as he broke another Tiger's neck. He held up his hands. "I do not know, either."

Those two could already be halfway back to Hyderabad.

Annja wiped the blade of her sword on the clothes of one of the Tigers. "We've still got a problem. Dunraj and the Tiger leader are missing."

Pradesh looked at her. "So, now what?"

"We go find them."

33

Annja took a moment to examine Frank's shoulder injury. The knife hadn't gone all that deep, and she cut some cloth from the fallen Tigers to make a bandage for him. Wrapping it, she nudged him.

"You did good back there."

Frank rolled his eyes. "I've been in fights before, Annja."

"For your life?"

"Well, no. Not until this time."

Annja nodded. "It's different when you fight for survival. No rules."

"I guess rules pretty much went out the window here, didn't they?"

"Exactly."

"Not to mention you've got a great big sword."

Annja smiled. "Well, yeah, but that's not the important difference."

"Are you sure? It seemed pretty important when you were able to cut that steel cable."

"I think it was only a matter of time before that cable snapped, anyway. I just helped it along."

"Well, it's a damned good thing you have it." Frank winced as she applied more pressure on his wound. "And don't worry, I won't tell anyone about it. I just want to get out of here and go home."

"We will," she said. "But we have to make sure we finish this."

"We can't just leave?"

"No."

"Is this even our fight?" Frank frowned. "Couldn't we just take off and leave Pradesh to handle it?"

Annja shook her head. "Yeah, we could do that. But that's now how I operate. The sword comes with a degree of responsibility. If I was to walk out and leave Dunraj free to keep killing, then I wouldn't be living up to that ideal. I'd be ignoring the problem instead of solving it."

"Is that what you do now, solve problems?"

Annja sighed. "Sometimes it feels like that." She finished wrapping his shoulder and patted it. "You're all set. Can you move it?"

Frank straightened his arm and Annja nodded. "All right, grab one of the guns from the Tigers, make sure you've got a full clip and let's get going."

"Full clip?"

Annja eyed him. "Never shot a gun before?"

"Uh, not unless you count on my Xbox."

"I don't." Annja picked up one of the guns left behind. It was a Heckler & Koch MP-5. She popped the clip, saw that it was almost full and slapped it back home, hit the charging handle and made sure the safety was on.

She flipped it over and handed it to Frank. "This is the selector switch. It's on safe right now—that means it won't fire."

"I know what the safety is, Annja."

"Just checking." She pointed at it. "The first option down is semiautomatic. One bullet per squeeze of the trigger. The next option down is full-auto spray-and-pray, as I like to call it. Try not to use full-auto unless absolutely necessary. You'll go through your magazine too fast, and I don't know how long we'll have to chase Dunraj."

"Okay, thanks."

Annja indicated the fallen Tigers. "Get another magazine of bullets and stick it in your pants. We're wasting time here."

Pradesh helped Frank find another magazine, and Kormi wandered over. "You sure about the boy?"

"He's not actually a boy, Kormi."

"He's not a man yet, either."

"True, but he acquitted himself pretty well here."

"What is the expression? Beginner's luck," Kormi said. "I don't wish the boy to have to face much more of this and risk his life. He is not born to be a warrior. You are. Pradesh, too. And me. We should go on alone."

Annja tensed. "I don't disagree with you, Kormi. There's nothing I'd like better than to keep Frank safe. But I don't want to send him back to the hotel when Dunraj and his man are out there on the loose somewhere. Besides, he's doing some serious growing up on the trip."

Kormi shook his head. "What is the value of growing up only to die so soon? When it could have been avoided."

Annja looked at him for a moment. Then she cleared her throat. "Frank. Come over here for a moment, would you?"

Frank walked over. "What's up?"

Annja smiled. "It occurs to me that I never asked if you'd be willing to come along. My fight shouldn't automatically become your fight. You've got a choice here. You can come with us to stop Dunraj or grab a car and head back to Hyderabad and bring help. That's *if* Dunraj hasn't made it out of here and back to Hyderabad first."

Pradesh spoke up. "I can tell you who to contact in my department. They will listen to you if I tell you what to say."

"You saying you don't want me to come along?"

"I'm not saying that at all. But you're not well versed in combat. And that's not necessarily a bad thing."

Frank nodded. "But I think I'm too deep in it to back out now. I need to see this through to the end. One way or the other."

"Stay behind me when the fighting starts," Kormi said. He looked at Annja. "I do not agree with this, but you gave the boy a choice."

"And he's chosen," she said. "Dunraj and the Tiger leader must have taken one of the paths out of here, but which way would they have gone?"

"If I was Dunraj," Pradesh said, "I'd want to get out of here quickly. The more distance he can put between himself and this place, the better."

"You're thinking he took the highway?"

Pradesh nodded. "It's what I would have done."

Annja led them down the slope toward the truck-processing area. There were wounded workers all over trying to patch one another up. They stared at Annja and the others, but the weapons they held kept any of them from trying to start a fight.

Annja pointed to where the statue lay in a million pieces. "Some of it took out the workers."

"It's dusty as hell in here," Pradesh said.

They walked among the dump trucks. Annja searched each of them, looking for any signs that Dunraj had been here. Most of them had no keys. And there was no evidence that any trucks had left since Dunraj called a halt to the work for his grand speech.

"He must still be around here."

"And he's still a threat," Pradesh said.

The truck yard suddenly seemed a lot more threatening than it had when they thought Dunraj might have already left.

"Was he armed?"

"I think we have to assume he was," Kormi said. "Plus the leader of the armed men also had a weapon."

"Wonderful," Annja muttered under her breath. "All right, we're going to have to split up."

"Are you sure that's wise?"

"It's the only way to check everything and make sure they're not moving around on us, possibly flanking for a better angle to open up, you know?"

Pradesh nodded. "I will take the left side."

"And I will take the right. With the boy." Kormi pulled Frank to his side. "Come with me, young warrior. And be careful with that weapon of yours."

Annja watched them head off on either side of her. That leaves the middle for me, she thought.

She crept among the giant wheels of the first dump truck. Even though there were ambient noises elsewhere in the work site, things seemed quieter in the immediate area.

She heard footsteps, of course, from both Pradesh and Kormi as they made their way down their respective search avenues. And she assumed that Frank would be behind Kormi, with his heart no doubt thundering in his chest.

Her own pulse was pounding, and Annja gripped the sword in front of her in a two-handed stance that she favored when she didn't know what was going to materialize in front of her.

Dunraj had wrought a lot of havoc here. And while he may not have done all the killing, he'd certainly enabled the horrific events to unfold by giving his brother free rein. As far as Annja was concerned, that made him just as guilty.

And the fact that he'd brought in the Tamil Tigers hired mercenaries only meant that Dunraj had no care for anything but his own lousy agenda.

She crept closer to the second dump truck. Its wheels were caked with mud and dirt, and it was in bad need of a wash.

Something moved.

Annja froze.

Dunraj?

Or the Tiger leader?

Either one would be deadly.

A noise nearby caused her to spin.

But there was nothing in her line of sight.

Annja forced herself to relax. Expanded her awareness outward.

Searching.

Feeling.

And when she rounded the side of the next dump truck, she wasn't surprised to see Dunraj leaning against it, a strange expression on his face.

"Hello again, Annja."

"Waiting for me?"

Dunraj shrugged. "I wasn't going anywhere, apparently."

Annja frowned. And then saw the leader of the Tigers move out from behind Dunraj. He had a gun aimed at Dunraj's head. "Put your sword away, little woman. Or else I kill him."

34

Annja had to keep from laughing. "You want to beat me to the punch?"

Dunraj sighed. "I tried to explain that to him. Really, I did. But this chap doesn't seem to understand how things work."

Annja nodded at the Tiger leader. "Go head. Put the bullet in his head. See if I care."

Dunraj raised his hand. "Although, if he does do that, then I'm afraid you will all be in a bit of a pickle."

"Yeah?"

"A rather explosive jar of pickles, actually." Dunraj smiled. "You didn't think that I've gotten as far as I have in life without being extremely careful, did you?"

"Could have fooled me," she said. "You're the one with the gun aimed at your head right now. So how come the honeymoon's over? I thought you guys were fast friends."

Dunraj looked pained. "I really wish you hadn't brought that up, Annja."

The Tiger leader nudged Dunraj with the gun. "Tell her. Tell her what you did to us."

Annja clucked. "Uh-oh, Dunraj. Sounds like you weren't playing fair and square with the Tigers. What's the matter? Did he find out that statue you promised them wasn't made entirely of gold?"

Dunraj gritted his teeth. "Severing the cable proved that, didn't it?"

"Solid-gold statues don't usually shatter into a million pieces, do they?"

"No," Dunraj said drily. "They do not."

"You double-crossed us," the Tiger leader accused him. "And now my men are dead and I have nothing to show for it."

Dunraj shrugged. "Yes, but I didn't kill your men. She did."

The Tiger leader looked at Annja. "Don't think you're going anywhere, either. You and I have unfinished business."

"Aren't you going to kill him first?" Annja asked. "Because, really, don't let me hold you up."

"Do that," Dunraj said, "and this whole cavern will explode into a fireball the likes of which no one will be able to survive. One of my subordinates will make sure of it. There's enough high explosive packed into these walls to melt steel. And in case you hadn't noticed, human flesh melts at a much lower temperature than steel."

Annja sighed. "And why should we believe you? After all, you've been lying in one way or another since we met."

"Don't believe me, then." Dunraj turned to the Tiger leader. "Shoot me in the head and get it over with. But if you do, then you'll never get out of here with the actual statue. And you'll die, as well."

Annja could see the Tiger leader's hesitation. He might have been a terrorist, but he wanted his money. God knew how many more terror operations it would finance in the south. And how many more people would lose their lives because of it.

She frowned. Was this the reason she'd been brought here? What had started out as a quest to find the creature responsible for killing people had led her to a twisted story of familial obligations and sociopaths, only to be involved with a known terrorist organization responsible for the slaughter of thousands.

And who was the man standing in front of her? Was he a high-ranking leader within the group? Or someone far lower in the chain of command?

The Tiger leader seemed to be mulling what Dunraj had said. After a moment he looked at Annja. "Do you believe him?"

Annja shrugged. "I don't even know your name. Why would you care what I think?"

"My name is Anup."

"You run the Tigers?"

Anup chuckled. "Not even close. I am a cell commander. When Dunraj hired us, I was ordered to come here and help him."

"How long have you been on his payroll?"

"Several months," Anup said. "And he promised us a gold statue that we could melt down and use to finance our struggle for independence."

"Several months?" Annja shook her head. "That's considerably longer than the time we've been in town."

She eyed Dunraj. "What have you been up to around these parts that you need assistance from a group like the Tigers?"

"None of your business."

"I could just ask Anup here. He doesn't seem all that friendly with you since you've betrayed his trust."

Anup seemed to agree. "Dunraj has had us engaged in a series of assassinations."

"Really? And who were your targets?"

"Developers in the area, mostly. One or two government officials. But their deaths were designed to look like accidents."

Annja studied Dunraj. "Taking care of the competition, were you? What's the matter, things getting a bit cutthroat in Hyderabad?"

"I had some outside competition that needed handling," he replied. "Nothing too terrible. And since they were done correctly, the papers never even noticed a trend. It just seemed like a rather fortuitous streak for me."

"Well, that's the problem with streaks," she said. "They always seem to come to an end." She looked back at Anup. "And how were you getting the statue out of here? On a truck?"

"Of course. How else could we manage it?"

"I'll bet the real one is still kicking around here someplace," she said. "Knowing Dunraj, he probably hid it under a pile of dirt in one of these trucks. And once he had you take the junk one away, he'd be free to melt the other one down."

Anup regarded Dunraj. "You are a fool."

"What would have happened when they tried to melt

it down, Dunraj? They would have discovered the ruse. What would have prevented them from coming after you then?"

Dunraj pursed his lips. "Nothing, I suppose," he said simply.

Annja frowned. That didn't seem like the Dunraj she knew. He wouldn't have been that careless.

"You're not telling us everything, are you?"

Dunraj smiled. "I don't know what you're talking about."

Annja shook her head. "There's no way you'd be that reckless. Once the Tigers found out you'd duped them, they'd put a contract out on you. You'd be a dead man walking and you wouldn't be able to go anywhere. You might dodge the hit teams for a while, but they'd eventually catch up with you."

"Everyone dies sometime," Dunraj said. "Look, I rolled the dice, and this time it didn't come up in my favor."

"I should kill him now," Anup said.

"Obviously," Annja replied. "But then we have that little problem of the bombs he's left behind."

Anup hesitated. "What do you suggest?"

"I don't know yet. I'm still intrigued by the idea that Dunraj was trying to trick you into taking that statue."

"You're wasting your time, Annja," Dunraj said. "It was a gambit that didn't pan out for me."

But she knew he was hiding something. And it was something he didn't want revealed, obviously, by the way he kept trying to skirt the issue.

Annja nodded at Anup. "You should come with me. And bring him. I want to check something out."

"What? What are you checking out?" Anup waved his pistol. "I'll shoot if I have to."

Annja held up her hand. "Relax. I just want to satisfy my own curiosity about something."

Dunraj sighed. "Do I need to remind you what happened to the cat that was too curious?"

"You're not in any position to give me advice right now." Annja walked away from the dump trucks and toward where the statue had fallen. Behind her, Anup was pushing Dunraj ahead of him so they were following.

Annja found the area of impact and set about looking at the fractured pieces of the statue. Anup watched closely.

"What are you looking for?"

Annja shook her head. "I don't know yet. But I have a feeling that I'll recognize it when I see it."

"Is this going to take a while?" Dunraj asked. "Because if it is, I'd like to sit down and rest a spell. My legs are aching."

Anup frowned disapprovingly. "Sit if you must."

"Thank you."

Dunraj sat twelve feet away from Annja and cleared his throat. Annja glanced at him.

"What?"

"Sorry?" Dunraj asked.

Annja shot him a look. "Leave me alone unless you've got something to tell us."

Dunraj glanced up at Anup and then back at Annja. "Nothing. Just that you should really think before blundering into things."

Annja was beyond irritated. "Shut up, Dunraj."

"Yes," Anup said. "Shut up."

Annja went back to studying the fragments of the statue. From what she could tell, the gold layered over the plaster certainly seemed real enough.

"This is quite the fake," Annja said. "It must have cost you a lot of money, Dunraj."

"Far less than I would get for the actual statue."

Annja nodded, studying the debris. The way the arms had broken off left no doubt that Dunraj had had this manufactured and then buried in the mountain to make it look genuine. He probably had the Tigers come out here when he was proposing the job to them. The sight of this thing partially uncovered in the dirt would certainly have been enough to convince them. And even if it wasn't, taking a sample of the gold from the arms would have convinced them. It was layered to a thickness of at least a half inch in some places.

But not others.

That meant Dunraj would have had to lead them to the exact point where they could take a sample. Probably he'd left the arm with the thickest layer of gold uncovered, and when the Tigers had seen it, it would have seemed natural for them to test that arm.

Clever.

But why?

Annja wasn't buying Dunraj's explanation. And the amount of effort that had gone into this. Why bother with the Tigers at all? Why get them involved in a situation like this? Surely Dunraj had other resources he could have tapped before resorting to a terrorist group.

She kept poking through the fragments and the plaster. The entire area was coated in a fine dust.

"Find anything interesting?"

Annja shook her head. "Not yet."

Anup frowned. "I don't have time for this. Let me force him to show me where he has hidden the explosives. Then I can kill him."

Annja smiled. "You really think he's going to tell you where he hid bombs if he knows you're going to shoot him?"

"I have ways to make him talk."

Annja nodded. "Very nice. I'm sure you have a catalog of nasty things you can do, but it's counterproductive. Give me a few more minutes here, and then we'll sort out the bomb business."

"Two minutes."

"Generous," Annja said. "Thanks."

She bent back to the pieces of the statue. And then something caught her eye. "Hello."

"Annja." Dunraj's voice was quieter now.

Insistent.

But it was too late. Anup had heard Annja's voice and come closer to look over her shoulder.

"Is that what I think it is?"

35

Annja hesitated. "I don't know. What do you think it is?"

Anup leaned closer. Annja followed his line of sight, not sure if he'd seen it yet. But judging from the look on his face, Anup had. And worse—for Dunraj at least—he was no dummy.

Anup leaned back. "It looks sophisticated. It is definitely not a thing you might purchase in a store. Is it?"

She shrugged. "I don't know all that much about it, to be honest. But judging from the placement and the microcircuitry, I'd have to agree with you. It looks very sophisticated."

Anup turned and hauled Dunraj to his feet. "Who are you working for? Who told you to put that into the statue?"

"I don't know what you're talking about. Honestly. I had that statue commissioned as a fake. If there's anything in it, it wasn't put there by me."

Annja brought out the rest of the wiring and held it aloft. "So what is it? A homing device?"

Dunraj glared at her. If looks could kill, Annja would have been well on her way to the next life. But to Anup, Dunraj merely looked puzzled. "I don't even know what that is."

"You are lying." Anup pitched Dunraj into the back side of a dump truck. Anup followed up with a right cross that set Dunraj on his heels before slumping down the side of the truck unconscious.

Annja nodded. "Nice shot."

Anup came back over. "Is there any way to tell who built this?"

"I doubt it. As I said, my knowledge of these things is only what I've seen in movies. But it's obvious you were set up. That's why Dunraj was willing to take a chance like this. He knew this statue would presumably be going—where, exactly?"

Anup frowned but didn't reply.

"Well, probably your headquarters or something, right? Some secret location, perhaps?"

"Perhaps."

"Don't you see?" she said. "That's what this was about. That's why you were hired. Dunraj didn't care about your targets. That was convenient cover to get you in here. And once you'd seen the statue, you were hooked. That kind of money could buy weapons, men, training— everything you'd need to start a full-fledged war with the Indian government."

"It would have allowed us to take the fight to them."

"And whoever put this inside the statue knew that. And you can bet once this statue had arrived at wherever you were planning to melt it down, the army would have shown up to kill every last one of you. The irony of this statue certainly isn't lost on me. You would have all been destroyed by the very goddess a lot of your men probably worship."

Anup was quiet for a moment. "I will kill the traitor now."

Annja caught his raised fist. "Wait—don't forget about the explosives. We don't have any way of knowing where they are."

"Are we so sure they even exist? He could be lying to us again. He does that quite often, apparently."

Annja held up the tiny circuit panel to which a very long wire was attached. "This must have been the antenna. They could run it the length of the statue to help improve its broadcast ability, I'm guessing."

Anup leaned closer as he looked back at Dunraj. "Who is this horrible man, anyway?"

"I don't know. But he certainly didn't want you to find out about this device, that much is certain."

"Only because I would kill him."

Annja shook her head. "He was aware of that, anyway. And it didn't bother him nearly as much as it should have."

Kormi and Frank and Pradesh hadn't yet returned from their search. Was it possible they had found another one of Dunraj's men in hiding? Or had something happened?

"Did you do anything to my friends?" she asked Anup.

"No, why should I have?"

"We were all looking for you and Dunraj." She gazed

past him toward the trucks. "And now they seem to be missing."

Anup lifted Dunraj off the ground by the shirt and held him there. "Perhaps this weasel knows where they are?"

Anup shook Dunraj hard. Dunraj's eyes fluttered. "You really shouldn't have meddled in this," he sputtered.

"You didn't leave me any choice," Annja replied. "You were trying to kill us. I took steps to make sure that didn't happen. Not my fault it caused you to run afoul of some very dangerous people."

Anup shook him again. "Where are her friends?"

"How would I know that? I have no idea what might be keeping them."

Annja frowned. "I'm really growing to not like you one little bit, Dunraj. Did you set a trap?"

He sighed. "How could I possibly set a trap when this lug here had me at gunpoint for betraying him? What was I supposed to do, run off and set an ambush and then come back to be his prisoner?"

Annja stood and tossed the circuit panel to Anup. "I need to go find them."

"We will accompany you." Anup shoved Dunraj ahead of him, and he fell into step with Annja.

"You don't know what you're dealing with here, Annja," Dunraj said adamantly. "You should have listened to me."

She stopped and turned on him. "At what point? When you were busy not telling me about any of this or later when you couldn't tell me again?"

"You didn't need to know."

"Maybe you should have considered changing your

mind about that when it became obvious I was going to be rooting through your precious fake statue. Who put you up to that, anyway? The manufacture of that statue alone would have cost tens of thousands of dollars. And it doesn't seem like something you would be willing to do for the hell of it."

"You're right. It's not."

"So who?"

"I suppose it depends on who would stand to gain the most from tracking the Tamil Tigers, wouldn't it?"

Annja moved closer to the dump trucks. They were still sitting idly by, their engines off. And again, a strange silence seemed to descend on the place.

"Maybe you should go first."

Dunraj was amused at her suspicions. "There's nothing here, Annja. I assure you I would know if there was an ambush about to occur."

"Then why don't I trust you?"

"Because you have issues with trust? Exactly what you accused me of earlier. A sad story in your childhood?"

Annja rolled her eyes. "Just keep moving."

They walked in between two dump trucks on the right side, where Kormi and Frank had taken the search. Annja reached out for the sword and held it up in front of her.

Dunraj shook his head. "That is truly a marvel. Do you mind my asking how it is you came by it?"

"Sorry, Dunraj, you don't have a need to know."

Behind them Anup held his pistol low and at the ready. Annja shook her head. How in the hell was she partnered up with a terrorist right now? What was her world coming to when something as bizarre as this had become her norm?

I need a vacation. A real one, she thought.

She rounded the corner and stopped. There were tracks in the dirt. Fresh tracks. "Hold it."

She crouched and examined them. One set was definitely Frank's. She could tell by the sheer size of the tread.

"Your friends?" Anup asked.

Annja nodded. "I think so."

"Then they were here."

"Yes, but I don't know what happened after this point. You see? The tread changes. It's no longer walking forward. And there are fresh drag marks in the dirt."

"They were taken by surprise," Anup suggested. "And then their captors dragged them away. Possibly unconscious?"

Annja squinted at the dirt. Who could have come upon them and managed to disarm them both? Sure, Frank was a newbie, but Kormi was a seasoned fighter. For someone to get the drop on them like this, it meant they had to be very good.

"I don't like this one bit," she said, standing and staring at Dunraj. "You sure you don't have something else you want to tell me?"

"I can't think of anything."

Annja held his gaze. "I get the feeling you're lying to me again, Dunraj. And I don't like that."

"I can't predict your suppositions. Honestly, the way you carry on gets tedious."

Anup shoved the barrel of his pistol under Dunraj's ear. "You are growing tiresome. I should execute you right now for your crimes against the Tamil Tigers."

Dunraj snorted. "Oh, yes, your grand plans for independence. How stirring. How revolutionary. Please. You're nothing but a poor excuse for a terrorist organization bent on its own agenda of opportunity. You're all hypocrites, deluded into believing what your leaders tell you."

Anup pulled the hammer back on his pistol. Annja held up her hand. "Anup, the explosives."

"I think he is lying about them, anyway. And in that event, it is time for him to meet his ancestors."

"Typical response from a terrorist," Dunraj said.

"You're not helping your situation," Annja snapped.

Anup leveled the gun on Dunraj's head. "I hereby sentence you to death for your crimes of betrayal against Tamil Tigers."

Annja sighed. "Are you sure about this, Anup?"

"I no longer care."

Annja looked at Dunraj. "Got any last words?"

Dunraj smiled wickedly. "Actually, yes, I do have a few last words. Well, one, anyway."

Anup hesitated, lowered the pistol slightly. "And what is that?"

"Boom."

Dunraj started to laugh. Annja looked at Anup but the Tiger was already bringing the pistol back up. Annja wasn't entirely sure she could blame him for wanting to end the man's life. But there was still the matter of finding Kormi, Frank and Pradesh.

Anup said something low in Hindi, but started to squeeze the trigger, anyway.

She heard the gunshot. It sounded like an explosion, but not quite as loud as she expected from being so close to the shooter.

But Dunraj's head didn't explode.

Anup's did.

And as his body crumpled to the ground, Dunraj smiled. "You see? I told you. Boom."

36

Annja turned and saw Pradesh step out from around a corner where he must've taken the kill shot. "You certainly took your time," Dunraj snarled. "This git was bloody close to ending me."

Pradesh shrugged. The expression on his face was one of absolute loathing as he stepped over the body of Anup. "I did it when it counted."

"What the hell is going on around here?" Annja asked. Pradesh and Dunraj together? She was giving strong consideration to simply cutting them both down and calling it a day.

Pradesh slid his gun back into his holster. "Surely you must have figured it out by now. Smart girl that you are."

"I have some ideas but I'd rather just cut to the chase. Speaking of which, where are Frank and Kormi? If you did anything to them—"

Pradesh held up his hand. "They're both fine. I had to hit Kormi on the head to get him under control, but

Frank helped me put him under cover. I couldn't be sure about Anup not going off half-cocked so I wanted them both out of the line of fire."

Annja frowned. "All right."

Dunraj pointed a finger at Annja. "She found the device. She ruined the entire operation."

Pradesh eyed Dunraj. "Calm down. As soon as she caused the statue to fall and shatter, the operation was over. There was no way they were going to fall for it once they saw that statue break into a million pieces."

"Exactly," Dunraj said. "It's her fault."

"And what was I supposed to do?" she asked. "You were going to have them shoot us. Including, I might add, Pradesh here. If you two have something going on, it doesn't seem very solid to me when one of you was willing to let the other get shot."

Pradesh nodded. "And don't think I didn't notice that, as well, Dunraj. We had an agreement, and you seemed only too willing to forget that. Rather convenient, wouldn't you say?"

"I told Anup not to shoot you. Just the others."

Annja shook her head. "I don't believe that for a second. I never heard Anup say anything to his men about only shooting us. Unless they had telepathy, you're lying."

Pradesh stared coldly at Dunraj. "We'll deal with that later. And you'd better have a good explanation or else you're in trouble, my so-called friend."

Dunraj fell silent and leaned against the dump truck, a sullen expression on his face.

"I'm sorry you got wrapped up in all of this," Pradesh

told her. "It's gone from chaos to worse than chaos. But I'll try to explain it as best I can."

Annja held up her hand. "Let me see if I can put it together. It's not my first time in the company of spooks."

Pradesh's eyes widened. He was clearly impressed. "It's not?"

"Unfortunately, no. You all seem to have the bad habit of springing up like weeds when least desired. Honestly, the intelligence world seems to bank on its ability to take a situation and completely ruin any chance of normalcy." She sighed. "So, you must be with, what—NIA?"

Pradesh shook his head. "Not even close. Research and Analysis Wing, actually."

"Never heard of it."

"Good. Not many people have unless you keep your finger on the pulse of the intel community."

"You're new?"

"No. We've been around for a while. In the shadows, where all the successful spooks live."

Annja indicated Dunraj. "And him? Is he with your organization, too?"

Pradesh sniffed. "Hardly. He does what we tell him to do, and that's it."

"Oh, goody. Another convenient relationship between an intelligence agency and a less-then-desirable individual. Let me guess—you knew all about his twin brother."

"His late twin brother, you mean."

"Whatever."

Pradesh grew somber. "Yes, we knew about him. It was how we cemented our relationship with Dunraj."

"And you put up with the fact that you had not one but two monsters on your payroll—why?"

Pradesh sighed. "The problem with criticizing intelligence agencies is that everyone always takes such a shortsighted view of things. And that's a direct contradiction to what intelligence is. It's long-term. You're thinking about Friday night, and we're thinking about Friday night ten years from now. Our worldview is so different that criticisms inevitably falter because by the time any judgment gets levied against us, we've proven our case over time."

"This whole thing was an operation?"

"Part of it. The rest was just what it should be to convince our targets it's real."

"And Dunraj. Explain how he became a part of it."

Pradesh relaxed his stance. "We knew that Dunraj had skeletons. And we also knew that he was hungry for success. That success couldn't possibly come without competition. So we entered into a relationship to facilitate his ascent into the richest segment of society. We got his hands wet with money. And naturally, he quite liked the lifestyle."

"Of course. He's narcissistic."

Dunraj snorted but Pradesh ignored him. "We had a plan, of course. Dunraj's wealth would naturally put him into conflict with others. It's inevitable. Developers try to outdo one another. The rich like to play their money games."

"But?"

"No buts. We knew a man like Dunraj would eventually have enemies. And he would need a means to deal with those enemies. The logical tool would be outside help. One way or another, his success would bring him into close proximity to a number of India's enemies. And that is exactly what we wanted."

"But you had no idea how long it would take. Or even who it might be. How could you afford to play that game?"

Pradesh looked at her. "You said that you've dealt with spies before. You're surprised by this?"

Annja wasn't. "I guess not. I just find the entire business unpalatable. The people you're forced to deal with. The alliances you make."

Pradesh gestured to where the statue had fallen. "Our goal was to track the Tigers back to their operations base—presumably in Sri Lanka, but we'd had reports of them having a forward operating base in southern India somewhere. Once we had the location, we were going in."

"To arrest them?"

Pradesh shook his head. "To wipe them out. You can't take a chance that they'd get out of prison and come back for vengeance. The best way to deal with terrorists is to put them down like animals."

"Charming," she said.

"None of this was ever supposed to be seen by civilians."

Annja rolled her eyes. "And what about the innocent people killed by Dunraj's crazy brother?"

"Unfortunate," Pradesh said. "But within the scope of the operation, acceptable."

"Not to their families."

"Their families will be well compensated by the government in some form. Dunraj's company will no doubt pay damages. My people will sort it all out and ensure that the families are taken care of. Money is the best way to ease the grief."

"Says you," Annja scoffed. "Some of those people would have been fathers or mothers or sons. No money will ever bring that back."

Pradesh frowned. "Annja, I told you it was a regrettable part of this affair. But we have to move beyond that. Once we figured out that Dunraj's brother was out of control, we sent Dunraj in to straighten him out, but by that point, you and Frank had already blundered in. Since then on, we've been scrambling to make sure the operation didn't fall apart."

Annja took in the chaos of the scene around them. "Oops."

"Yes, it's all bunged up now, isn't it?" He sighed. "We've had this in motion for over a month now."

"Just a month? I thought you got to Dunraj ages ago."

"Oh, we did. But the Tiger connection only started about a month ago. As I said, we think long-term. Try to fake something like Dunraj having competition and it looks fake a mile away. But when you get media coverage backing it up, and certain projects get derailed, and even sprinkle in some shadowy skeletons into his past…"

Dunraj shuffled a few feet away, his hands in his pockets. Annja nodded at him. "He doesn't like being talked about like that."

"He's an asset. They never like hearing about their status as a pawn in a larger game. He'll be all right."

"So, what happens now? The Tiger operation is blown, but you can't put Dunraj back out into the cold again, can you? The other Tigers will come looking for him."

"We'll roll this up in such a way that he's still viable. I've done things like this before."

"Does it always work out?"

"Usually."

"Usually?"

Pradesh shrugged. "Sometimes it doesn't. And our assets become…negligible."

"Which means what—you yank support?"

"We have no choice," Pradesh said, lowering his voice so Dunraj wouldn't hear. "We can't risk exposure. Our mandate is that we only answer to the prime minister. And that's caused us problems in the past. The less the Indian people know of our activities, the better."

Annja shook her head. "You're not quite the police officer I thought you were."

"If it makes you feel any better, I started out as a cop. That's why the cover fits me so well."

"Your poor mother," Annja said. "If she only knew what things you get up to in the name of your country."

Pradesh chuckled. "My mother's dead, Annja. I'm an orphan."

"You took us out to dinner! That place!"

"That woman is part of my cover. Legending, we call it. A little more in-depth than your usual backstopping material like fake credit cards. But effective at selling a story. She's a wonderful old actress in our employ, and she does a very respectable job at cooking, too."

"Why would she agree to stay there?"

"She gets a great salary from us, plus whatever her business makes. It's all hers tax-free. When we need her, she's there to supply a convincing story and that's it. She's never in danger and she likes the thrill of it."

"You guys have this country sewn up pretty well, don't you?"

"It's not about sewing anything up," Pradesh denied. "It's about protecting our interests. Surely you have some sense of nationalistic pride? You wave the flag for America, don't you?"

"I'm a patriot," she confirmed. "But being a patriot doesn't mean I blindly follow whatever my government does. America was founded because people questioned authority. The way to a better, more perfect union is through constant debate and evolution—not the absence of it."

"I agree."

"But you tow the party line."

Pradesh shrugged. "I see things a little differently because of my job."

Annja sighed. "Can we go collect Frank and Kormi and get out of here? I'm a little worried about where Dunraj has gone."

"Absolutely."

A gunshot interrupted their conversation.

Annja and Pradesh sprinted toward the trucks.

37

Annja rounded the corner first, her sword held high, ready to strike down whoever was threatening. What she saw when she got there wasn't what she expected.

Kormi lay in a pool of blood.

Frank was next to him, trying to stem the flow, but even from a distance, Annja could tell it was going to be a losing battle.

"What the hell happened?"

"Dunraj!" Frank cried. "He pulled out a gun and shot Kormi."

Kormi grimaced through the pain. "I'll be fine."

Annja looked at Frank and saw the concern etched on his face. Kormi had been shot in the upper abdomen, and the bullet had likely punched into his heart. The blood flow, typical of an abdominal wound, was tremendous. She knelt next to him.

"I owe you a tremendous debt of gratitude, Kormi.

You saved my life. And Frank's. And you kept watch over him. You lived up to your pledge."

He smiled, but she could see him weakening by the second. "I have done my best. I only hope it is enough to outweigh the bad in this lifetime."

"You should be proud," Annja said. "I'm certain you will be properly rewarded."

Kormi gestured for Frank to stop. "My time is here. Allow me to go with dignity."

Frank pulled his bloody hands away. "Kormi, I can—"

Kormi shook his head. "No. You can't. My heart…" He smiled. "It's all right. I die happy."

Annja watched as his eyes closed and Kormi slumped to one side. Frank turned to Annja. "What the hell did Dunraj shoot him for? And how come he didn't shoot me?"

"I don't know." She glanced at Pradesh. "Still think your asset is under your control?"

Pradesh checked his pistol. "I told you I had to roll this operation up. Well, I think the time has come to do just that."

"And Dunraj?"

Pradesh stared into her eyes. "It's a terrible thing when unlicensed construction projects suffer tragic mishap. You never know who could be buried under all the debris."

"We find him," Annja said, "and then we take him to the police. The real ones." She glanced at Frank, who looked very confused. "You need to get the hell out of here." She held up a hand as he started to protest. "I don't want to hear it. I know Kormi liked you and thought it was his duty to protect you. Well, it's my duty now. And you work for me on this assignment. So do as I say, grab a truck and leave. Head for Hyderabad, go to the hotel and order room service. Get drunk or something. Find a cute waitress. I don't care. Just get gone from this mountain."

Frank started to say something and then stopped. He took a breath. "Yeah. All right."

He went to wipe his hands in the dirt of the ground. "No sense heading through the lobby with hands that look like I committed murder."

"Good plan."

"What about you guys?"

"Don't worry about us," Annja said. "We'll find Dunraj."

"All right—"

A volley of automatic gunfire raked the area. Annja bent and twisted as she dropped. Pradesh scrambled for cover.

But a round caught Frank.

"Annja!" Frank rolled over and squirmed his way next to a thick rubber tire for cover. "He got me!"

Not Frank. She'd never forgive herself if Frank didn't come through alive.

She dashed over and crouched near where Frank was clutching his thigh. "Is it bad?"

He shook his head. "I don't know."

Annja pried his hand away and sagged in relief. The bullet had grazed the outside of his thigh. There was blood and probably a lot of pain. But Frank would survive.

Well, provided she and Pradesh could find Dunraj before this got any worse.

"How's Frank?" Pradesh called.

"He'll live."

"Dunraj has got to be around somewhere." Pradesh stuck his head up and instantly another volley of automatic gunfire sprayed the area. He ducked as several rounds caught the windshield of the truck closest to him and showered the agent with glass.

"You're right. He's out of control."

"You think?" She frowned. Damned spies and their games. She turned back to Frank. "All right, when Pradesh and I figure out where Dunraj is, you're only going to have a limited time to get a truck and head for the tunnel. If he figures out that you're escaping, then he'll shoot you."

Frank bit his lip. "Yeah, okay. I got it."

"Get in the cab and wait until you hear me shout for you to go and then hit the gas and do not stop until you're clear of this mountain. I'll come find you later, all right?"

"Take care of yourself, Annja."

"You, too."

Annja scurried over to Pradesh. Another few bullets whizzed by overhead.

"What's he waiting for?" she asked. "He could charge us with the AK and kill us before we knew what hit us."

Pradesh shook his head. "He's not a soldier. It's one thing being up close with a pistol on Kormi. But using an assault rifle is quite another. And he knows we're armed." Pradesh frowned. "No, he's up to something—I just don't know what."

Annja took a breath. "The explosives."

"Huh?"

"Explosives. When Anup had the drop on him, Dunraj mentioned he'd had this place wired to blow."

Pradesh sighed. "I'm going to need a serious vacation after this."

"Me first," Annja said. "Where do you think he is?"

Pradesh nodded ahead of them. "There's a small dirt pile beyond that last truck there. It would give him the tactical advantage of higher ground. The gunfire seems to be coming from that direction."

"Then we'll need to hit him from two sides."

"I'll go left," Pradesh said. "Give me thirty seconds to get into position and then we hit at the same time."

"You'll need to start since you've got the gun. Distract him with a few shots and then I'll move in close."

"You sure?"

Annja's eyes narrowed. "Yeah. I'm sure. I'm not going to hurt him unless I absolutely have to. It's long past time this guy was in custody."

Annja threaded her way through one of the tires and then got low to the ground. She figured the lower her profile, the less chance of Dunraj seeing her.

Across the way, Pradesh had the same idea. He snaked along the ground, trying to cut the distance to where they thought Dunraj was hiding.

Annja tasted dirt in her mouth, crunching in the back of her teeth. She spat and kept slithering along the dirt track. The trucks loomed over her but provided excellent cover.

Unless, of course, Dunraj wasn't where they thought he was.

Let's not think about that. She took a moment to look back at where she'd left Frank, but he was gone from his spot. He would be climbing into a truck cab right then, waiting for her to shout to move out.

Annja drew closer to the hill of dirt and rocks.

Was Dunraj there?

Was he wiring up his bomb to go off?

Out of the corner of her eye, she spotted movement and knew it would be Pradesh squirming along at about the same pace as her. It was critical they reach their staging points at the same time.

Annja kept moving, breathing and sweating. She blinked and felt sweat run into her eyes but she quelled the sting by blinking some more.

Her heart thundered into the ground.

Directly ahead of her, she saw the base of the pile of dirt and rocks. She was coming to the last cover the trucks afforded her.

This was it.

She steeled herself and bunched her legs under her, set to sprint for the base of the hill and to try to cover the open ground as quickly as possible. The less time she was exposed, the less chance Dunraj would have of squeezing off a shot.

Or fifty.

She took a breath.

Flexed her legs.

Now!

Annja dashed from cover at the exact same moment as Pradesh, yelling for Frank to leave as she did. They hit the base of the hill at the same time. Annja looked down the way, and Pradesh gave her a thumbs-up.

She nodded.

Okay, Dunraj, she thought, here we come.

Pradesh checked his pistol.

Annja reached for the sword, feeling its power in her hands. In her body. She pulsed with the energy of the blade.

Annja took a breath. And then started clambering up the hill.

38

Pradesh reached the top first and let loose two shots. Annja heard an engine start up across the way and knew Frank had heard. Then she was already coming over the top of the hill, with her sword at the ready.

But Dunraj was nowhere to be seen.

Annja stumbled in the loose dirt and rocks. Pradesh caught up with her, the look on his face more annoyed than anything else. "Where the hell did he go?"

Annja shook her head. "Damned if I know. I could have sworn he was here. After all, the shots came from this area, didn't they?"

Pradesh nodded. "Yes, so I thought. But if he's not here, then where would he be?"

Dunraj's voice boomed out from somewhere across the work site. "Haven't found me yet, have you?" He laughed. "I'm having a lot of fun with this now. Imagine, the intrepid intelligence agent and the fearless archae-

ologist with the sword being unable to locate one man.
I love it."

Frank's truck trundled toward the exit. Annja watched
it hit the on-ramp and then it was through the tunnel.

"And where does your young friend think he's going?"
Dunraj boomed. "Back to the city? Not if I can help it!"

Annja heard the explosion and then felt the concussion
wave a second later even as Pradesh was pulling her to
the ground. A massive cloud of dust exploded out of the
tunnel.

"Frank!"

Annja tried to get out of Pradesh's grasp but he held
her firmly. "Don't, Annja, that's what he wants. Once
you're in the open, he'll be able to get a shot on you.
Don't give him that satisfaction."

Annja felt herself weaken. "Frank. Oh, Frank. Dammit." She took a shuddering breath. "This is all my fault."

Pradesh shoved Annja. "If we don't stop Dunraj, he's
going to bring this whole mountain down on top of us.
And he'll get away. We can't let that happen."

Annja took another look at the tunnel. The back side
of Frank's truck still jutted out into the work area. But
she couldn't see the cab, and judging from the thick black
smoke issuing forth from the tunnel, it was a firestorm
in there.

"The fire might bring down the tunnel," she said.
"We'll have to find our way out through Dunraj's
brother's condominium and the secret passage out onto
the mountain."

"Did you say *condominium?*"

"Long story," Annja said. "But if Dunraj has blown

this exit, then my bet would be that's where he's heading."

Pradesh's face was grim. "Then that's where we're going, too." He checked his pistol. "You lead. I'll follow."

Annja took point as she came around the pile of dirt and rocks. She halfway expected to be on the receiving end of more gunfire, but nothing greeted her as she stuck her head out.

She dashed for the cover of the trucks. Far away, she thought she heard a metallic clank somewhere up the slope where Dunraj had buried the fake Kali statue. Was he already moving back into the mountain's depths?

"We need to move faster," she said. "Otherwise, he'll start blowing the tunnels behind him."

"Does he have that much explosive?" Pradesh asked. "I didn't think he had any schooling in this stuff."

"He told me that he'd been a paramedic back during his college days. Maybe he picked it up somewhere in England?"

Pradesh shook his head. "It's possible, I suppose, but nothing we had in our files indicated it."

"Wouldn't be the first time an intelligence agency got something wrong, though, would it?"

"No, it wouldn't." Pradesh nodded at the slope. "You think it's clear?"

"One way to find out. She ran up the slope with her sword at the ready. But upon cresting it, she found only the scattered wreckage of the work site. All of the workers who weren't dead or injured had already fled. And those that were left were too close to death to even care.

"The workers have abandoned the sinking ship," she said. "And they left these guys behind."

"They couldn't be evacuated," Pradesh said. "That guy's injuries are too severe. This whole place is going to be a write-off. Everyone that was able to get out left before now."

"Except for Frank," Annja said quietly.

"I'm sorry about your friend," Pradesh said. "I liked him. Really good-natured sort. It's a tragedy, for sure."

"I'll sort things out with Dunraj when I catch up with him," she said. "Let's keep moving."

Up past the site where the fake Kali statue had been buried, she paused. She had to round a corner and remembered from the first time she'd stumbled out here that there were plenty of places to take cover. Dunraj could be behind any one of them, ready to shoot the two of them at will.

"What are we awaiting for?" Pradesh asked.

Annja pointed. "You see that rock?"

"Yes."

"That's where I hid when I found this place. It gave me a great vantage point to observe everything happening out here."

"You think Dunraj is there?"

"He might be."

"Well, we can't stay here forever." Pradesh stood and ran into the open.

Annja braced for the explosion of bullets, but nothing happened. Pradesh reached the rock and checked behind it, his gun out. "Nothing."

So Dunraj had already moved back into the mountain. Unless there was another way to get out of the work site. And she didn't think there was. She'd found what she thought were all of the secret little spaces this mountain provided for concealment.

Still, it was good that she was dealing with Dunraj instead of his brother. His brother had lived here, and if anyone knew more of its nooks and crannies, it would have been him.

But he was dead.

And only Dunraj was left.

She looked at Pradesh. What was it about intelligence agencies that made them so keen to get into bed with the lowest caliber of people? Dunraj was an industrialist with tons of skeletons. So he was able to be manipulated. That's what made him perfect for targeting by the Indian spy agency.

She understood it, of course, but it didn't make it any easier to deal with. Especially when the fallout resulted in crap like what they were immersed in right now.

Not to mention the fact that a lot of innocent people were dead because of Dunraj's influence.

Pradesh waved her on. "Let's keep moving!"

Annja paused and took one final look at the work site. Was that movement down by the tunnel?

She held up her hand. "Wait."

It was.

Dunraj?

Was he trying to get out of the tunnel he'd just blown up? How could he hope to do that?

No.

Not Dunraj.

She saw the person turn and hold up a giant hand.

Frank!

"Oh, my God!"

Pradesh looked back. "Annja?"

"It's Frank! He's alive!"

She gave up all thought of herself and ran back down the slope through the trucks. Frank's face was covered in smoke and grime but he was walking and stumbling.

Annja caught him up in a hug. "I thought you were dead!"

"Yeah, me, too." He coughed.

Annja let him go. "What happened?"

"The place exploded in front of me, so I slammed on the brakes and tried to reverse. By then it was too late so I waited for the debris to stop falling. I figured I was safer in the cab than outside of it. It took me a while, but I got out. I had to move a few stones, but I managed."

Annja grinned. "Thank God."

Pradesh came running up a moment later. "You all right, Frank?"

"Pretty good, yeah, Pradesh, thanks."

"You had this one crying over you, that's for sure."

Annja shook her head. "I was thinking about how inconvenient it would be to have to drag a coffin back through customs into the States."

"Gee, thanks," Frank said.

Annja laughed. "How's your leg?"

"I forgot about the gunshot wound when the bomb went off, actually. But it's fine. Just a little sore. I can deal with it."

"Good." She sighed. "Well, as much as I hoped I'd be able to pack you safely away, it appears you're stuck with us."

Frank clapped his hands. "Good. I've got a few things I'd like to do to that punk when we catch up with him."

"Wait in line."

Pradesh gestured back up the slope. "The longer a head start we give him, the more chance there is of him escaping."

Annja looked at Frank. "Can you move?"

"Try to stop me."

Annja looked at Pradesh. "Let's go."

They got back up the slope quickly, pausing only while Frank helped himself to an MP-5 that one of the Tigers had left behind when he was busy dying.

At the top, they again paused while Annja scouted ahead. The area where the fake statue had been buried was deserted. But something inside her told her that Dunraj wasn't that far away.

I wonder if he's still placing the explosives. Or has he already had them set this whole time?

They regrouped near the entrance to the condominium. Pradesh looked at the rock wall in front of him. "It's carefully disguised. Are you sure this is the way back inside?"

Annja nodded. "I came out this way twice. This is the way we get back into his brother's condominium."

"I remember it, too," Frank said. "Although I kinda wish I didn't."

Annja patted him on the arm. "Soon enough, this will all be a bad memory."

"That I'd prefer neither of you ever talk about again," Pradesh said.

"Don't worry about that," Frank said. "I plan on sticking this particular journey in a closet somewhere and never, ever revisiting it."

Pradesh examined the door. "It doesn't seem to be

wired or anything. What are the odds it will swing right open when we try it?"

"Only one way to find out." Annja reached for her sword and watched its gray light reflect on their faces.

"Are we ready?"

39

They positioned themselves outside of the entrance. Pradesh volunteered to take the lead since he had the pistol. Annja would come second and Frank would bring up the rear.

On a count of three, Pradesh yanked the door open and plunged into the room through the walk-in closet. Annja went to the left of the room, clearing as much as she could.

But the bedroom was empty.

Pradesh put a finger to his lips and motioned them to keep moving. If they got bottled up, Dunraj might have booby traps or explosives to take them out.

They moved into the living area next. And in this way, they leapfrogged from room to room.

But with each room they cleared, Annja grew more and more concerned that they had missed the psychotic industrialist.

As they got to the kitchen and it became apparent

that Dunraj was not there, Annja slumped into one of the seats. "He could be anywhere by now."

"I'm telling you," Pradesh said, "he's still here."

"What makes you so sure?"

"Because he hasn't blown us up yet." Pradesh looked grim. "Either he's bad with bombs or he's still here. And since the tunnel exploded when he wanted it to, I'm guessing he knows what he's doing when it comes to explosives. He's still here. Somewhere."

"But how are we going to find him?" Frank asked. "I don't know about you guys but the thought of running around this place in the pitch-dark doesn't sound like a fun way to spend my night. Plus, my leg is smarting like a bastard."

"We should get you out," Annja said. "And this time, I mean it. We can exit the condo and take you to the exit that Kormi showed us. You can follow the game trail down to the foot of the mountain and get some help at the residential complex. Someone there can see to you." She glanced at Pradesh. "Can your people assist or is that asking a bit much?"

"He's better off with the cops." He looked at Frank. "You know who to call and what to say?"

"Yeah."

"If my people—my real people—find out that you guys know about this operation, then it won't go over well at all. I'm supposed to be deniable, you know? And so are my activities for the nation."

Annja nodded. "All right."

She led them out of the condo and back into the passage that they had to crawl through. Then Annja took them back to the slope that revealed the exit in the rock.

She breathed in the fresh air. "I could get used to breathing that after having been in this place for a few days."

Pradesh nodded. "The sooner we find him, the sooner we can both be breathing clean air."

Annja took Frank by the hand. "You all set?"

He hefted the MP-5. "I was going to ditch this, but then I thought there might be a chance I'd meet Dunraj on the way down. I'm taking this puppy and keeping it until I see you again."

"Just don't shoot me."

"Don't sneak up on me, then." He smiled.

"I'll find you when we're done," she said.

Frank nodded.

She watched him crawl out through the doorway built into the rock, and then she shut the door. She waited a moment until her eyes started to readjust to the dark. Then she came down the slope where Pradesh was waiting.

"Now what?"

"I've been thinking," Pradesh said. "What would keep Dunraj here when he could be anywhere else?"

"I don't know.... He likes being inside a mountain?"

"Dunraj doesn't do anything unless he's sure he's going to make some money off the deal. When we approached him, that's how we got our hooks into him. We made sure he understood how much cash he stood to gain if he played ball."

"And what—you think he's got something still here that he wants?"

Pradesh nodded. "That's exactly what I think. But what would it be? It would have to be something of significant value. After all, if he's going to blow this place up, that means he loses that highway and the thoroughfare that would open him up to being first to develop the region. That means it's got to be worth an awful lot of money."

Annja thought hard. "The only thing I can think of that has any worth at all was that supposedly golden statue of Kali you guys were going to give to the Tigers."

Pradesh paused. "Yes."

"But that's not actually based on something real, is it?"

Pradesh looked around. "When we broached the idea of it, Dunraj suggested we come up with some way to implant the tracker on something valuable. But we suggested the statue idea."

"Are you sure?"

"What do you mean?"

"As much as you guys were playing Dunraj, it sounds like he might have slipped a little something past you. What if he actually found an amazing statue but he knew there was no way he'd be able to get it out of here without you knowing about it? So he comes up with a neat idea that lets you guys think you thought of it. But it's something he wanted you to develop."

"It's possible...I guess."

"Let me ask you this—who designed the statue?"

Pradesh gave it some thought. "Dunraj did a sketch. It wasn't anything amazing, but we were in the conference room and he sketched something on a napkin. Ten arms. Jewels. Golden." Pradesh shook his head. "Aw, dammit. This thing just keeps getting worse."

"Come on," said Annja.

"Where are we going?"

"To the only place where Dunraj can get something like that out of here—the work site."

"But the tunnel's blocked."

"If I know Dunraj, and I think by now I've got a fairly decent idea of the way his wacky mind works, then I'm guessing he's able to unblock it. In fact, I'm willing to bet that explosion there was all for show. He got us to do exactly what he wanted—he got us away from the very place he needs to be."

They raced back through the passageway and into the condominium. Annja led them through the closet and then back out into the passage that took them to the work area.

Even as they got close they could hear the sound of heavy machinery.

Annja was startled. "He's already got things going."

Pradesh nodded. "We've really underestimated him. I won't make this mistake ever again."

"I just hope we're not too late."

"Stay low," Pradesh advised. "We don't want him getting advance notice that we're back."

Annja led them down to the large outcropping that she'd used for cover the first time she was here. The sounds of heavy machinery grew louder. Annja thought she heard two separate engines.

How many people were still here?

"I thought the workers all left," she said.

"Except the ones who looked like they were dying," Pradesh said. "But they couldn't be doing this work. They were too badly injured."

"Well, someone is."

They peered out from behind the rocks. And Annja saw what she expected to see. The crane that had lifted the Kali statue when she and Frank and Kormi had been close to being executed by the Tigers was back in operation.

And overhead, she saw an exact replica of the first statue.

"There it is."

"Only this is the real thing," Pradesh said, mouth open in awe. "It's even more beautiful than the fake we had manufactured to fool the Tigers."

And it was. The ten-armed statue of Kali gleamed in the bright work lights. Even from the distance, Annja could see there were significantly more jewels bedecking the statue than the fake had possessed.

"Look at that."

Pradesh seemed humbled by its presence.

"What do you think that's worth? Honestly?"

Pradesh shrugged. "Depends. If he melts it down and pries all the jewels off, it would certainly be a lot of money. But I think it would be worth more if he keeps the statue intact. A collector would pay an incredible amount for that."

"But who would buy it?"

Pradesh sniffed. "This is India. We've got plenty of billionaires now. Any one of them would be inclined to snatch up something like this on the black market. And Dunraj would certainly be able to hide for as long as he liked."

"If that's his plan," she said, "I don't think he's going to hide at all. I think he's going to go public with news of your operation here. That's how he'll get his life back."

"We'd kill him first."

"Don't be so sure," Annja said. "If you've got him working for you, then this will be the only way he sees possible to get out from under you. Expose your agency and what you were about to do. Expose this work site and the victims here. Even if his claims are outlandish, they'll put you guys under such a microscope the agency won't survive without a massive reorganization. You told me that your group had already had problems in the past because you report to the prime minister, yes?"

"Yes."

"Then that's it. Dunraj gets a nice payday, he keeps his reputation and business, and he gets out from under your organization. It's a win-win-win."

"All this time we thought we were playing him," Pradesh said. "And the Tigers?"

Annja shrugged. "I'm sure the way Dunraj spins the story, he'll come out looking clean, and then the Tigers will have good reason to continue their activities against the governments in both Sri Lanka and Delhi."

Pradesh checked his pistol again. "Well, then, there's a very simple way to put an end to this."

He started to stand but Annja jerked him back down to cover. "Wait."

"What is it?"

"Look!"

She pointed. A large dump truck was rolling up the slope. If Pradesh had stood, the driver would have seen him.

"Wait until it stops. Dunraj will probably be distracted then."

"Which one do you want?"

"Dunraj."

"I'll take the truck driver, then," Pradesh said. "At the same time."

Annja nodded, realizing there was no way out of this but through the violence she'd hoped she could avoid. "And the statue?"

"Can we talk about that later?"

Annja smiled.

But then her smile died when she saw the driver of the truck get out.

She looked back at the crane's driver seat. Dunraj sat there manipulating the controls.

Annja looked back at the dump truck driver.

It was Dunraj all over again.

"The twin," she said quietly. "He's not dead, after all."

40

"How's that possible?"

Annja looked at Pradesh. "Did you see the corpse?"

He nodded. "I did. And he sure as hell looked dead when the medical team paraded him past us."

"Clearly that wasn't the truth. I wonder how much of anything has been." Annja gripped her sword. "We need to make sure Dunraj doesn't have this place wired. If we hit them fast enough and hard enough, we ought to be able to ensure he doesn't set this place off."

"Agreed. We go?"

"We go."

As Dunraj—or was it the brother?—came around from the dump truck, Pradesh made his move. He slunk forward like a stealthy snake. Annja didn't wait to see what happened next—she was already heading for the crane's cab.

She jumped the last few feet and landed on the tracks

next to the cab compartment. The look on Dunraj's face was one of absolute surprise, but it didn't stay long.

He immediately shot a hand out and slammed the cab's door into Annja as she tried to gain purchase on the treads. The blow knocked her off, and she had to roll to dissipate the shock of the fall.

In her peripheral vision, she saw that Pradesh was involved in a fistfight with the other brother. Where was his gun? Had Pradesh thrown it away? Maybe it had jammed.

But then she was up and heading back for the first brother.

A bullet hit her blade, and the impact made her almost drop it. Dunraj shot at her again, and she ducked as the bullet went wide to the right.

This was getting far too dangerous.

Dunraj was out of the cab now, although the crane was still moving, with the hoisted statue of Kali still dangling overhead. He fired another shot at Annja. And he was shouting for his brother.

"Kill the cop and then get her!"

Annja frowned as Dunraj ducked back into the cab. He threw the crane into gear, and it shuddered as the tracks started grinding up the dirt around it. It spun directly at Annja.

The sudden movement almost caught her off guard. Still gripping her sword, she dived to the right as the crane trundled past her.

But Dunraj knew how to manipulate the crane. It stopped and turned on a dime and headed right back at her.

Annja had to dive again to escape being ground under

the caterpillar tracks. She was out of breath and running to get away from it.

But then she turned and waited. The crane bore down on her. Overhead the statue still dangled, precariously waving back and forth from the motion of the crane now that Dunraj was using it to try to run her over.

She could see Dunraj smiling through the crane's windshield. He gunned the engine. Annja was trapped between two parts of the wall, and the crane was coming right at her.

One chance, she thought.

She flipped the sword over and took a running step toward the crane. At the right moment, she launched the blade like a javelin, aiming it right at the windshield.

The sword arced through the air. At the apex of its flight path, weight took over, and with the help of gravity, it plunged downward.

Dunraj must have seen it because his eyes went wide, and then the sword punched through the glass, shattering it before embedding in Dunraj's chest.

He fell forward and must've hit the control panels because the crane lumbered to a stop inches away from Annja.

She heard another gunshot.

Pradesh was squatting, with the other brother in his sights. But the brother was weaving and ducking, and Pradesh couldn't get off a clean shot.

The villainous man was running for the tunnel. If he got to the trucks he could escape. He wouldn't go far, but Annja couldn't let him even get close.

She looked back at the crane. And then she was running for it, climbing aboard and tossing the body out of the cab. She visualized the sword and it was back in her hands.

Annja looked at the crane's controls and pushed the throttle forward, gunning the engine.

She waved Pradesh aboard. "Come on!"

Pradesh swung himself up next to her in the cab. In front of them, the fleeing figure dashed ahead. But he was too fast, and the crane didn't have as much speed on the straightaway.

"We're not going to catch him," Pradesh said.

The statue swung back and forth like a giant pendulum as Annja pressed the gas pedal again.

But Pradesh was right. Dunraj's brother would reach one of the trucks before they could catch up with him. He was still weaving, and Pradesh couldn't get a decent shot off in time.

"We've got to stop him!"

Annja nodded. "Take the controls."

Pradesh swung into her seat, and Annja studied the panel. As they got close to the truck yard, Annja found the control she wanted and studied the fleeing figure ahead of them.

"You think he has the detonator on him?"

"There might not even be one," Pradesh said. "We've got to make a move!"

"If he's wired, we'll kill ourselves in the process."

"But what choice do we have?"

"We don't."

She studied their quarry's rhythm.

"Annja! Now!"

She punched the release button on the crane's cable.

There was a sudden lurch as the weight dropped from the crane. But had she guessed the right moment?

Annja watched the statue fly through the air, and then its shadow loomed large over the fleeing brother.

The man stopped, turned and in that split second saw the reality before the statue came down directly on top of him, crushing him like a bug.

Pradesh killed the engine.

Silence dropped over the work site. A dark stain blossomed around the edge of the statue.

Annja swallowed. "Ouch."

Pradesh took a breath. "I'm thinking that might just be one of the most terrible ways to die. Death by the statue of Kali."

"Agreed. But we didn't have any choice. I'm just glad it's over."

"It sure as hell had better be."

They climbed out of the crane's cab, and Annja ran back to check on the first brother she'd stabbed through the chest. His eyes were wide open, but he was very much dead.

"He's done for," she said when Pradesh came walking over.

He whistled. "That was some throw you made."

"He was trying to run me down," she said defensively. "It was either launch the sword or dive under the crane. I'm not a fan of throwing myself under large machinery."

"I can't say I'd be in a rush to do that, either. But it was a great shot."

"Thank you."

Pradesh thumbed over his shoulder. "We should probably check on the other one."

Annja frowned. "That's going to be messy."

"Yes. It will be."

Annja pointed at the crane. "Shame we couldn't use the crane to simply lift it off of him."

"You released the cable. No way to string it back up without help." He looked puzzled. "How did you know how to do that?"

"I didn't. I guessed."

He whistled. "Lucky for us it worked."

As they wandered over to where the statue was embedded in the ground, Pradesh nodded. "I see a hand."

Annja looked at the statue of Kali and shook her head. "It's incredible how upright this thing is standing. Almost as if this is where it was supposed to be the entire time."

"Are you finding religion now, Annja?"

She smiled. "I respect all religions, Pradesh. The fewer deities I piss off, the happier I'll find myself when my time finally arrives." She winked. "I hope."

"Well said." He turned and looked at her. "This has been some adventure for you, hasn't it?"

"It's…been interesting."

"I get the feeling you've had plenty of others. You and that incredible sword of yours. It's a gift from God, and I don't think you're going to find yourself apart from it for a very long time to come."

Annja nodded. "The responsibility of wielding it can sometimes get to be too much, but I can't ever imagine being without it." She grinned. "Do me a personal favor, though?"

"If I can."

"Don't ever tell anyone about this. There's nothing

top secret or superspy about it. I was chosen to possess it for some time and that's all there is. It's just me and the sword. I don't need to know that the world's intelligence agencies are gunning for me because of it."

He held up his hands. "Every adventure you have with that sword is your trial by fire. The entire journey you're on is extraordinary."

"You might be right."

"And I give you my word that I won't mention the sword's existence to anyone. It's the least I can do."

"Thanks." Annja glanced around. "So, what happens now?"

"Now? Now I clean this mess up. Literally, it looks like." He sighed. "I'll grab a truck and head back into Hyderabad and get the cleanup crews out here. This site needs to be expunged from the earth. The operation has to vanish."

"And the Tigers who were here?"

Pradesh shrugged. "Unfortunate accidents of Dunraj's betrayal. I walk away from this, as does my agency."

"Back into the shadows."

"Exactly." His smile was firmly in place.

"You ever get to New York, look me up," she said. "I'd tell you my address, but you probably already know it."

"I might."

Annja frowned. "Wait—which one? You know it or you might look me up?"

Pradesh laughed. He pointed at the trucks. "Would you like a lift back?"

Annja thought about it and then shook her head. "You know what? I'm going to find Frank and walk down the mountain with him. Our car's still down there some-where. We'll drive back. The normal way."

"Flying home tonight?"

"I might have time for one more meal before we say goodbye to Hyderabad."

"I know a place...."

"I'll bet you do," she said. "Say, three hours?"

Pradesh checked his watch. "I might be able to fit you in."

Annja walked up the slope and found her way through the condominium. After so much time in the tunnels, the differences in light didn't seem to bother her as much anymore.

At the secret entrance in the rock, Annja paused one final time to look back into the inky darkness. She'd spent so much time in there over the past few days, it felt strange to finally walk out for good.

I guess Kali has certainly lived up to her name, she thought.

She closed the door behind her and stood in the valley. The sun was just beginning its trek toward the western horizon. It would soon be evening.

It was time to head home.

But first, she had to find Frank.

And then she had to think up a story to explain to her producer, Doug, why they had no TV footage for *Chasing History's Monsters*.

* * * * *

TAKE 'EM FREE
2 action-packed novels plus a mystery bonus

NO RISK
NO OBLIGATION TO BUY

JAMES AXLER

DEATH LANDS

Palaces of Light

A treacherous quest through tomorrow's post-nuclear reality.

Steeped in beauty and mysticism, the canyons of Mesa Verde, Colorado, survived the blast that altered the American West. Ryan Cawdor and his band follow the trail to a legendary city carved in stone, older and stronger than the nukecaust—the palaces of light. The inhabitants are masters of mind games, poised to push the companions over the edge....

Available May wherever books are sold.

Don Pendleton's Mack Bolan.

Road of Bones

A high-speed death chase through Russia's most brutal terrain

Dispatched on a high-priority search-and-rescue mission, Mack Bolan is on a motorcycle hell ride along the Road of Bones—a mass grave to thousands of slaves buried during Stalin's iron rule. It's a one-way trip effectively sealed at both ends by death squads. Every mile survived brings him closer to freedom...or certain doom.

**Available April
wherever books are sold.**
